JAMES PATTERSON

LONDON BRIDGES

headline

First published in Great Britain in 2004
by HEADLINE BOOK PUBLISHING

This edition published in 2014
by HEADLINE PUBLISHING GROUP

9

Cataloguing in Publication Data is
available from the British Library

ISBN 978 0 7553 4938 8

Printed and bound in Great Britain by
Clays Ltd, St Ives plc

Headline's policy is to use papers that are natural, renewable
and recyclable products and made from wood grown in
sustainable forests. The logging and manufacturing processes
are expected to conform to the environmental regulations of
the country of origin.

HEADLINE PUBLISHING GROUP
An Hachette UK Company
338 Euston Road
London NW1 3BH

www.headline.co.uk
www.hachette.co.uk

LONDON BRIDGES

For Larry Kirshbaum.
Here's to the *tenth* Alex Cross.
None of this would have happened without your
commitment, your wise counsel, and your friendship.

THE WEASEL RETURNS, AND WHAT A NICE SURPRISE

Chapter One

Colonel Geoffrey Shafer loved his new life in Salvador, Brazil's third-largest city and, some would say, its most intriguing. It was definitely the most fun.

He had rented a plush six-bedroom villa directly across from Guarajuba Beach, where he spent his days drinking sweet caipirinhas and ice-cold Brahma beers, or sometimes playing tennis at the club. At night, Colonel Shafer – the psychopathic killer known as the Weasel – was up to his old tricks, hunting on the narrow, winding streets of the 'Old City'. He had lost count of his kills in Brazil, and nobody in Salvador seemed to care, or to keep count either. There hadn't been a single newspaper story about the disappearances of any young prostitutes. Not one. Maybe it was true what they said of the people here – *when they weren't actually partying, they were already rehearsing for the next one.*

At a few ticks past two in the morning, Shafer returned to the villa with a young and beautiful street-walker who called herself Maria. What a gorgeous face the girl had, and a stunning brown body, especially for someone so young. Maria said she was only thirteen.

The Weasel picked a fat banana from one of several plants in his front garden. At this time of year he had his choice of coconut, guava, mango and pinka, which was sugar apple. As he plucked the fresh fruit, he had the thought that there was always something ripe for the taking in Salvador, which he believed was paradise. *Or maybe it's hell and I'm the devil,* Shafer thought and chuckled to himself.

'For you, Maria,' he said, handing her the banana. 'We'll put it to good use.'

The girl smiled knowingly and the Weasel noticed her eyes – what perfect brown eyes. *And all mine now – eyes, lips, breasts.*

Just then, he spotted a small Brazilian monkey called a mico trying to work its way through a screened window and into his house. 'Get out of here, you thieving little bastard!' he yelled. 'G'wan! Beat it!'

There came a quick movement from out of the bushes, then three men jumped him. *The police,* he was certain, *probably Americans. Alex Cross?*

The cops were all over him, powerful arms and legs everywhere. He was struck down by a bat, or a lead pipe, yanked back up by his full head of hair, then beaten unconscious.

'We caught him. We caught the Weasel first try. That wasn't very hard,' said one of the men. 'Bring him inside.'

Then he looked at the beautiful young girl, who was clearly afraid, rightly so. 'You did a good job, Maria. You brought him to us.' He turned to one of his men. '*Kill her.*'

A single gunshot ruptured the silence. No one seemed to notice or care in Salvador.

Chapter Two

The Weasel just wanted to die now. He was hanging upside down from the ceiling of his own master bedroom. The room had mirrors everywhere and he could see himself in several of the reflections.

He looked like death. He was naked, bruised and bleeding all over. His hands were tightly cuffed behind his back, his ankles bound together, cutting off the circulation. Blood was rushing to his head.

Hanging beside him was the young girl, Maria, but she had been dead for several hours, maybe as much as a day, judging by the terrible smell. Her brown eyes were turned his way, but they stared right through him.

The leader of his captors, bearded, always squeezing a black ball in one hand, squatted down so that he was only a foot or so from Shafer's face. He spoke softly, a whisper.

'What we did with some prisoners when I was active – we would sit them down, rather politely, peacefully – and then nail their fucking tongues to a table. That's absolutely true, my weasely friend. You know what else? Simply plucking hairs . . . from the *nostrils* . . . the *chest* . . . *stomach* . . . *genitals* . . . it's more than a little bothersome, no? *Ouch,*' he said, as he plucked hairs from Shafer's naked body.

'But I'll tell you the worst torture, in my opinion anyway. Worse than what you would have done to poor Maria. You grab the prisoner by both shoulders and shake violently until he *convulses.* You literally rattle his brain, the sensitive organ itself. It feels as if the head will fly off. The body is on fire. I'm not exaggerating.

'Here, let me show you what I mean.'

The terrible, unimaginable violent shaking – while Geoffrey Shafer hung upside down – went on for nearly an hour.

Finally, he was cut down. 'Who are you? What do you want from me?' he screamed.

The head captor shrugged. 'You're a tough bastard, but always remember, *I found you.* And I'll find you again if I need to. Do you understand?'

Geoffrey Shafer could barely focus his eyes, but he looked up to where he thought the captor's voice came from. Finally, he whispered, *'What – do you – want? Please?'*

The bearded man's face bent close to his. He almost seemed to smile. 'I have a job, a most incredible job for you. Believe me, *you were born for this*.'

'Who are you?' the Weasel whispered again through badly chapped and bleeding lips. It was a question he'd asked a hundred times during the torture.

'I am the Wolf,' said the bearded man. 'Perhaps you've heard of me.'

PART ONE

THE UNTHINKABLE

Chapter Three

On the sunny, blue-skied afternoon when one of them would die, unexpectedly, needlessly, Frances and Dougie Puslowski were hanging sheets and pillowcases and the kids' play clothes out to dry in the noonday sun.

Suddenly, US Army soldiers began to arrive at their mobile-home park, 'Azure Views', in Sunrise Valley, Nevada. *Lots* of soldiers. A full convoy of US jeeps and trucks came bouncing up the dirt road they lived on, and stopped abruptly. Troops poured out of the vehicles. The soldiers were heavily armed. They definitely meant business.

'What in the name of Sweet Jesus is going on?' asked Dougie, who was currently on disability from the Cortey Mine outside Henderson and was still trying to get used to the 'domestic scene', as he called it. But Dougie knew that he was failing pretty badly.

He was almost always depressed, always grumpy and mean-spirited, and always short with poor Frances and the kids.

As they climbed out of their trucks, Dougie noticed that the soldier boys and girls were outfitted in battle-dress uniform: leather boots, camouflage pants, olive T-shirts – the whole kit and caboodle, as if this were Iraq and not the ass-end of Nevada. They carried M-16 rifles and ran toward the closest trailers with muzzles raised. Some of the soldiers even looked scared themselves.

The desert wind was blowing pretty good, and their voices carried all the way to the Puslowskis' clothes-line. Frances and Dougie clearly heard, 'We're evacuating the town! This is an emergency situation. Everyone has to leave their houses now! *Now,* people!'

Frances Puslowski had the presence of mind to notice that all of the soldiers were pretty much saying the same thing, like they had rehearsed it, and that their tight, solemn faces sure showed that they wouldn't take no for an answer. The Puslowskis' three-hundred-odd neighbors – some of them *very* odd – were already leaving their mobile houses, complaining about it, but definitely doing as they were told.

The next-door neighbor, Delta Shore, ran over to Frances. 'What's happening, hon? Why are all these soldiers *here*? My good God Almighty! Can you believe it? They must be from Nellis or Fallon or someplace. I'm a little scared, Frances. You scared, hon?'

The clothes-peg in Frances's mouth finally dropped to the ground as she spoke to Delta. 'They say that they're evacuating us. I've got to get the girls.'

Then Frances ran inside the mobile home, and at 240 some pounds, she had believed her sprinting, or even jogging days were far behind her.

'Madison, Brett, c'mere you two. Nothin' to be scared of. We just have to leave the house for a while! It'll be fun. Like a movie. Get a move on, you two!'

The girls, aged two and four, appeared from the small bedroom where they'd been watching *Rolie Polie Olie* on the Disney Channel. Madison, the oldest, offered her usual, 'Why? Why do we have to? I don't want to. I won't. We're too busy, Momma.'

Frances grabbed her cell phone off the kitchen counter – and then the next really strange thing happened. She tried to get a line to the police, but there was nothing except loud static. Now that had *never* happened before, not that kind of annoying, buzzy noise she was hearing. Was some kind of invasion going down? Something nuclear maybe?

'Damn it!' she snapped at the buzzing cell phone, and almost started to cry. *'What is going on here?'*

'You said a bad word!' Brett squeaked, but she also laughed at her mother. She kind of liked bad words. It was as if her mother had made a mistake, and she loved it when adults made mistakes.

'Get Mrs Summerkin and Oink,' Frances told the girls, who *would not* leave the house without their two favorite lovies, not even if the infernal plague of Egypt had come to town, and Frances prayed that it hadn't – but what *had*? Why was the US Army swarming all over the place, waving scary guns in people's faces?

She could hear her frightened neighbors outside verbalizing the very thoughts racing around in her head: *What's happened? Who says we have to leave? Tell us why! Over my dead body, soldier! You hear me, now?*

That last voice was Dougie's! Now what was *he* up to?

'Dougie, come back in the house!' Frances yelled. 'Help me with these girls! Dougie, I *need* you in here.'

There was a gunshot outside! A loud, lightning-bolt *crack* exploded from one of the rifles.

Frances ran to the screen door – here she was, running again – and she saw two US Army soldiers standing over Dougie's body.

Oh my God, Dougie wasn't moving. Oh my God, oh my God! The soldiers had shot him down like a rabid dog. For practically nothing! Frances started to shiver and shake, then she threw up lunch.

Her girls screeched, 'Yuk, Mommy. Mommy, yuk. You threw up all over the kitchen!'

Then suddenly a soldier with a couple of days' facial growth on his chin kicked open the screen door and he was right in her face and he was *screaming,* 'Get out of this trailer! Now! Unless you want to die too.'

The soldier had the business end of a gun pointed right at Frances.'I'm not kidding, lady,'he said.'Tell the truth, I'd just as soon shoot you as talk to you.'

Chapter Four

The job – the operation – the mission – was to wipe out an entire American town. In broad daylight.

It was some eerie, psycho gig. *Dawn of the Dead*, either version, would be mild compared to this. Sunrise Valley, Nevada, population three hundred and fifteen brave souls. Soon to be population zero. *Who was going to believe it? Well, hell, everybody would in less than about three minutes.*

None of the men on board the small plane knew *why* the town was being targeted for extinction, or anything else about the strange mission, except that it paid extremely well, and all of the money had been delivered to them upfront. Hell, they didn't even know one another's names. All they had been told was their individual tasks for the mission. Just their little *piece* of the puzzle. That's what it was called – their *piece*.

Michael Costa from Los Angeles was the munitions

expert on board and he'd been instructed to make a 'bootleg fuel-air bomb with some real firepower'.

Okay, he could do that easy enough.

His working model was the BLU-96, often called a 'Daisy Cutter', which graphically described the end result. Costa knew that the bomb had originally been designed to clear away minefields, and also jungles and forests for military landing zones. Then some really crazy and sick dude had figured out the Daisy Cutter could wipe out people as easily as it could trees and boulders.

So now here he was inside an old, beat-to-hell cargo plane flying over the Tuscarora Mountain range toward Sunrise Valley, Nevada, and they were very close to T for target.

He and his new best friends were assembling the bomb right there on the plane. They even had a diagram showing them how to do it, as if they were idiots. *Assembling Fuel-Air Bombs for Dummies.*

The actual BLU-96 was a tightly controlled military weapon and relatively hard to obtain, Costa knew. Unfortunately for everybody who lived, loved, ate, slept and shit in Sunrise Valley, Daisy Cutters could also be assembled at home out of readily obtainable ingredients. Costa had purchased a thousand-gallon supplement fuel bladder for starters. Then he'd filled it with high-octane gas, fitted a dispersing device, and inserted dynamite sticks as the initiator. Next, he made a motion brake and trigger assembly using a parachutist's altitude deployment device for parts. Simple stuff like that.

Then, as he'd told the others on board the cargo plane, 'You fly over the target. You push the bomb out the payload door. You run like your pants are on fire and there's an ocean up ahead. Trust me, the Daisy Cutter will leave nothing but scorched earth below. Sunrise Valley will be a burnmark in the desert. A memory. Just you watch.'

Chapter Five

'**E**asy does it, gentlemen. No one is to be hurt. Not this time.'

Nearly eight hundred miles away, the Wolf was watching in 'live time' what was happening in the desert. *What a flick!* There were four cameras 'on the ground' at Sunrise Valley, and they were pumping video footage onto four monitors in the house in the Bel Air section of Los Angeles where he was staying. For the moment anyway.

He watched closely as the inhabitants of the mobile-home park were escorted by Army personnel into waiting transport trucks. The clarity of the footage was very good. He could see the patches on the soldiers' arms: *Nevada Army Guard Unit 72nd*.

Suddenly, he spoke out loud. 'Shit! Don't do that!' He started to rapidly squeeze the black handball in his fist, a habit when he was anxious or angry, or both.

One of the male civilians had pulled a gun and had it pointed at a soldier. Incredibly dumb mistake!

'You *imbecile!*' the Wolf shouted at the screen.

An instant later the man with the handgun was dead, face down in the desert dust, which actually made it easier to get the other retards from Sunrise Valley into the transport trucks. *Should have been part of the plan in the first place,* the Wolf thought. But it hadn't been, so now it was a small problem.

Then one of the handheld cameras focused in on a small cargo plane as it approached the town and circled overhead. This was just gorgeous to behold. The handheld was obviously on board one of the Army trucks, which were, hopefully, speeding out of range.

It was amazing footage – black and white – which somehow made it even more powerful. Black and white was more realistic, no? *Yes* – absolutely.

The handheld was steady on the plane as it glided in over the town.

'Angels of death,' he whispered. 'Beautiful image. I'm such an artist.'

It took two of them just to push the bladderload of gas out the payload door. Then the pilot banked a hard left, firewalled the engines, and climbed out of there as fast as he could. That was his job, his *piece* of the puzzle, and he'd done it very well. 'You get to *live,*' the Wolf spoke to the video again.

The camera was on a wide angle now, and captured the bomb as it slowly plummeted toward town. Stunning footage. Scary as hell, too, even for him to see. At approximately a hundred feet from the ground, the bomb detonated. 'Ka-fucking-boom!' said the Wolf. It just came out of his mouth. Usually, he wasn't this emotional about anything.

As he watched – couldn't take his eyes away – the Daisy Cutter leveled everything within four to five hundred yards of the drop site. It also had the capacity to *kill* everything within an area that large, which it did. This was utter devastation. Up to ten miles away windows blew out of buildings. The ground and buildings shook in Elko, Nevada, about *thirty-five* miles away. The explosion was heard in the next state.

And actually, much farther away than that, like right there in Los Angeles. Because tiny Sunrise Valley, Nevada, was just a 'test run'.

'This is just a warm-up,' said the Wolf. 'Just the beginning of something great. My masterpiece. *My payback.*'

Chapter Six

When everything started, I was blessedly out of the loop, on a four-day vacation to the West Coast, my first in over a year. First stop, *Seattle, Washington*.

Seattle is a beautiful, lively city that, in my opinion anyway, nicely balances the funky-old and the cyber-new, with possibly a tip of a Microsoft cap to the future side of things. Under ordinary circumstances I would have looked forward to a visit there.

These were kind of shaky times, though, and I only had to look down at the small boy tightly holding on to my hand as we crossed Wallingford Avenue North to remember why.

I only had to listen to my heart.

The boy was my son, Alex, and I was seeing him for the first time in four months. He and his mother lived in Seattle now. I lived in Washington, D.C., where I was an FBI agent. Alex's mom and I were involved in a 'friendly' custody struggle over our son – at least it was evolving that way after a very stormy couple of encounters.

'You having fun?' I asked Little Alex, who still carried around 'Moo', a spotted black-and-white cow that had been his favorite toy when he had lived with me in Washington. He was almost three, but already a smooth talker and even smoother operator. God, I loved this little guy. His mother believed that he was a gifted child – high intelligence, high creativity – and since Christine was an elementary-schoolteacher, and an excellent one, she would probably know.

Christine's place was in the Wallingford area of Seattle, and because it's a pleasant 'walking neighborhood', Alex and I had decided to stay close to home. We started out playing in the back yard that was bordered with Douglas firs and had plenty of room, not to mention a view of the Cascade Mountains.

I took several pictures of The Boy, per my instructions from Nana Mama. Alex wanted me to see his mother's vegetable garden and, as I expected, it was very well done, full of tomatoes, lettuce and squash. The grass was neatly mown. Pots of rosemary and mint covered the kitchen windowsills. I took more pictures of Alex.

After our tour of the yard, we walked over to the Wallingford Playfield and had a catch-and-batting session; then it was the zoo; and then another hand-holding walk along nearby Green Lake. Alex was pumped up about the upcoming Seafair Kiddies Parade and didn't understand why I couldn't stay for it. I knew what was coming next and I tried to brace myself for it.

'Why do you always have to go away?' he asked, and I didn't have a good answer. Just a sudden, terrible ache in my chest that was all-too familiar. *I want to be with you every minute of every day, buddy,* I wanted to say.

'I just do, buddy,' I said, 'but I'll be back soon. I promise. You know I keep my promises.'

'Is it because you're a policeman?' he asked. 'Why you have to go away?'

'Yes. Partly. That's my job. I have to make money to buy VCRs and PopTarts.'

'Why don't you get another job?' asked Alex.

'I'll think about it,' I told him. Not a lie. I would. I had been thinking about my future with the FBI a lot lately. I'd even talked to my doctor about it – my *head* doctor.

Finally, around two-thirty, we made our way back to his house, which is a restored Victorian, painted deep blue with white trim, in excellent condition. It's cozy and light, and I must admit, a nice place to grow up in – as is Seattle.

Little Alex even has a view of the Cascades from his room. What more could a boy ask for?

Maybe a father who was around more than once every few months? How about that?

Christine was waiting on the porch, and she welcomed us back warmly. This was such a switch from our last face-to-face in Washington. Could I trust Christine? I guess I had to.

Alex and I had a final couple of hugs on the sidewalk. I took a few more snapshots for Nana and the kids.

Then he and Christine disappeared inside, and I was on the outside, alone, walking back to my rental car with my hands stuffed deeply in my pockets, wondering what it was all about, missing my small son already, missing him badly, wondering if it would always be as heartbreaking as this, knowing that it would be.

Chapter Seven

After the visit with Alex in Seattle I took a flight down to San Francisco to spend some time with Homicide Inspector Jamilla Hughes. She and I had been seeing each other for about a year. I missed Jam and needed to be with her. She was good at making things all right.

Most of the way, I listened to the fine vocals of Erykah Badu, then Calvin Richardson. They were good at making things right too – better, anyway.

As the plane got close to San Francisco we were treated to a surprisingly clear view of the Golden Gate Bridge and the city's skyline. I spotted the Embarcadero, and the Transamerica Building, and then I just let the scene wash over me. I couldn't wait to see Jam. We've been close ever since we worked a murder investigation together; the only problem – the two of us live on different coasts. We like our respective cities, and our jobs, and haven't figured out where to go with that yet.

On the other hand, we definitely enjoyed being together, and I could see the joy on Jamilla's face as I spotted her near an exit at busy San Francisco International Airport. She was in front of a North Beach Deli, grinning, clapping her hands over her head, then jumping up and down. She has that kind of spirit, and can get away with it.

I smiled and felt better as soon as I saw her. She always has that effect on me. She was wearing a buttery soft leather car coat, light blue tee, black jeans, and looked like she'd come straight from work, but she looked *good*, really good.

She'd put on lipstick – and perfume, I discovered as I took her into my arms. 'Oh *yes*,' I said. 'I missed you.'

'Then hold me, hug me, kiss me,' she said. 'How was your boy? How was Alex?'

'He's getting big, smarter, funnier. He's pretty great. I love that little guy. I miss him already, Jamilla.'

'I know you do, I know you do, baby. Give me that hug.'

I picked Jam up off her feet and spun her around. She's five-nine and solid, and I loved holding her in my arms. I noticed a few people watching us, and most were smiling. How could they not?

Then two of the spectators, a man and a woman in

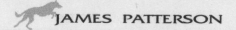

dark suits, walked up to us. *Now what was this?*

The woman held up her badge for me to see: *FBI.*
Oh no. No. Don't do this to me.

Chapter Eight

I groaned and gently set Jamilla down, as if we had been doing something wrong instead of something very right. All the good feelings inside me evaporated in a hurry. Just like that. Wham, bam! I needed a break – and this wasn't going to be it.

'I'm Agent Jean Matthews, this is Agent John Thompson,' the woman said, gesturing toward a thirty-something blond guy munching a Ghirardelli chocolate bar. 'We hate to interrupt, to intrude, but we were sent out here to meet your plane. You're Alex Cross, sir?' she thought to check.

'I'm Alex Cross. This is Inspector Hughes from the SFPD. You can talk in front of her,' I said.

Agent Matthews shook her head. 'No, sir, I'm afraid I can't.'

Jamilla patted my arm. 'It's okay.' She walked away, leaving me with the two agents, which was the opposite of what I wanted to happen. I wanted *the two of them* to walk away – far, far away.

'What's this about?' I asked Agent Matthews. I already knew it was something bad, and that was an ongoing problem with my current job. FBI Director Burns had my schedule and itinerary at all times, even when I was off-duty, which effectively meant that I was *never* off-duty.

'As I said, sir, we were told to meet you. Then to put you right on a plane to Nevada. There's an emergency out there. A small town was bombed. Well, the town was blown off the map. The Director wants you on the scene, like *an hour ago*. It's a terrible disaster.'

I was shaking my head, feeling incredible disappointment and frustration as I walked over to where Jamilla stood. I felt like there was another hole at the center of my chest. 'There's been a bombing in Nevada. They say it's on the news. I have to go out there,' I told her. 'I'll try to get back soon as I can. I'm sorry. You have no idea how sorry I am.'

The look on her face said it all. 'I understand,' she said. 'Of course I understand. You have to go. Come back if you can.'

I tried to hug her, but Jamilla backed away, finally giving me a small, sad wave. Then she turned and left without saying another word, and I think I knew that I had just lost her too.

Chapter Nine

I was on the move, but the whole scene felt more than frustrating – it was actually surreal. I flew by private jet from San Francisco to a place called Wells, Nevada, and from there caught a ride in an FBI helicopter to what had once been Sunrise Valley.

I was trying not to think about Little Alex, trying not to think about Jamilla, but so far it wasn't working. Maybe once I got to the bombsite? Once I was there in the action, in the middle of the shit.

I could tell by the way the local agents deferred, and fussed around me, that my reputation, or the fact that I worked out of Washington, was making them nervous and edgy. Director Burns had made it clear that I was one of the Bureau's troubleshooters, that I was *his* troubleshooter. I wouldn't carry tales back to Washington, but the agents in the field offices didn't know that. How could they?

The helicopter ride from Wells to the bombing site took only about ten minutes. From the air, I could see emergency lights all around Sunrise Valley, or what *had been* Sunrise Valley. The town was gone now. There was still smoke, but no fire was visible from the air, possibly because there was nothing left to burn.

It was a little past eight o'clock. What the hell had happened out here? And why would somebody go to the trouble of destroying a hole-in-the-wall town like Sunrise Valley?

I had been briefed as soon as I stepped inside the FBI helicopter. Unfortunately, there wasn't too much information available. At four that afternoon, the residents – except for one male who'd been shot – had been 'evacuated' by what appeared to be US Army national guardsmen. The townspeople were then driven forty miles away to a point halfway from the nearest large town, Elko. Their location was called in to the Nevada state police. By the time the troopers arrived to assist the badly frightened townies, the Army trucks and jeeps were gone. And so was the town of Sunrise Valley. Blown off the map.

I mean, there was nothing down there but sand, sage and scrub.

I could see fire-trucks, vans, offroad vehicles, maybe a half-dozen helicopters. As our 'copter began to settle down I spotted techies in chemical-protective overgarments.

Jesus, what had happened here?

Chemical warfare?

War?

Was that a possibility? In this day and age? Of course it was.

Chapter Ten

I t was probably the scariest thing I'd ever seen in my years as a police officer – total desolation, *without apparent rhyme or reason.*

As soon as we touched down, and I climbed out of the helicopter, I was outfitted in chemical-protective overgarments, C-POGs, including a gas mask and other gear. The rubber mask was state-of-the-art with dual eyepieces and an internal drinking tube for replenishing liquids. I felt like a character in a scary Philip K. Dick story. But it didn't last too long. I took the unwieldy mask off as soon as I saw a couple of Army officers roaming around without theirs.

We got a possible break soon after I arrived. A couple of rock-climbers had spotted a man using a video camera to film the explosion. He looked suspicious, and one of the climbers had photographed the man with his digital camera. The climbers also had shots of the town's evacuation.

Two of our agents were interviewing the climbers, and I wanted to talk to them also, as soon as the agents had finished. Unfortunately the local police had gotten to the camera first, and they were holding it until their chief arrived at the scene. He was late, because he'd been away on a hunting trip.

When the chief finally got there, in an old black Dodge Polaris, I was all over him. I started talking before he had even climbed out of his car.

'Chief, your men are holding important evidence. We need to see it,' I said, not raising my voice at the sixtyish, potbellied man, but making sure he got the point. 'This is a federal investigation now. I'm here representing both the FBI and Homeland Security. We've lost valuable time because of your men.'

To his credit, the police chief himself was exasperated. He began yelling at his officers. 'Bring the evidence over here, you morons. What the hell are you two trying to pull? What were you thinking? *Do* you think? Bring the evidence.'

His men came running, and the taller of the two, who I later learned was the chief's son-in-law, handed over the camera. It was a Canon PowerShot and I knew how to get at the pictures.

So what did we have here? The first shots were well-composed nature photos. No people in any of them. Close-ups and wide shots.

Then came shots of the actual evacuation. Unbelievable.

Finally, I got my first look at the man who had filmed the explosion.

His back was to the camera. At first he was standing, but in the next few shots, he was down on one knee. Probably to get a better angle.

I don't know what had prompted the rock-climber to take the initial few shots, but his instinct was pretty good. The mystery man was videotaping the deserted town – then suddenly it went up in flames that rose several hundred feet high. It seemed pretty clear that he had known about the attack *before* it *happened*.

The next photograph showed the man turning in the direction of the climbers. He actually began to walk toward them, or so it appeared on film. I wondered if he'd spotted one of them taking his picture? He seemed to be looking their way.

That was when I saw his face, and I couldn't believe what I was looking at. *I recognized him.* And why not? I'd been chasing him for years. He was wanted for over a dozen murders here and in Europe. He was a vicious psychopath, one of the worst of his kind still on the loose anywhere in the world.

His name was Geoffrey Shafer, but I knew him better as the Weasel.

What was he doing here?

Chapter Eleven

There were a couple more crystal-clear shots as the hateful Weasel got closer to the photographer.

Just the sight of him sent my brain reeling, and I felt a little sick. My mouth was dry, and I kept licking my lips. *What was Shafer doing here? What connection would he have to the bomb that had leveled this small town a few hours ago? It was crazy, felt like a dream, completely unreal.*

I'd first come across Colonel Geoffrey Shafer in Washington three years ago. He'd murdered more than a dozen people there, though we could never prove it. He would pose as a cab driver, usually in Southeast where I lived. The prey was easy to grab, and he knew D.C. Police investigations weren't as thorough when the victims were poor and black. Shafer also had a *day job* – he was an Army colonel working inside the British Embassy. On the face of it, he couldn't have been much more respectable. And yet – he was a horrible murderer, one of the worst pattern-killers I'd ever come across.

A local agent named Fred Wade joined me near the helicopter I'd come in on. I was still studying the climber's photos. Wade told me he wanted to know what was going on, and I couldn't blame him. So did I.

'The man who videotaped the explosion is named Geoffrey Shafer,' I told Wade. 'I know him. He committed several murders in D.C. when I was a homicide detective there. The last we heard of him, he'd fled to London. He murdered his wife in front of their children in a London market. Then he disappeared. Well, I guess he's back. I have no idea why – but it makes my head hurt just to think about it.'

I took out my cell phone and put in a call to Washington. As I described what I'd discovered, I was reviewing the last few photographs taken of Colonel Shafer. In one of the photos he was climbing into a red Ford Bronco.

The next was a rear shot of the Bronco as it rode away. *Jesus.* The license plate was visible.

And that was the strangest thing of all so far: *the Weasel had made a mistake.*

The Weasel I'd known didn't make them.

So maybe it wasn't a mistake after all?

Maybe it was part of a plan.

Chapter Twelve

The Wolf was still in Los Angeles but reports were coming in from the Nevada desert on a regular basis. Police were arriving near Sunrise Valley – then helicopters – the US Army – finally, the FBI.

His old friend Alex Cross was out there now too. *Good for Alex Cross. What a good soldier.*

Nobody understanding a goddamn thing, of course.

No coherent theory about what had happened in the desert.

How could there be?

It was chaos, and that was the beauty of it. Nothing scared people more than *what they didn't understand*.

Case in point, a local LA hot-shit named Fedya Abramtsov and his wife, Liza. Fedya wanted to be a big Mafiya gangster, but also lead the life of a movie-star type out here in Beverly Hills. This was Fedya and Liza's house that he was staying in now, but really, the

Wolf thought of it as his house; after all, *their* money was *his* money. Without him, they were nothing but small-time punks with big ambitions.

Fedya and Liza didn't even know that he was at their house. The couple had been at their place in Aspen and they finally got back to LA at just past ten that evening.

Imagine their surprise.

A powerful-looking man sitting by himself in the living room. Just sitting there. So peaceful. Rhythmically squeezing a rubber ball in his right hand.

They had never seen him before.

'Who the hell are you?' demanded Liza. 'What are you doing here?'

The Wolf spread his arms. 'I am the one who gave you all of this wonderful stuff. And what do you give me in return? Disrespect like this? I am the Wolf.'

Fedya had heard enough already. He knew that if the Wolf was here, letting himself be seen, then he and Liza were as good as dead. *Best to run and hope to God the Wolf was here alone, unlikely as that might be.*

He took a single step, and the Wolf raised a handgun from out of the seat cushion. He was good with a gun. He shot Fedya Abramtsov once in the back, once in the back of his neck.

'He's very dead,' he spoke calmly to Liza, which he knew to be a nickname of hers.

'I prefer Yelizaveta,' he said. 'Not so common, so

Americanized. Come and sit. Come. Please.' The Wolf patted his lap. 'Come. I don't like to repeat myself.'

The girl was a pretty one, smart too, and apparently ruthless as a snake. She walked across the room and then she sat in the Wolf's lap. She did as she was told anyway. Good girl.

'I like you, Yelizaveta. But what choice do I have – you've disobeyed me. You and Fedya stole my money. Don't argue – I know it's true.' He looked into her beautiful brown eyes. 'Do you know *zamochit*?' he asked. 'The breaking of bones?'

Apparently Yelizaveta did because she screamed at the top of her voice.

'This is good,' said the Wolf as he grabbed the woman's slender left wrist. 'Everything is going so well today.'

He started with Yelizaveta's little finger, just the pinkie.

Chapter Thirteen

Had a war started? If it had, who was the enemy?

It was pitch dark, and it was freezing cold in the desert. Scary and disorienting, to put it mildly. No moon out tonight. Was that part of the plan? What was supposed to happen next? Where? To whom? Why?

I tried to collect my thoughts and make a rough plan to take us through the next few hours in at least a semi-organized manner. Difficult to do, maybe impossible. We were looking for a small convoy of Army trucks and jeeps that seemed to have disappeared, to have been gobbled up by the desert. But also a Ford Bronco with the Nevada license tag 322JBP and a sunset design.

And we were looking for Geoffrey Shafer. Why would the Weasel be here?

While we waited for something to break, maybe a

message, or a warning, I walked around what had been Sunrise Valley. Where the bomb had actually detonated, buildings and vehicles hadn't just been flattened, they'd practically been vaporized. Little bits of death and destruction, sparks and ash, were still floating in the air. The night sky was masked by a dark and oily cloud of smoke, and I was struck by the unsettling idea that only man could create something like this, and only man would want to.

As I wandered through the mounds of debris, I also talked to agents and techs involved in the investigation, and I began to make a few crime-scene notes of my own:

Bits and pieces of the mobile-home camp are scattered everywhere.

Witnesses describe canisters dropped from a prop plane . . .

One falling can seemed about to strike a trailer-home, then exploded in mid-air above the town . . .

At first, the explosion was like a 'white, undulating jellyfish cloud'. . . then the cloud ignited . . .

High winds from the heat of the fire, convection whirls, apparently blew at gale force for several minutes . . .

So far we had discovered only one body in the rubble. Everyone was wondering the same thing: Why only one? Why spare the others? Why blow up this trailer-park town at all?

It just didn't make sense. Nothing did so far. But

especially Shafer's presence.

One of the local FBI agents, Ginny Moriarity, called out my name and I turned. She waved excitedly for me to come over. Now what?

I jogged back to where Agent Moriarity was standing with a couple of local cops. They all seemed exercised about something.

'We found the Bronco,' she told me. 'No Army trucks, but we located the Bronco in Henderson.'

'What's in Henderson?' I asked Moriarity.

'An airport.'

Chapter Fourteen

'**L**et's go!'

I was back in the FBI helicopter, and headed to Henderson in a hurry, hoping to catch up with the Weasel. It seemed like a long shot, but we didn't have anything else for now. Agents Wade and Moriarity traveled with me. They didn't want to miss this – *whatever was waiting in Henderson.*

As we pulled up and away from what remained of Sunrise Valley I was aware of the 'high desert'; the former town was at an elevation over 4,000 feet.

Then I tuned the surroundings out and started thinking about Shafer, trying once again to figure what could possibly tie him to this mess, this disaster, this murder scene. Three years before, Shafer had kidnapped Christine Johnson. It had happened during a family vacation in Bermuda; at the time, Christine and I were engaged to be married. Neither of us knew it, but she was pregnant with Alex when Shafer abducted her. We were never the same after her rescue. John Sampson, my best friend, and I found her in Jamaica. Christine was emotionally scarred, and of course I couldn't blame her. Then she moved out to Seattle, where she lived with Alex. And I blamed Shafer for the custody struggle.

Who was he working with? One thing was obvious, and probably useful to the investigation: the fire-bombing at Sunrise Valley had involved a lot of people. So far we didn't know who the men and women posing as US Army were, but we did know that they weren't real Army national guardsmen. Sources at the Pentagon had helped confirm that much. Then there was the matter of the bomb that had leveled the town. Who made it? Probably somebody with military experience. Shafer had been a colonel in the British Army but he'd also served as a mercenary.

Lots of interesting connections, but nothing very clear yet.

The helicopter pilot turned toward me. 'We should be in visual contact with Henderson as soon as we clear these mountains up ahead. We'll see lights anyway – but so will they. I don't think we can sneak up on anybody out here in the desert.'

I nodded to him. 'Just try to land as close as you can to the airport. We'll coordinate with the state troopers. *We might draw fire,*' I added.

'Understood,' the pilot said.

I started to discuss our options with Wade and Moriarity. Should we try to land at the airport itself – or nearby in the desert? Had either of them fired their weapons before, or been fired on? I found out that they hadn't. Neither of them. Terrific.

The pilot turned to us again. 'Here we go. Airport should be coming up on our right. There.'

Suddenly I could see a small airfield with a two-story building and what looked like two airstrips. I spotted cars, maybe a half-dozen, but I didn't see a red Bronco yet.

Then I saw a small private plane taxiing and getting ready for takeoff.

Shafer? It didn't seem likely to me, but neither did anything else so far.

'I thought we shut down Henderson,' I called to the pilot.

'So did I. Maybe this is our boy. If it is, he's *gone*. That's a Learjet 55 and it moves pretty damn good.'

From that moment on, there was very little we could do but watch. The Learjet shot down one of the runways, then it was airborne, winging away from us and making it look ridiculously easy. I could imagine Geoffrey Shafer on board, looking back at the FBI helicopter, maybe giving us the finger. Or was he giving me the finger? Could he know that I was here?

A few minutes later we were on the ground at

Henderson. Almost immediately I got the jolting news that the Learjet was *off-radar*.

'What do you mean, off-radar?' I asked the two techies inside the tiny Henderson control room.

The older of the two answered. 'What I mean is that the jet seems to have disappeared off the face of the earth. It's like it was never here.'

But the Weasel had been here – *I'd seen him*. And I had photographs to prove it.

Chapter Fifteen

Geoffrey Shafer drove a dark blue Oldsmobile Cutlass full-bore through the desert. He *wasn't* on board the jet that had flown out of Henderson, Nevada. That would have been too easy. Weasels always have several escape routes planned.

As he drove, Shafer was thinking that everything about the oddly brilliant plan in the desert had worked well, and there had certainly been backup contingencies just in case something didn't go right. He had also learned that Dr Cross, now with the FBI, had shown up in Nevada.

Was that part of the big picture too? Somehow, he expected that it was. But why Cross? What did the Wolf have in mind for him?

Shafer eventually made a stop in Fallon, Nevada, where he was scheduled to make his next contact. He didn't know exactly *who* he was contacting, or *why* or *where* this whole operation was leading. He just knew his 'piece' – and his explicit orders were to call in from Fallon and get the next set of instructions.

So he followed his orders, registered at the Best Inn Fallon, and went straight to his room. He used a cell phone which he'd been told to destroy after he made the call. There were no pleasantries exchanged, no unnecessary words. Just the business at hand.

'This is the Wolf,' he heard as contact was made, and Shafer wondered if that was so. According to rumor the real Wolf had impersonators, maybe even body doubles. All of them with their 'piece', right?

Next, he heard disturbing news. 'You were seen, Colonel Shafer. You were spotted and photographed near Sunrise Valley. Did you know that?'

At first, Shafer tried to deny it, but he was ignored.

'We're looking at copies of the pictures right now. That's how the Bronco was followed to Henderson. Which is why we told you to exchange vehicles outside town and drive to Fallon. Just in case something went wrong.'

Shafer didn't know what to say. How could he have been spotted out in the middle of nowhere? Why was Cross there?

The Wolf finally laughed. 'Oh, don't worry your pretty head, Colonel. You were supposed to be spotted. The photographer worked for us.

'Now proceed to your next contact point in the

morning. And have some fun tonight in Fallon. Paint the town, Colonel. I want you to go and kill somebody out in the desert. You choose a victim. Do your stuff. *That's an order.'*

Chapter Sixteen

The level of frustration and tension I was feeling was increasing by the hour, and so was the general confusion about the case. I'd never seen so much chaos, so fast, in my entire life.

Almost a full day after the bombing there was nothing but a hole in the ground in the Nevada desert, plus a couple of questionable leads. We had talked to the three hundred or so residents of Sunrise Valley, but none of the survivors had a clue either. Nothing unusual had happened in the days before the bombing; no stranger had visited. We hadn't found the Army vehicles, or discovered where they had come from. What had happened in Sunrise Valley still didn't make sense. Neither did Colonel Geoffrey Shafer's being there. But it sure shook us up.

No one had even taken credit for the bombings yet. After two days, there wasn't too much more I could do out in the desert, and I caught a ride home to Washington. I found Nana, the kids, even Rosie the cat out on the front porch waiting for me.

Home Sweet Home again. Why didn't I just learn a lesson and stay there?

'This is real nice,' I beamed as I came bounding up the steps.'A welcoming committee. I guess everybody missed me, right? How long you been out here waiting for your Pops?'

Nana and the kids shook their heads pretty much in unison, and I smelled conspiracy.

Nana said, 'Of course we're glad to see you, Alex,' and finally cracked a smile. They all did. *Conspiracy, for sure.*

'Gotcha!' said Jannie. She had on a crocheted sun hat with her braids hanging out.'Of course we're your welcoming committee. Of course we missed you, Daddy. Who wouldn't?'

'Got you bad!' Damon taunted from his perch on the rail. He's twelve and looks the part. Sean John T-shirt, straight-leg jeans, Hiptowns.

I pointed a finger at him.'I'll get *you*, you break my porch rail.'Then I smiled. *'Gotcha!'* I said to Damon.

After that, I had to answer all sorts of questions about Little Alex and show around my digital camera with dozens of pictures of our beloved little man.

Everybody was pretty much laughing now, which was better, and it was definitely good to be home again, even if I was still waiting for more news about the bombing in Nevada; and about Shafer's involvement.

Nana had held dinner for me, and after a delicious meal of roast chicken with garlic and lemon, squash, mushrooms and onions, the family congregated in the kitchen over cleanup and bowls of ice cream. Jannie showed off a pen and ink of her heroes Venus and Serena Williams, which was *sensational*; eventually, we watched the Washington Wizards on TV. Finally, everybody started to wander off to bed, but there were hugs and kisses first. Nice, very nice. Much, much better than yesterday, and I was willing to bet, better than *tomorrow.*

Chapter Seventeen

Around eleven, I finally climbed the steep stairs to my office in the attic. I reviewed my case file on Sunrise Valley for twenty minutes or so in preparation for tomorrow, then I called Jamilla in San Francisco. I'd talked to her a couple of times in the past two days, but I'd mostly been too busy. I figured she might be home from work by now.

All I got was a voice message, though.

I don't like to leave messages myself, especially since I'd already left a couple from Nevada, but I finally said, 'Hi, it's Alex. I'm still trying to sell you on the idea of forgiving me for what happened at the airport in San Francisco. If you want to come East sometime soon, I'm buying the plane ticket. Talk to you soon. I miss you, Jam. Bye.'

I hung up the phone, then I let out the sigh I'd been holding in. I was blowing it again, wasn't I? *Hell yes,* I was. *Why would I do such a thing?*

I went downstairs and ate a double-size piece of cornbread that Nana had made for the next day. It didn't help, just made me feel even worse, guilty about my eating habits. I sat on a kitchen chair with Rosie the cat in my lap, stroking her.

'You like me, right? Don't you, Rosie? I'm kind of a nice guy?'

The phone calls weren't over for the night. Just past midnight I received a call from one of the agents I'd worked with out in Nevada. Fred Wade had something he thought I might find interesting. 'We just got this from Fallon, Nevada,' he told me. 'Receptionist in a Best Inn there was raped and murdered two nights ago. Her body was left in the brush near the motel parking lot – like we were supposed to find it. We got a description of a guest who could be your Colonel Shafer. Needless to say, he's long gone from Fallon.'

Your Colonel Shafer. That said it all, didn't it? And, *he's long gone from Fallon. Of course he is.*

Chapter Eighteen

I didn't sleep much that night. I had awful nightmares about the Weasel. And about the holocaust in Sunrise Valley, Nevada.

Early the next morning I had to sign permission slips so the kids could go on a field trip to the National Aquarium in Baltimore. I signed the slips at 4:30 before they were up, and then, while the house was still dark, I had to sneak off to work. I didn't get to say goodbye, and I don't like that, but I left love notes for Jannie and Damon. *Such a nice pops, right?*

I drove to work with Alicia Keys and Calvin Richardson on the CD, good company for the trip, and whatever lay ahead.

These days, 'Major Threats' was being run out of FBI headquarters in D.C. Since 9/11, the Bureau had shifted dramatically – from what some people felt was a reactive, investigative organization, to a much more proactive and effective one. A recent addition, a six-hundred-million-dollar software package at the Hoover Building, included a forty-million-page terrorism database dating back to the 1993 bombing of the World Trade Center.

We had a blizzard of information; now it was time to see if any of it was worth a damn.

About a dozen of us met on the subject of Sunrise Valley that morning in the Strategic Information Operations Center Suite on the fifth floor. The obliteration of the small town had been listed as a Major Threat, even though we had no way to tell whether it was. So far, we didn't have a single clue as to what Sunrise Valley was really about.

There still hadn't been any contact with the bombers, not a word from them.

Surreal. And probably scarier than if we had heard from them.

This particular conference room was one of the jazzier and more comfortable ones: lots of blue leather armchairs, a dark wood table, wine-colored rug. Two flags – an American and a Department of Justice; lots of crisp white shirts and striped ties around the table.

I had on jeans and a navy windbreaker that read: *FBI Terrorism Task Force.* And I felt that I was the only one dressed correctly for the day. This case sure wasn't going to be 'business as usual'.

The room was loaded with heavy hitters though.

The highest-ranking person was Burt Manning, one of the five Executive Assistant Directors at the Bureau. Also present were senior agents from the National Joint Terrorism Task Force, as well as the top analyst from the new Office of Intelligence, which combined experts from the Bureau and the CIA.

My partner for the morning was Monnie Donnelley, a superior analyst, and a good friend from my time at Quantico.

'I see you got your personal invitation,' I said as I sat down beside her. 'Welcome to the party.'

'Oh, I wouldn't miss this. It's like sci-fi or something. It's *so* weird, Alex.'

'Yeah, it's all of that.'

On the screen at the front of the room was the special agent in charge from the Las Vegas field office. The SAC was reporting in about the mobile crime lab that had been set up inside the town limits of what had been Sunrise Valley. She didn't have much new, though, and the meeting quickly moved on to 'threat assessment'.

This was where everything got a lot more interesting.

First, there was a discussion of domestic terrorist groups like the National Alliance and the Aryan Nations. But nobody really believed those simpletons could be responsible for something as well-planned as this. Next up was the latest on al Qaeda and Hezbollah, the radical jihad movement. These groups received a solid couple of hours of heated discussion. They were definitely suspects. Then formal assignments were given out by Manning.

I *didn't* get an assignment, and that made me wonder if I would be hearing from Director Burns soon. I didn't particularly want to hear from him on this one. I particularly didn't want to travel out of Washington again, especially back to Nevada.

And then, it got really wild.

Every pager in the conference room went off – simultaneously!

Within seconds, everybody had checked their pagers, myself included. For the past several months all terror threats got flashed to senior agents – whether it was a suspicious package on a New York subway, or an anthrax threat in LA.

The message on my pager read: *Two surface-to-air missiles missing at Kirtland Air Force Base in Albuquerque. Connection to Sunrise Valley situation being investigated. Will keep informed.*

Chapter Nineteen

No rest for the righteous, read a placard on the wall near the canteen and soda machines. At ten to six that night, we were called back to the conference room on the fifth floor. The same august group as before. Some of us were guessing that the Bureau had finally been contacted by whoever was responsible for the bombing of Sunrise Valley. Others thought this might have to do with the missile thefts from Kirtland Air Base in New Mexico.

A few minutes later, half a dozen agents from the CIA arrived. All in suits with briefcases. *Uh-oh*. Then came a half-dozen hitters from Homeland Security. Things were definitely getting more serious now.

'This is getting hinky,' Monnie Donnelley whispered to me. 'It's one thing to talk the talk about interagency cooperation. But the CIA is *really* here.'

I smiled over at Monnie. 'You're sure in a good mood.'

She shrugged, 'As General Patton used to say about the battlefield, "God help me, I do love it so!" '

Director Burns entered the room precisely at six. He walked in with Thomas Weir, the head of the CIA, and Stephen Bowen from Homeland Security. The three heavies looked extremely uneasy – maybe just being there together did it – which succeeded in making all of us nervous too.

Monnie and I exchanged another look. A few agents continued to talk, even as the Directors took their places at the front. It was the veterans' way of showing that they'd been here before. Had they? Had anyone? I didn't think so.

'Can I have your attention,' Director Burns said and the room immediately went quiet. All eyes were glued to the front.

Burns let the quiet settle in, and then he continued.

'I want to bring you up to speed. The first contact that we received on this situation was two days before the bombing in Sunrise Valley, Nevada. The initial message concluded with the words: "*It is our hope that no one will be injured during the violence.*" The nature of "the violence" wasn't revealed or even hinted at. We were also instructed not to mention the initial contact to anyone. If we did, we were warned there would be serious consequences, though these consequences were never spelled out for us.'

Burns paused and looked around the room. He

made eye-contact with me, nodded, then moved on. I wondered how much he knew that none of us did. And who else was involved? The White House? I would think so.

'We have been contacted every day since then. One message went to Mr Bowen, one to Director Weir, and one to me. Until today, nothing of consequence had been revealed. But this morning each of us received a film of the bombing in Nevada. The film had been edited. I'll share it with you now.'

Burns made a rapid, circular hand signal and a video began to play on the half-dozen monitors around the room. The film was in black and white; it was grainy and looked handheld, like news footage. Like war footage, actually. The room was very quiet as we watched the video.

From a distance of a mile or more, one camera angle revealed the Army trucks and jeeps arriving in Sunrise Valley. Moments later the mystified residents were escorted from their mobile homes into the trucks.

A man pulled a handgun and was shot dead in the street. *Douglas Puslowski*, I knew.

The convoy then drove off quickly, raising great clouds of dust.

In the next shot, a large, dark object tumbled into view from the sky. While it was *still in the air*, there was an incredible explosion.

The film of the actual bombing had also been edited but it showed only footage from a single camera. The editing was mostly a series of jump-cuts. Jarring, but effective.

This was followed by a long shot of the explosion. The plane that delivered the bomb was never in the shot.

'They filmed the whole damn thing.' Burns spoke again. 'They wanted us to know that they were there, that they are the ones who bombed the town out of existence. In a few minutes they're going to tell us why this is happening. They'll call on the phone.

'The person making the calls has been using phone cards from public phones. Crude but effective. The calls so far originated at grocery stores, movie theaters, bowling alleys. Pretty much untraceable, as you know.'

We sat mostly in silence for a minute or two. There were only a few private conversations going on.

Then the quiet was broken – as the phone at the front of the room began to ring.

Chapter Twenty

'**T**his will be on speaker for everyone to hear,' Burns told us. 'They said it was permissible, even advisable for all of you to be here. In other words, they expected an audience. They're very big on rules, as you'll see.'

'Who the hell is *they*?' Monnie whispered up close to my ear. 'See, it *is* sci-fi. Aliens, maybe? That's my bet going in.'

'We'll know in a minute, won't we? I'm not betting against you.'

Director Burns pushed a button on his console and a male voice came over the speakers. The voice was heavily filtered.

'Good evening. This is the Wolf,' we heard.

The hair on the back of my neck rose immediately. I knew the Wolf; I'd chased him for nearly a year. In fact, I'd never known a more ruthless criminal or killer.

'I'm the one responsible for the destruction of Sunrise Valley. I'd like to explain myself – at least as much as you deserve to know. Or should I say, as much as I want you to know at this time.'

Monnie looked over at me and she shook her head. She knew the Wolf too. The news couldn't have been worse if the call came straight from Hell.

'It's good to be able to talk to all of you, so many self-important people gathered together just to listen to my ramblings. The FBI, CIA, Homeland Security,' the Wolf continued. 'I'm so very impressed. Humbled, actually.'

'Do you want us to talk, or listen?' Burns asked.

'Who am I speaking to? Who was that just now? Would you mind identifying yourself?'

'It's Director Burns, FBI. I'm with Director Weir of the CIA and Stephen Bowen of Homeland Security.'

There was a crackling sound over the speakers that might have been a laugh. 'Well, I'm just so very honored again, Mr Burns. I'd have thought you would assign a lackey to speak to me. At first anyway. Someone like Dr Cross. But you know, it's better that we talk top-to-top. That's always best, don't you think?'

Weir from the CIA said, 'You specifically requested "the first team" in your earlier contact. Believe me, this is the first team. We're taking the bombing incident in Nevada seriously.'

'You actually listened. I'm impressed. I've heard that about you, Mr Weir. Although I foresee some problems between us in the future.'

'Why is that?' Weir asked.

'You're the CIA. Not to be trusted. Not for a minute . . . Don't you read your Graham Greene? Who else is on your *first team*?' the Wolf asked. 'Stand up and be counted.'

Burns went around the room listing off who was present. He omitted a couple of agents, and I wondered why.

'Excellent choices for the most part,' the Wolf said once Burns had finished the roll call. 'I'm sure you know who to trust, and who not to, who you can depend on – with your very lives. Personally, I'm not keen on the CIA, but that's just me. I find them to be liars and unnecessarily dangerous. Does anyone there disagree?'

No one spoke and the speakers crackled with the Wolf's laughter. 'That's interesting, don't you think? Even the CIA doesn't disagree with my scathing indictment.'

Suddenly the Wolf's tone changed. 'Now listen closely to what I have to tell you, you morons. That's the important thing now, you have to *listen* to me. Many lives can be saved if you do. And you must obey.

'Does everyone get that? *Listen and obey!* I want to hear you. Please, speak up. Do all of you fucking *understand*?'

Everyone spoke at once, and although it seemed absurd and childish, we understood that the Wolf was showing us he was in control, total control.

Burns suddenly spoke in a loud voice. 'He's gone! He hung up! He's off the line, the son of a bitch!'

Chapter Twenty-One

We waited like his puppets in the conference room, but the Russian mobster didn't make contact again. I knew the bastard well, and I didn't expect him to call us back. *He was playing with us now.*

Eventually, I went back to my office, and Monnie Donnelley headed to Virginia. I still hadn't been assigned to the case, not officially anyway. But the Wolf had known I would be there in the crisis room. He'd singled me out for a gratuitous insult. Just his style.

What was he up to? *A mobster using terror tactics? Starting a war? If a small group of madmen in the desert could do it, why not the Russian Mafiya? All it seemed to take was a ruthless enough leader, and money.*

I waited and wondered if the terrible uncertainty I felt was part of the Russian's plan to increase the pressure and stress. To control us? Test our patience?

And, of course, I thought about Geoffrey Shafer and how he might be connected. What was that all about? I'd already pulled up most of the recent data on Shafer. We had put an old girlfriend of Shafer's – his therapist – under surveillance. Her name was Elizabeth Cassady and I was trying to get a look at the notes from her therapy sessions with Shafer.

Later, I checked in at home and talked to Nana. She accused me of eating her cornbread and I blamed it on Damon, which got a cackle out of her. 'You have to take responsibility for your actions,' she scolded.

'Oh, I take full responsibility,' I told her. 'I ate the cornbread, and I'm glad. It was delicious.'

Shortly after I got off the phone I was called down to a meeting in the crisis room. Tony Woods from the Director's office addressed a room full of agents. 'There have been new developments,' he began in a solemn tone. 'All hell has broken loose in Europe.'

He went on: 'There were two more terrible fire-bombings about an hour ago. Both were in Western Europe.

'One bombing took place in the northern part of England, in Northumberland near the border with Scotland. The village of Middleton Hall – population four hundred plus – is no more.' Wood paused. 'This time, the townspeople *weren't* evacuated. We don't know why. There were close to a hundred casualties. It was a horrible bloodbath. Whole families died – men, women and some children.

'We have already received a filmed segment from Scotland Yard. A local policeman took it from the Cheviots, which are a range of nearby hills. I'll put it on for you to see.'

We sat and watched the short film in total, stunned silence. At the end, the local policeman himself spoke to camera. 'My name is Robert Wilson, and I grew up here in Middleton Hall, which is gone. There was a high street, a couple of pubs and shops, the houses of people I knew. There used to be an old Royal Engineers bridge into town, but that was blown up. Our local pub – gone. As I stand here looking over this wasteland, I am reminded of why I am a Christian. What I feel most is hopelessness about our world.'

Following the moving tape, Tony Woods told us about the bombing that had taken place in Germany. He said he had no accompanying videotape as yet.

'The damage in Lübeck was not quite as horrifying, but it's bad. A group of college students apparently resisted. Eleven of them were killed. Lübeck is in the Schleswig-Holstein region of Germany, near the border with Denmark. It's a farming area. Secluded. The Wolf has made no contact about the bombings, nor were we warned ahead of time. All we know is – *it's escalating.*'

Chapter Twenty-Two

W hat next? And how soon would it happen?

The tension during the next waiting period was excruciating. A madman was out there, blowing up small towns, and wouldn't tell us why, or if the attacks would continue and get worse.

For the time being, I concentrated my attention on a close study of the psychopathic Weasel – reading and re-reading everything in his thick files. More than I wanted to, I could see his face, hear his voice, and I still wanted to bring him down. I went through notes from the psychiatrist who'd treated Shafer when he'd lived in Washington. Dr Elizabeth Cassady had not only been Shafer's shrink, she'd been his lover.

The notes were mind-boggling to say the least, especially given the nature of their relationship and how it developed – and also, how wrong she'd been about Shafer. As I read, I made notes on Dr Cassady's notes.

First encounter:

XX-year-old male, self-referred with stated Chief Complaint – 'I'm having trouble at work focusing on my projects.' States that what he does is 'Classified.' Also describes people at work telling him that he has been behaving 'strangely'. Client says that he is married, father of three: twin girls and a boy, and states that he is 'happy' at home and with his wife.

Impression:

Well-dressed, very attractive, *articulate male, somewhat restless, and with considerable presence. Grandiose in describing his past accomplishments.*

Rule out:

 Schizoaffective Disorder
 Delusional Disorder
 Substance-Induced Mood Disorder (primarily alcohol or recreational drugs)
 Attention Deficit Hyperactivity Disorder
 Borderline Personality Disorder
 Unipolar Depression

Interview #3:

10 minutes late for appointment today. Irritable when questioned about this. States that he feels 'spectacular', and yet seems ill-at-ease and anxious in session.

Interview #6:

When questioned about home-life and earlier discussion of problems with sexual functioning, became somewhat inappropriate: chuckling, pacing, making sexually explicit jokes and asking about my personal life. Stated that when he and his wife are together, he engages in fantasies about me, and that this causes him to ejaculate prematurely.

Interview #9:

Quiet today, almost with flattened affect, but denies any depression. Feels that people around him 'don't understand me'. Continues to describe sexual problems with wife. States that he had an episode of impotence last week with her, despite fantasizing about me. The sexual fantasies are very detailed and he refuses to curtail them when asked. Admits to being 'obsessed' with me.

Interview #11:

Marked change in affect today. Very energetic, euphoric, and almost overwhelmingly charismatic (possibility of Sociopathic Disorder). Questioned the need for further sessions, and states, 'I feel terrific.' When asked about issues with his wife, states: 'Things couldn't be better. She adores me, you know.'

Discussed an episode of risky behavior this past week involving driving his car very fast, and intentionally leading police on a high-speed chase. Alluded to participating in sexual behavior with another partner, possibly a prostitute, and spoke of 'rough sex'. Manner of relating today is flirtatious, and almost openly seductive. He is convinced that I 'want' him.

Interview #14:

Missed last appointment: no call, no show. Apologetic today, but later became angry and restless. States that he feels the need to 'reward himself'. Discussed increase in libido again, and mentioned calling several high-priced escort services to engage in sexual activity, and discussed desire to engage in sado-masochistic behavior.

Says that he is probably 'in love' with me. No affect when he reveals this to me. None whatsoever. I must say, I am a little speechless myself. Colonel Shafer seems to be attending these sessions almost solely for the purpose of seducing me. And unfortunately, it's working.

Chapter Twenty-Three

After reading Dr Cassady's notes, I have to admit, I was a little speechless too. More than a little, actually. The strange case-notes began to *side* with Shafer after the sixteenth visit; they no longer contained any of his personal feelings that must have led to the affair.

Then Dr Cassady stopped making notes on the sessions altogether. How incredibly odd, not to mention unprofessional. I assumed that their affair had begun by then. If I needed any more proof of what a clever and highly disturbed psychopath Shafer was, I had it in Dr Cassady's notes.

Late that night I got a call to head down to the crisis room again. I was told that the Wolf would be calling very soon. This had to be something. The countdown must be about to start.

When the call came through, he began in a low-key

manner. 'Thank you for getting together again on my behalf. I'll try not to disappoint you, or waste anyone's valuable time. Directors Burns, Bowen, Weir – do you have anything you'd like to say before I begin?'

'You told us to *listen*,' said Burns. 'We're listening.'

There was a burst of laughter from the Wolf. 'I like you, Burns. I suspect you'll be a worthy adversary. By the way, is a Mr Mahoney there in the room?'

The head of the Hostage Rescue Team and a friend of mine glanced at Ron Burns, who nodded to him to speak.

Ned Mahoney sat hunched forward in his chair, and he was giving the Wolf the finger. 'Yes, I'm right here. I'm listening.' He still had his middle finger extended. 'What can I do for you?'

'You can *leave* now, Mr Mahoney. I'm afraid that you won't be needed. You're too unstable for my tastes. Too dangerous. And yes, I'm quite serious.'

Burns motioned for Mahoney to go.

'There will be no need for the FBI's Hostage Rescue Team,' said the Wolf. 'If it comes to that, all is lost, I assure you. I hope you're beginning to understand how my mind works. I don't want HRT mobilized, and I don't want any further investigation. Call off the dogs.

'Are you all *listening*? No one is to try to find out who I am – or who *we* are. Do you really understand? Please respond if you do.'

Everyone in the room called out, 'Yes'. They under-stood. Once again, it seemed that the Wolf was trying to make us feel like children; or maybe he just enjoyed humiliating the FBI, CIA and Homeland Security.

'Anyone who *didn't* respond just then, please leave the room,' said the Wolf. 'No, no, sit back down. I'm just having fun at your expense. I'm what you might call a "creative type". But I am serious about Mr Mahoney, and about there being no formal investigation. I'm deadly serious about it, in fact.

'Now then, let's get down to today's business, shall we? This is an interesting juncture, actually. I hope someone is taking notes.'

There was a pause of approximately fifteen seconds. Then the Wolf resumed. 'I want you to know the *targeted cities*. It's time for that.

'There are four – and I would advise that these cities prepare for the worst possible case scenarios. The cities should, in fact, prepare for total destruction.'

Another pause, then – 'The targeted cities are . . . *New York . . . London . . . Washington . . . Frankfurt*. These cities should prepare for the worst disasters in history. And not a word of this goes public. *Or I attack immediately.*'

Then he was gone again. And he still hadn't given us any deadline.

Chapter Twenty-Four

The President of the United States was up at five-thirty that morning. Unfortunately, he had already been in meetings for almost two hours. He was on his fourth cup of black coffee.

The National Security Council had been in his office since a little past three-thirty. Those present included the heads of the FBI and CIA, plus several Intelligence experts. Everyone was taking the Wolf very seriously.

The President felt he was sufficiently briefed for his *next* challenging meeting, but he could never tell about these things, not for sure, especially when politics came into play in a real emergency situation.

'Let's get this unfortunate circus started. Let's do it,' he finally turned to his Chief of Staff.

A couple of minutes later he was talking with the German Chancellor and the British Prime Minister. They were all on screen, all slightly out-of-synch in the strange land of video-conferencing.

The President found it a little hard to fathom, but none of the countries' Intelligence Services had anything concrete on who the Wolf was, on where he might be living at this time. He said as much to the others.

'Finally, we agree on something,' the German Chancellor said.

'Everyone is aware that he exists, but no one has a clue where he is,' the Prime Minister stated. 'We *think* he's former KGB. We *think* he's in his late forties. But all we *know* is that he's very clever. It's maddening.'

They all agreed on that single fact; and finally they agreed on one other thing.

There could be no negotiations with the terrorist.

Somehow, the Wolf had to be hunted down – and terminated with extreme prejudice.

PART TWO

MISDIRECTIONS

Chapter Twenty-Five

All large cities were becoming the same boring and antiseptic place to the Wolf now, as capitalism and multinational businesses spread everywhere, and major crime followed and spread as well. The Wolf spent part of the night walking in one of the world's most important cities; it didn't matter which one, since the Russian was equally uncomfortable in nearly all of them.

But tonight, he happened to be in Washington, D.C. Plotting next steps.

No one understood the Wolf, not one person in the world. Of course, no one was ever understood by anyone else, were they? Any rational person knew that. But no one could possibly comprehend the Wolf's extraordinary level of paranoia — something burned into his heart long ago, in Paris of all places. Something almost physical — a poison in the system. His

Achilles heel, he suspected. And this paranoia, the *certainty* of an untimely death, led to a passion – not exactly a love of life, but a need to play fiercely at it, to win at all costs, or at the least, *never to lose*.

So the Wolf walked the streets of downtown Washington, and he planned even more murders.

Alone. Always alone. Frequently squeezing his black rubber handball. A good luck charm? Hardly. But ironically, a key to everything about him. *The little black ball.*

Time to think, to plan, to execute, he reminded himself. He was sure that the governments wouldn't listen to his demands – they *couldn't* give in. Not yet; not so easily.

They needed another lesson. Possibly more than one lesson.

And so – a late-night drive out to FBI Director Burns's home in the Washington suburbs.

What a desirable life the man seemed to live with his family. The Wolf genuinely felt that way.

An attractive, well-kept ranch-house – modest enough, consistent with American dreams of a sort. A blue Mercury sedan in the driveway. Bike-rack with three two-wheelers. Basketball hoop with a glass backboard and a bright white half-square above the rim.

Should this family die? A simple enough task to execute. Pleasurable in a way. Richly deserved.

But was it the most effective lesson?

The Wolf wasn't sure. So the answer was probably *no*.

Besides, there was another target to consider.

A grudge to settle.

What could be better than that?

Revenge, a dish best served cold, thought the Wolf, squeezing his rubber ball again and again.

Chapter Twenty-Six

Welcome to the process-obsessed federal government and its completely bizarre way of doing things. That was my mantra lately, something I told myself nearly every time I entered the Hoover Building. And never truer than during these last few days.

What happened next followed the prescribed 'protocol' under a couple of recent Presidential Decision Directives that affected the Bureau. The response to the Wolf would fall into *two* distinct categories: 'Investigation' and 'Consequence Management'. The FBI would oversee the Investigation; the Federal Emergency Management Agency (FEMA) would be in charge of Consequence Management.

Very neat and orderly, and *unworkable*. In my opinion anyway.

Because the threat was to a major US metropolitan area – *two*, actually, New York City and Washington –

the Domestic Emergency Support Team was deployed, and we met with them on the fifth floor of the Hoover Building. I was starting to feel like I worked out of the crisis center; still, it was anything but dull.

The morning's first subject was *threat assessment*. On account of the three bombed towns, we were taking the 'terrorists' very seriously, of course. The discussion was led by the new Deputy Director of the Bureau, a man named Robert Campbell McIllvaine, Jr. The Director had recently talked him out of retirement in California because he was so good at what he did. Some of the talk was about 'false alarms', since there had been many of them in the past couple of years. It was agreed that this *wasn't* a false alarm. Bob McIllvaine was certain of it and that was enough for most of us.

The second topic was 'Consequence Management', so FEMA ran the session. The ability of healthcare providers to deal with a big blast in Washington, New York, or both cities simultaneously, was called into question. The dangers of sudden evacuation was now a major issue since the sheer panic to get out of either city, but especially New York, could kill thousands.

The theoretical but very frank talk that morning was the scariest I'd ever been a part of, and it only got worse. After a thirty-minute lunch – for those with an appetite – and a break for phone calls, we launched into 'Suspect Assessment'.

Who was responsible? Was it the Wolf? The Russian Mob? Could it be some other group? And what did they want?

The initial list of alternatives was long – but it was quickly whittled down to al Qaeda, Hezbollah, the Egyptian Islamic Jihad, or possibly a 'freelance' group operating for profit and maybe working with one of the organized terrorist units.

Finally, the talk turned to 'action steps' to be spear-headed by the Bureau. Both mobile and fixed, or static, surveillance was being set up on several suspects around the US, but also in Europe and the Middle East. We had begun a huge investigation already, one of the largest in history.

All of it against the explicit and very threatening orders given by the Wolf.

Late that evening, I was still going over some of the most recent data that had been collected on Geoffrey Shafer here and in Europe. *Europe?* I wondered. *Is that where this plot is coming from? Maybe England, where Shafer had lived for so many years? Maybe even Russia? Or one of the Russian settlements inside the US?*

I read a few reports about Shafer's years working as a procurer of mercenaries in Africa.

Then something hit me.

When he had traveled back to England recently, he'd used a disguise – he'd come into the country in a wheelchair. He'd apparently traveled around London using the wheelchair disguise. It was also doubtful he knew that *we* knew.

It was a clue, and I put it into the system immediately. I flagged it as something important.

Maybe the Weasel was using a wheelchair in Washington.

And maybe, we were suddenly one step ahead of him, instead of two steps behind.

On that note, I finally called it a night. At least I hoped the day was finally over.

Chapter Twenty-Seven

Very early the following morning, the Weasel made his way through crowded and noisy Union Station in a black, collapsible wheelchair, and he was thinking mostly happy thoughts. He liked to win, and he was winning at every twist and turn.

Geoffrey Shafer had very good military contacts in Washington, D.C., which made him extremely valuable to the operation. He had contacts in London too, one of the other target cities, but that wasn't as important to the Wolf. Still, he was a player again, and he liked the feeling of being somebody.

Besides, he wanted to hurt a lot of people in America. He despised Americans. The Wolf had given him an opportunity to do some real damage here. *Zamochit.* The breaking of bones. *Mass murder.*

Lately, Shafer had been wearing his hair cut short and he'd also dyed it black. He couldn't disguise the

fact that he was six foot two, but he had done something better – actually he'd gotten this idea from an
old associate. During daylight at least, he traveled
around Washington in the wheelchair, a state-of-the-
art model he could easily throw in the back of the
Saab station wagon he was driving. If he was noticed
occasionally – and he was – it was for all of the wrong
reasons.

At six-twenty that morning, Shafer met with a
'contact' inside Union Station. They both got on
a queue – the contact standing behind Shafer – at a
Starbucks. They struck up what appeared to be
a casual conversation.

'They're on the move,' said the contact, who worked
as an assistant to a higher-up in the FBI. 'Nobody
listened to the warnings not to investigate. They've
already moved surveillance into the targeted cities.
They're looking for you here, of course. Agent Cross is
assigned to you.'

'I wouldn't have it any other way,' Shafer said and
smiled crookedly, as he always did. He wasn't surprised about the surveillance. The Wolf had predicted
it. So had he. He stayed on the queue, and bought a
latte. Then he pressed a button and the wheelchair
rolled to a row of pay phones near the railway station's ticket booths. He sipped his hot drink as he
placed a local call.

'I have some scutwork for you. Pays very well,' he

said to the woman who answered. 'Fifty thousand dollars for just an hour or so of your time.'

'Well then, I'm your scut,' said the woman, who happened to be one of the world's very best snipers.

Chapter Twenty-Eight

The meeting with the 'subcontractor' took place just before noon in the food court at the Tysons Corner mall. Colonel Shafer met Captain Nicole Williams at a small table directly across from a Burger King restaurant.

They had burgers and sodas laid out in front of them but neither ate what Shafer referred to as 'godawful Yankee artery cloggers'.

'Nice wheels,' Captain Williams smirked when she saw him arrive in the wheelchair. 'You have no shame, do you?'

'Whatever works, Nikki.' He returned her smile. 'You know me well enough by now. Whatever the job takes, I get it done.'

'Yeah, I know you, Colonel. Anyway, thanks for thinking of me for this.'

'Wait until you hear about the job before you thank me,' he said.

'That's why I'm here. To listen.'

Actually, Shafer was already a little concerned; he was surprised that Nikki Williams had let herself go so much since the last time they'd worked together. He doubted that she was five feet six, but she must weigh close to two hundred pounds now.

Still, Nikki Williams exuded the confidence of a highly skilled professional – which Shafer knew she had always been. They'd worked together for six months in Angola, and Captain Williams was very good at her 'specialty'. She'd always delivered what was asked of her before.

He only told Nikki Williams her part of the job, and repeated the fee, which was fifty thousand dollars for less than an hour's work. The thing he liked best about her was that Nikki never complained about the difficulty of any job, or even its risks.

'What's the *next* step for me? When do we go?' were her only two questions after he had detailed the basics, though not the actual target.

'Tomorrow at one you're to be at Manassas Regional Airport in Virginia. An MD-530 helicopter will set down there at five past the hour. We'll have an HK PSG-1 on board for you.'

Williams frowned and shook her head. 'Unh-uh. If you don't mind, I'll bring my own. I prefer the

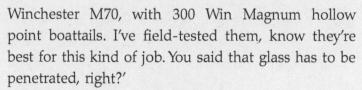
Winchester M70, with 300 Win Magnum hollow point boattails. I've field-tested them, know they're best for this kind of job. You said that glass has to be penetrated, right?'

'Yes, that's right, Captain. You have to shoot into an office building.'

Shafer didn't object to the change in weapons. He had worked with snipers plenty of times, and knew they were always idiosyncratic, had their own peculiar way of doing things. He'd expected modifications from her, and was surprised there weren't more, actually.

'So who's going to die tomorrow?' Nikki Williams finally asked. 'I need to know that of course.'

Shafer told Captain Williams the target, and to her credit, she never raised an eyebrow. Her only reaction was, 'My price just went up. It just doubled.'

Shafer slowly nodded. 'Agreed. That will be just fine, Captain.'

Then Nikki Williams smiled. 'Did I settle too low?'

Shafer nodded again. 'Yes, you did. But I'm going to give you one fifty anyway. Just don't miss him.'

Chapter Twenty-Nine

We might have a decent break in the case — finally *something*, and it had started with a tip from me. The wheelchair! We had a lead.

At ten in the morning, I raced across Washington to the Farragut apartment building on Cathedral Avenue. Three years before, a partner of mine named Patsy Hampton had been murdered in the underground garage of the Farragut. Geoffrey Shafer had killed her. The Farragut was where his old therapist lived.

We'd had Dr Elizabeth Cassady under surveillance for the past thirty-six hours and it seemed to have paid off. *The Weasel had shown up.* He parked in the underground garage near where Patsy had been brutally killed. Then he went upstairs to the penthouse apartment, 10D, where Dr Cassady still lived.

He'd come in a wheelchair!

I boarded an elevator with four other agents. We

had our guns drawn and ready. 'He's extremely dangerous. Please take what I'm saying very seriously,' I reminded them as we stepped from the elevator on the therapist's floor.

It had been painted since the last time I was there. So much of this was familiar, hauntingly so. I was getting angry all over again about Patsy Hampton's death, about the Weasel.

I pressed the bell at 10D.

Then I called out, 'FBI, open the door. FBI, Dr Cassady.'

The door opened, and I was staring at a tall, attractive blonde woman whom I recognized.

Elizabeth Cassady recognized me too. 'Dr Cross,' she said. 'What a surprise. Well no, not really it isn't.'

As she spoke I heard a wheelchair rolling up behind her. I raised my gun, pushing Dr Cassady out of the way.

I aimed my weapon!

'Stop right there! Stop!' I shouted.

The wheelchair, and the man seated in it, came into full view. I shook my head and slowly lowered the gun. I held back a curse. I smelled a rat, or should I say, a Weasel.

The man in the wheelchair spoke. 'I'm obviously *not* Colonel Geoffrey Shafer. Nor have I met him. I'm a stage actor named Francis Nicolo, and I *am* physically impaired so no rough treatment, please.

'I was told to come here and I am being paid handsomely to do so. I was instructed to tell you that the colonel says hello, and that you should have listened to the explicit instructions you were given. Since you are here, you *didn't* listen.'

The man in the wheelchair then bowed from the waist. 'That's my part, my *piece*. It's all I know. How was my performance? Acceptable? You may applaud if you wish.'

'You're under arrest,' I told him. Then I turned to Elizabeth Cassady. 'So are you. Where is he? Where's Shafer?'

She shook her head and looked incredibly sad. 'I haven't seen Geoffrey in years. I'm being used, and so are you. Of course for me it's harder – I loved him. I strongly suggest that you get used to it. This is how his mind works, and I should know.'

So should I, I was thinking. *So should I.*

Chapter Thirty

This is impressive, thought Captain Nikki Williams. *And not the airfield meeting itself. The whole plan was dazzling. Audacious.*

Manassas Regional was a small, nondescript airport, spread over eight hundred acres, with two parallel runways. There was a Main Terminal building and an FAA Control Tower, but it was a very good spot for the mission.

Somebody is really thinking things through. This is going to work.

A couple of minutes after Captain Williams arrived at the airfield, she saw her helicopter setting down. She had two instant notions: *Where the hell had these people gotten an MD-530?* And – *It was just right for the job she'd been given.*

This was definitely going to work. It might not even be that hairy.

Nikki Williams hurried to the helicopter, and she was carrying the Winchester M70 in a cloth sling-bag. The pilot had the other critical puzzle pieces for her. He was apparently the man with the final plan.

'I'm all fueled. We're headed northeast, over Route 28. I'm gonna set down for half a minute or so in Rock Creek Park,' he told her.

'Rock Creek Park? I don't follow,' Captain Williams said. 'Why would you put down again once we're airborne?'

'The Park stop is just to get you up on the skid. That's your position for the hit. All right with you?'

'Perfect,' Williams said. 'I get it now.'

The scheme was daring, but it made sense to her. Everything about it did. They had even picked an overcast day with very slight winds. The MD-530 was fast and highly maneuverable. It was also stable enough to shoot from. In her Army days, she'd fired thousands of rounds from them in all kinds of weather, and practice made perfect.

'You ready?' the pilot called back once she was on board. 'We're going to be in and out of D.C. in less than nine minutes.'

Williams gave it a thumbs-up, and the MD-530 corkscrewed up fast, flew northeast, and was soon crossing the Potomac. It never got higher than thirty to forty feet off the ground, and was traveling at about eighty knots.

The helicopter set down for less than forty seconds in Rock Creek Park.

Captain Williams took a position on the right skid, behind and just below the pilot. Then she signaled for him to lift off. 'Let's go. Let's do it.'

Not only is this smart, it is cool as hell, she couldn't help thinking as the helicopter took off again – and closed on her target. *In and out of harm's way in less than nine minutes. He'll never know what hit him.*

Chapter Thirty-One

I was back at my desk before noon, feeling edgy and ragged, tapping into the National Crime Information Center computer database, drinking about a gallon of black coffee – which was the worst thing to do. *The goddamn Weasel – he knew we had found out about the wheelchair. But how? They had somebody inside, didn't they? Somebody had warned Shafer.*

At around one, I was still at my desk when a shrill, ear-splitting alarm sounded in the building.

At the same time my pager signaled a *terrorist alert.*

I heard loud voices up and down the hall. 'Look out your window! Go to your window, quick!'

'Oh good God! What the hell are they doing down there?' somebody else yelled.

I took a look outside, and was stunned to see two men in fatigues running across the pink granite cobblestone of the inner courtyard. They were just passing the bronze sculpture, *Fidelity, Bravery, Integrity*.

My first wild thought was that the men might be human bombs. How else could just two of them hope to damage the building or anybody inside?

An agent named Charlie Kilvert, from next door, peeked his head inside. 'You catching this, Alex? You believe it?'

'I see it. I don't believe it.'

I couldn't take my eyes off the action down in the courtyard, though. Within seconds, heavily armed security agents had appeared on the scene.

At first there were only three guards, then at least a dozen. The guards from the sidewalk booth suddenly came tearing up the driveway, too.

All of the guards below had their guns pointed at the two men in fatigues. Both of them had stopped running now. They appeared to be surrendering.

The agents weren't coming any closer, though. Maybe they shared my idea about 'human bombs', but more likely, they were following procedure.

The suspects were holding their arms high over their heads. Then, slowly and deliberately, they lay flat on their stomachs. What the hell?

Then I spotted a helicopter drift around the south side of the Hoover Building. Just about all I could see was the nose and rotor.

The ominous hovering of the 'copter caused the agents in the courtyard to aim their weapons into the sky. This was a 'no fly' zone, after all. The agents on the ground were yelling and threatening with their guns.

Then the helicopter banked sharply away from the Hoover Building. It disappeared from sight.

Seconds later, Charlie Kilvert was in the doorway again. 'Somebody's been shot upstairs!'

I almost knocked Charlie over, getting out the door.

Chapter Thirty-Two

The MD-530 was really moving as it got to Washington; the pilot was using office and apartment buildings for cover now, sliding between them like somebody playing the craziest game of hide-and-seek.

The flying tactics would avoid radar detectors and also confuse the hell out of casual observers, Nikki Williams figured. Besides, this was all happening incredibly fast. No one would be able to react – and an Air Force jet wouldn't fly in this close to these office buildings anyway.

She could see the target now. Hot damn! The disturbance on the ground had been planned and lots of people were at their windows at the target building – which she knew was FBI headquarters. *This was really something!* She loved it! There had been some major league action while she was in the Army, but not enough of it, and there were always a thousand rules you were supposed to follow.

Only one rule now, baby: shoot this guy dead and get the hell out of Dodge before anybody can do a goddamn thing about it.

The pilot had the coordinates on the targeted window and sure enough – two men in dark suits were standing there looking down on the street action – the diversion built into the plan. Captain Williams knew what her target looked like, and by the time he saw her rifle – only a hundred feet away – he'd be dead and she'd be on her way out of there.

One of the men behind the window appeared to shout a warning, and tried to push the other one away. Quite the hero.

No matter – Williams pulled the trigger. *Easy does it.* Then – escape!

The helicopter pilot used the same flying technique for exfil and headed directly to the drop zone in Virginia. It took just three and a half minutes from the FBI building all the way out to the drop area. Nikki Williams was still buzzing from the shot and kill, not to mention the big fee she'd be getting. Double fee, and God knows, she was worth every penny.

The helicopter set down easily and she jumped down off the skid. She flipped a salute to the pilot, and he reached out his right arm toward her – and *shot her twice*, once in the throat, once in the forehead. The pilot didn't like it, but he did it. Those were his orders, and he knew enough to obey them. The female sniper had apparently told someone else about her mission. The pilot knew nothing more than that.

Just his *piece* of the big picture.

Chapter Thirty-Three

This much we knew.

The two men captured down in the courtyard had been hustled inside the FBI building and were now being held on the second floor. But who the hell were they?

The serious rumor circulating was that Ron Burns had been shot – and that my boss and my friend was dead.

Sources had it that a successful sniper attack had been made and that Burns's office was the target. I couldn't help thinking of the assassination of Stacy Pollack earlier that year. The Wolf had never actually taken responsibility for the murder of the head of SIOC, but we knew he was the one who ordered it. Burns vowed revenge, though none had been taken. Not to my knowledge anyway.

About a half-hour after the sniper attack, I got a call

to go down to the second floor. That was good – I needed to do *something* or go crazy in my office.

'Anything on the shooting upstairs?' I asked the ACAS who called me.

'Nothing I know of. We've heard the rumors, too. No one will deny or confirm anything. I spoke to Tony Woods in the Director's office, and he won't say anything. Nobody's talking, Alex. Sorry, man.'

'Something happened, though? Somebody got shot?'

'Yeah. Somebody got shot up there.'

Feeling sick about everything that had happened in the last few days, I hurried down to the second floor and was led, by a guard, to a row of holding cells I hadn't even known existed. The agent who met me explained that he wanted me to conduct the interview without a briefing, to get my take on the prisoners.

I walked into one of the small interview rooms and found two scared-looking black men dressed in cammies. Terrorists? That was doubtful. They looked to be in their mid-thirties, maybe early-forties, but it was hard to tell. They needed haircuts and shaves, their clothes were soiled, wrinkled, and the room already stank with perspiration and worse.

'We already tol' our story,' one of the men screwed up his wrinkled face and complained bitterly as I entered the room. 'How many times we got to tell y'all?'

I sat down across from the two of them. 'This is a *homicide* investigation,' I said. I didn't know whether they'd been told that, but it was where I wanted to start. 'Somebody is dead upstairs.'

The man who hadn't spoken yet covered his face with his hands and started to moan and sway from side to side. 'Oh no, oh no, oh, God no,' he groaned.

'Take your hands away from your face and listen to me!' I yelled at him.

Both men looked at me. They shut up; now they were listening at least.

'I want to hear your story. Everything you know, every single detail. And I don't care that you told it before. You hear me? *You understand?* I don't care how many times you think you told it. Right now, you two are murder suspects. So I want to hear your side of things. Talk to me. I am your lifeline, your only lifeline. Now *talk*.'

They did. Both of them. They rambled, incoherently at times, but they talked. A little more than two hours later I left the interview room feeling that I'd heard the whole truth, at least their sketchy version of it.

Ron Frazier and Leonard Pickett were drifters who lived near Union Station. Both were Army veterans. They'd been hired off the street to run around the FBI Building like the crazies that they probably were in real life. The camouflage outfits were theirs, the same clothes they said they wore every day in the park and panhandling on the streets of D.C.

Next, I went into another interviewing room to brief two very senior agents from upstairs. They looked about as tense as I felt. I wondered what they knew about Ron Burns?

'I don't think those two know much of anything,' I told them. 'They may have been approached by Geoffrey Shafer. Whoever hired them had an English accent. The physical description fits Shafer. And whoever it was paid them all of two hundred bucks. Two hundred dollars to do what they did.'

I looked across at the senior agents. 'Your turn. Tell me what happened upstairs. Who was shot? Is it Ron Burns?'

One of the two agents, Millard, took a deep breath, then spoke. 'This doesn't go out of the room, Alex. Not until we say so. Understood?'

I nodded solemnly. 'Is the Director dead?'

'Thomas Weir is dead. Weir is the one who was shot,' said Agent Millard.

Suddenly I felt weak-kneed and woozy. *Somebody had killed the Director of the CIA.*

Chapter Thirty-Four

C haos.

Once word got out about the murder of Thomas Weir, it was on every TV channel and the press corps began to circle the Hoover Building. Of course nobody could tell them what we thought had really happened, and every reporter knew in their gut we were holding back information.

Later that afternoon we'd learned that the body of a woman had been found in the woods of northern Virginia. We believed that she might have been the sniper who killed Tom Weir. A Winchester M70 rifle was found with the body and it was almost definitely the murder weapon.

At five o'clock the Wolf made contact again.

The phone in the crisis room rang. Ron Burns himself picked up.

I had never seen the Director look graver, and

more vulnerable. Thomas Weir had been a friend of his; the Weir and Burns families went on vacations to Nantucket in the summertime.

The Wolf began, 'You're an extraordinarily lucky man, Director. Those bullets were meant for you. I don't make many mistakes, but I also know they're inevitable in a military operation this complex. I accept that mistakes happen in any war. It's simply a fact of life.'

Burns said nothing. His face was expressionless, a pale mask, impossible to read, even by any of us.

The Wolf continued, 'I understand how you're feeling, how all of you are feeling. Mr Weir was a *family man*, yes? Basically a decent human being? So now you're angry at me. You want to put me down like a mad dog. But think about it from my perspective. You were told the rules and you still chose to go your own way.

'As you can see now, your way led to disaster and death. It always will lead to disaster and death. It's inevitable. And the stakes are much higher than just a single life. So let's move on. The clock is ticking.

'You know, it's difficult to find people today who will listen. Everyone is so self-absorbed these days. Take Captain Williams, for example, our assassin. She was instructed not to tell anyone about the job she was hired to do, but she told her husband. Now she's dead. I understand that you found the body. News flash: the husband is dead too. You might want to retrieve the body at their home. It's in Denton, Maryland. Do you need an address? I can help with that.'

Burns spoke. 'We already found her husband's body. What's the point of your call? What do you want from us?'

'I should think it would be obvious, Mr Director. I want you to know that I mean exactly what I say. I expect compliance, and I will get it. One way or the other, I will get my way. I always do.

'So, that having been said, let me give you the gory details – the numbers. Our price *to go away*. I hope someone has a pencil and paper?'

'Go ahead,' said Burns.

'All right, here we go then.

'New York, *six hundred fifty million US dollars*. London, *six hundred million. In dollars*. Washington, *four hundred fifty million*. Frankfurt, *four hundred fifty million*. A grand total of two billion, one hundred and fifty million US dollars. *Plus*. There are fifty-seven political prisoners I want released. You will be provided with the names in the next hour. For what it's worth, all of the prisoners are from the Middle East. *You* figure it out. Interesting puzzle, don't you think?

'You have four days to deliver the money *and* the prisoners. That's plenty of time, no? More than fair? You'll be told how and where. You have four days from . . . right . . . *now.*

'And yes, I'm perfectly serious. I also realize I'm asking for a great deal of money, and that it will be deemed "impossible" to raise. I expect to hear as much. But don't bother with the excuses or the whining.'

There was a short pause.

'That's the fucking *point* of the call, Mr Burns. Deliver the money. Deliver the prisoners. Don't mess up again. Oh, and I suppose there is one other thing. I don't forgive and forget. You *are* going to die before this is over, Director Burns. So keep looking over your shoulder. One of these days, I'll be there. And *boom*! But for right now – *four days!*'

Then the Wolf hung up.

Ron Burns stared straight ahead and spoke through clenched teeth, 'You've got that right, *boom!* One of these days, I'll be there for you.'

Then Burns's eyes slowly went around the room, and stopped at me. 'We're on the clock, Alex.'

Chapter Thirty-Five

Burns went on, 'I'd like Dr Cross to give us his impressions of the Russian maniac. He knows all about him. For those of you who don't know Alex Cross, he came to us from the Washington PD. Their loss, believe me. He's the man who put Kyle Craig away.'

'And who let Geoffrey Shafer escape, once or twice,' I spoke up from my seat. 'My impressions so far? Well, I won't belabor the obvious too much. There's his need for complete control and power. I can tell you this: he wants to do things on a large scale, work on a big stage. He's a creative, obsessive planner. He's an "executive type", meaning that he organizes, delegates well, doesn't have problems making difficult decisions.

'But most of all – he's vicious. He likes to hurt people. He likes to *watch* people get hurt. He's giving us plenty of time to think about what could happen.

That's partly because he knows we won't, *can't* pay him easily. But also because he's preying on our minds. He knows how hard it will be to catch him. Bin Laden is still free, isn't he?

'I'll tell you what *doesn't* track for me – the assassination attempt on the Director. I don't see how it fits his pattern. Not this early in the game anyway. And I especially don't like it that he missed, that he failed.'

The words came out wrong and I looked at Burns, but he waved me off. 'Do you think he missed? Or was Tom Weir the real target?' he asked.

'My guess . . . Weir was the target. I don't think the Wolf made a mistake. Not one this big. I do think he lied about what happened.'

'Any idea why? Anybody?' Burns glanced around the room.

No one spoke up, so I continued. 'If Director Weir *was* the target, it's the best clue we have. Why would Thomas Weir be a significant threat to the Wolf? What could he have known? I wouldn't be surprised if Weir and the Wolf knew one another from somewhere, even if Weir wasn't aware of it. Weir is important. But where would Thomas Weir have come across the Russian? That's a question we need to ask.'

'And then answer in a hurry,' said Burns. 'Let's get on it. Everybody, and I mean everybody, in the Bureau!'

Chapter Thirty-Six

The man who had made the most recent phone calls for the Wolf had his instructions and he knew enough to follow them very precisely. He was to be *seen* in Washington. That was his 'piece'.

The Wolf was to be seen, which would definitely cause a stir. Wouldn't it?

The phone call he'd made to FBI headquarters and elsewhere would soon be traced to the Four Seasons Hotel on Pennsylvania Avenue. It was part of the current plan, and the plan had been nearly flawless thus far.

So he calmly walked down to the hotel lobby and made certain he was noticed at the concierge desk and also by the couple of doormen out front. It helped that he was tall, blond, bearded, and wore a long cashmere coat. All according to the plan he'd been given.

Then he took a leisurely stroll along M Street,

checking out restaurant menus in the front window, and the latest fashions of Georgetown.

He found it somewhat comical that he could actually see police cruisers, and the FBI, as they sped toward the Four Seasons Hotel from several directions.

Finally, the man stepped into a white Chevy van that was waiting for him at the corner of M and Thomas Jefferson.

The van sped away in the direction of the airport. In addition to the driver, there was a second man. He sat in back beside the one who'd made the phone calls from the Four Seasons.

'It went well?' the driver asked once they were a few miles from M Street and the commotion going on there.

The bearded man shrugged. 'Of course it did. They have an "accurate" description. Something to go on, a little hope, whatever they want to call it. It went perfectly. I did what was asked of me.'

'Excellent,' said the second man. He then pulled out a Beretta and shot the blond man in the right temple. He was brain-dead before he would have heard the explosion.

Now the police and FBI had a physical description of the Wolf – *but no one alive matched it.*

Chapter Thirty-Seven

There was more intrigue, or at least confusion, that afternoon. According to our telecommunications people, the Wolf had called us from the Four Seasons Hotel in D.C. and had been spotted there. The 'description' we had of him was already being sent around the world. It was possible that he'd slipped up, but I didn't know if I could believe it. He'd always called on cell phones before, but this time he used a hotel phone. Why?

I got a surprise when I arrived home at a little before nine-thirty that night. Dr Kayla Coles was in the living room with Nana. The two of them were huddled together on the sofa, conspiring about God only knew what. I was a little concerned that Nana's doctor was there so late in the evening.

'Everything okay?' I asked. 'What's going on?'

'Kayla was in the neighborhood. She just stopped

by,' Nana answered. 'Isn't that right, Dr Coles? No problems that I know of. Except you missed supper.'

'Well, actually,' Kayla spoke up, 'Nana was feeling a little faint again. So I stopped by as a precaution.'

'Now, Kayla, don't exaggerate, please. Let's not get carried away,' Nana scolded in her usual way. 'I'm just fine. Fainting's just a part of my life now.'

Kayla nodded and smiled pleasantly. Then she sighed out loud, and leaned back on the couch. 'I'm sorry. You tell it, Nana.'

'I felt a little faint a few days *last* week. As you know, Alex – no big thing. If we still had Alex Junior around to take care of, then maybe I would be more concerned.'

'Well, I'm concerned,' I said.

Kayla smiled and shook her head. 'Right. Like Nana said, I was in the neighborhood and I just stopped by, Alex. Strictly social. I did take her blood pressure. Everything seems to be in working order. However, I would like her to go for a few blood tests.'

'Fine, I'll go for tests,' said Nana. 'Let's talk about the weather now.'

I shook my head. At both of them. '*You* still working too hard?' I asked Kayla.

'Look who's talking,' she said, then smiled brightly. Kayla had tremendous spirit and could always light up a room. 'Unfortunately, there's too much work to do around here. Don't get me started about the number of people in the *capital* of this wealthy nation of ours who can't begin to afford to see a good doctor, or who wait for hours and hours at St Anthony's and several other hospitals I could name around this town.'

I had always liked Kayla, and maybe, to be honest, I was even a little intimidated by her. *Why was that?* I wondered as we talked. I noticed that she'd lost some weight, what with all her running around and do-gooding in the neighborhood and elsewhere. The truth was, she looked better than ever. I almost felt embarrassed to have noticed.

'What are you standing there gawking at?' Nana asked. 'Sit down and join us.'

'I have to go,' Kayla said, and stood up from the couch. 'It is late, even for me.'

'Don't let me break up the party,' I protested. Suddenly, I didn't want Kayla to leave. I wanted to talk about something other than the Wolf and the terror attacks that had been threatened.

'You're not breaking up the party, Alex. Wouldn't happen. But I still have two more house calls to make.'

I looked at my watch. 'Two more calls at this hour? You're something else. Wow. You're crazy, you know that?' I grinned.

'Maybe I am,' Kayla said and shrugged. 'Probably true.' Then she kissed Nana with obvious affection. 'You take care. Blood tests – don't forget.'

'My memory is *fine*.'

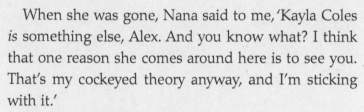

When she was gone, Nana said to me, 'Kayla Coles *is* something else, Alex. And you know what? I think that one reason she comes around here is to see you. That's my cockeyed theory anyway, and I'm sticking with it.'

The thought had occurred to me too. 'Then why does she leave so fast when I get here?'

Nana frowned and raised an eyebrow at me. 'Maybe it's because you never ask her to stay. Maybe it's because you gawk at her when she's here. Why is that? You know, she just could be the one for you. Don't argue with me. She scares you, and that might be a good thing.'

I thought about it, and I didn't have a response. It had been a long day and my brain wasn't firing on all cylinders right now. 'So you're okay?' I asked Nana. 'You're sure you're feeling all right?'

'Alex, I'm eighty-three years old. More or less. How okay can I be?' she said. Then Nana kissed me on the cheek and headed off to bed.

'You're not getting any younger yourself,' she turned and chirped over her shoulder.

Good one, Nana.

Chapter Thirty-Eight

Not everyone was heading off to bed. The night was still young in some quarters.

The Weasel had never been any good at controlling his so-called baser desires and physical needs. This fact scared him sometimes because it was an obvious weakness and vulnerability, but it also turned him on. The danger, the adrenaline rush. Actually, it made him feel more alive than anything else in his life did. When he went for the kill, he felt so good, so powerful, that it took over everything and he lost himself completely in the moment.

Shafer knew Washington, D.C., very well from his earlier posting at the British Embassy, and he knew the poorer sections, because it was where he had most often hunted in the past.

The Weasel was *hunting* tonight. And he was feeling alive again, like his life had a purpose.

He drove a black Mercury Cougar along South Capitol. A cool drizzle was falling, and there were only a couple of skanks walking the streets. But one of the girls had already caught his eye.

He cruised around the block a couple of times, checking her out in the most obvious ways, playing at being a john.

He finally slowed the Cougar beside a petite black girl showing off her wares near the Hot Nation night-club. She wore a silver bustier, matching short skirt, and platform heels.

The very best part: *he had been instructed to go hunting in Washington tonight. He was following orders from the Wolf. Just doing his job.*

The young black girl thrust her chest forward pro-vocatively as he leaned across the front seat to talk to her. She probably thought that her pert young nipples put her in control of the situation. This encounter would be interesting, he was thinking. Shafer had on a wig tonight, and he had colored his face and hands black. A dumb old rock tune was playing inside his head: *The name of the song is 'I Like It Like That'.*

'Those real?' he asked as the girl leaned in close.

'Last time I checked they were. Maybe you should touch for yourself? You interested in a feel? It could be arranged, you know. A private tour, just for you, darlin'.'

Shafer smiled pleasantly, playing the game too, the

street hustle. If she'd noticed he was wearing black-face, the girl wasn't letting on. Nothing bothered this one, did it? Well, we'd see about that.

'Hop in,' he said. 'I'd like to check you out. Breast to toe, as it were.'

'It's a hundred,' she said and suddenly stood back from the car. 'Y'okay with that? 'Cause if you're not . . .'

Shafer continued to smile. 'If they're real, a hundred is fine. It won't be a problem.'

The girl opened the door and hopped into the car. She was wearing way too much perfume. 'See for yourself, sweetheart. They're kind of small-like, but they're *soooo* nice. And they're all yours.'

Shafer laughed again. 'You know, I like you a great deal. Remember what you said, though. I'll hold you to it.' *They're all mine.*

Chapter Thirty-Nine

I was on duty again at midnight, and I felt like I was back in Homicide. I arrived in a familiar neighborhood that was mostly white clapboard row houses, many of them deserted, on New Jersey Avenue in Southeast. A crowd had already gathered at the murder scene, including some local gang members, and little kids on bikes still up at that late hour.

A man in a Rastafarian hat full with dreadlocks was shouting at the police from behind the yellow crime-scene tape. 'Hey, ya hear dat music?' he called in a loopy, wheezy voice. 'Ya like dat music? Dat mah people music.'

Sampson met me outside one of the dilapidated row houses and we went in together.

'Just like the bad old times,' John said. 'That why you're here, Dragonslayer? Are you nostalgic for the old days? Want to come back to the Washington PD?'

I nodded and gestured around. 'Yeah. I missed this. Bad homicide scenes in the middle of the night.'

'Bet you do, too. I would.'

The building where the body had been found was boarded up in front but it was easy enough for us to get inside. There was *no front door*.

'This is Alex Cross,' Sampson said to the patrolmen standing just outside the open doorway. 'You heard of him? This is *the* Alex Cross, brother.'

'Dr Cross,' said the man as he stepped aside to let us enter.

'Gone,' said John Sampson, 'but not forgotten.'

Once we were in, the scene was sadly familiar and reprehensible. Garbage was strewn in the hallways and the smell of decaying food and urine was overpowering. Maybe it was because I hadn't been inside one of these vacated rat traps in a while, over a year now.

We were told that the body was on the top floor, the third, so Sampson and I began to climb.

'Dumping grounds,' he muttered.

'Yeah, I know. I remember the drill pretty well.'

'At least we don't have to visit the goddamn basement,' Sampson grumped. 'So, *why* did you say you're here? I didn't catch that part.'

'I just missed hanging with you. Nobody calls me Sugar any more.'

'Uh-huh. You Feebies aren't into nicknames? So why are you here, *Sugar*?'

Sampson and I had made our way to the third floor. There were Washington PD uniforms everywhere up there. This really was déjà vu, *all over again*. I put on plastic gloves and so did Sampson. I did miss working with him and sadly, this brought it all home, the good and the bad.

We stopped outside the second door on the right – just as a young black patrolman was leaving. He had his hand over his mouth, a white handkerchief wrapped over the fist. I think he was going to be sick any second. That part doesn't change either.

'Hope he didn't barf all over our crime scene,' Sampson said. 'Goddamn rookies.'

Then we went inside. 'Oh man,' I muttered. You see things like this over and over in Homicide, but you never get used to it, and you don't forget the details, the sensations, the smells, the taste it leaves in your mouth.

'He called it in to us first,' I told Sampson. 'That's why I'm here.'

'Who's *he*?' he asked.

'You tell me,' I said.

We walked over closer to the body that lay on the bare wooden floor. Young woman, probably still in her teens. Petite, pretty enough. Naked except for one platform hanging off the toes of her left foot. Golden ankle charm on her right foot. Her hands were tied behind her back with what looked like plastic cable. A black plastic bag had been stuffed inside her mouth.

I'd seen this kind of murder before, exactly this kind. So had Sampson.

'Prostitute,' Sampson sighed. 'Patrolmen seen her around on South Capitol. Eighteen, nineteen years old, maybe even younger. So who is *he*?'

It looked to me as if the girl's breasts had been sliced right off her chest. Her face had been attacked too. A checklist of deviant behavior ran through my head, the kind of things I hadn't thought about for a while: expressive aggression (*check*), sadism (*check*), sexualization (*check*), offense planning (*check*). *Check, check, check.*

'It's Shafer, John. It's the Weasel. He's back in Washington. But that's not the worst of it. I wish to hell it was.'

Chapter Forty

We knew a bar that was open and Sampson and I went for a beer after we left the slaughter scene on New Jersey Avenue. We were officially off-duty, but I had my beeper clipped on. So did John. There were only two other guys drinking in the gin mill, so we pretty much had the place to ourselves.

Didn't matter one way or the other. It was just good to be with John. I needed to talk to him. I *really* needed to talk to him about something.

'You sure it's Shafer?' he asked me, once we had our beers and some nuts in front of us. I told him about the disturbing tape I'd seen from Sunrise Valley, Nevada. But not about the other threats, or the ransom. I couldn't, and that bothered me a lot. I'd never lied to Sampson and this felt like a lie.

'It's him. No doubt about it.'

'That's messed up,' John said. 'The Weasel. Why

would he come back to Washington? He almost got caught here the last time.'

'Maybe that's why. The thrill of it, the challenge.'

'Yeah, and maybe he misses us. I won't miss *him* this time. Put one right between his eyes.'

I sipped my beer. 'Shouldn't you be home with Billie?' I asked.

'It's a work night. Billie is cool with it, with my job. Her sister's staying with us for a while anyway. They're both asleep by now.'

'How's that working out? Married life? Billie's sister at the house?'

'I like Trina, so it's okay. Funny, things I couldn't imagine getting used to aren't a problem. I'm happy. First time, maybe. Floatin' on a cloud, man.'

I grinned at Sampson. 'Ain't love grand?'

'Yes, it is. You ought to try it again sometime.'

'I'm ready,' I said and smiled.

'You think so? I wonder about that. Are you really ready?'

'Listen, John, there's something I need to talk to you about.'

'Figured that out already. Something about those bombings. Then the murder of Thomas Weir. Shafer back in town.' Sampson looked into my eyes. 'So what is it?'

'This is confidential, John. They've made a threat against Washington. It's pretty serious. We've been warned about an attack. They demanded a huge ransom to stop it.'

'Which can't be paid?' Sampson asked. 'The United States doesn't negotiate with terrorists.'

'I don't know that. I'm not sure if anybody does, except maybe the President. I'm on the inside, but not that far inside. Anyway, now you know as much as I do.'

'And I should act accordingly.'

'Yeah, you should. But you can't talk about this to anybody. Not to anyone, not even Billie.'

Sampson took my hand. 'I got it. Thank you.'

Chapter Forty-One

On the way home late that night I was guilt-tripping and a little shaky about what I'd told Sampson, but I felt I'd had no choice. John was my family, simple as that. Also, maybe I was on burn-out because we were working eighteen- and twenty-hour days. Maybe the stress was getting to me. There was a lot of disaster planning going on behind the scenes, but nobody I talked to knew where we were on the ransom demands. Everybody's nerves were frayed, including mine. About twelve hours were gone on our four-day deadline.

Other questions burned in my mind. Was Shafer the one who had murdered and maimed the woman we'd found on New Jersey Avenue? I was almost sure he was; and Sampson agreed. But why commit that type of grisly murder now? Why risk it? I sure as hell doubted it was a coincidence that the young woman's

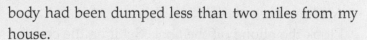

body had been dumped less than two miles from my house.

It was late and I wanted to think about something else, anything else, but I couldn't get my head off the case. I drove the old Porsche faster than I needed to on the mostly empty streets, knowing I had to focus on the driving. It didn't really work too well though.

I pulled into my driveway and sat in the car for a few minutes. I tried to clear my head before I went inside. *Things to do*. I needed to give Jamilla a call – it was only eleven on the coast. I felt like my head was ready to explode though. And I knew when I'd felt this way before – *the last time the Weasel went on a killing spree in Washington*. Only this was so much worse.

I finally trudged inside the house – past the old piano on the sun porch. I thought about sitting down and playing. A little blues? Broadway? At two in the morning? Sure, why not. I couldn't sleep anyway.

The phone began to ring and I ran to get it. *Awhh Jesus, who the hell?*

I snatched up the phone on the kitchen wall near the fridge.

'Hello? Cross.'

Nothing.

And then a hang-up.

Seconds later, the phone rang again. I picked up after one ring.

Another hang-up.

And another after that.

I took the phone off the hook. Set it on the counter inside Nana's oven mitt to muffle the sound.

I heard a noise behind me and I turned around quickly.

Nana was standing there in the doorway, all five foot, ninety-five pounds of her. Her brown eyes were fired up.

'What's wrong, Alex? What are you doing up?' she asked. 'This isn't right. Who's calling the house this late at night?'

I sat down at the kitchen table, and over some tea, I told Nana everything that I could.

Chapter Forty-Two

The next day, I was paired off with Monnie Donnelley, which was good news for both of us. Our assignment was to gather information on Colonel Shafer and the mercenaries being used in the attacks; our timetable – *fast, incredibly fast*.

Monnie, as usual, already knew a lot on the subject, and she talked nonstop while she retrieved even more data for the case. Once Monnie gets going, it's difficult to get her to stop, almost impossible. The woman is relentless about *facts* being the way to *truth*.

'Mercenaries, the "dogs of war", so-called. They are mostly former soldiers from Special Forces – Delta Force, Army Rangers, SEALs, SAS if they're Brits. Many are totally legit, Alex, though they operate in a kind of legal netherworld. What I mean is that they aren't subject to the US military's code of conduct or even our laws. Technically, they're subject to the laws of the countries where they serve, but some of those hot spots have piss-poor judicial systems, if they have any system at all.'

'So they're pretty much on their own. That would appeal to Shafer. Most mercenaries work for private companies now?'

Monnie nodded. 'Yes they do, grasshopper. Private military companies, PMCs. Earn as much as twenty thousand a month. Average probably closer to three or four. Some of the larger PMCs have their own artillery, tanks. Even fighter jets if you can believe that.'

'I can believe it. These days, I can believe anything. Hell, I even believe in the Big Bad Wolf.'

Monnie turned away from her computer screen and looked at me. I sensed that one of her infamous 'stats' was on the way. 'Alex, the Defense Department currently has over three thousand contracts with US-based PMCs. These contracts are valued at over three hundred billion dollars. You believe *that*?'

I whistled. 'Well, that sort of puts the Wolf's demands in perspective, doesn't it?'

'Pay the man,' said Monnie. '*Then* we'll go catch him.'

'It's not my call. But I don't entirely disagree. At least that could be a plan.'

Monnie went back to her computer. 'Here's a tidbit on the Weasel. Worked with an outfit called Mainforce International. Listen to this – offices in London,

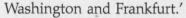

Washington and Frankfurt.'

That got my attention. 'Three of the targeted cities. What else do you have on Mainforce?'

'Let me see . . . Clients include financial institutions, oil of course, precious stones.'

'Diamonds?'

'Are a mercenary's best friend. Shafer was going under the name Timothy Heath. Worked in Guinea to "free" some mines taken over by "the populace". Heath/Shafer was arrested in Guinea, charged with trying to bribe local officials. He had a *million pounds* on him, cash, when he was arrested.'

'How did he get out of that one?'

'Says he *escaped*. Hmmm. No detail. No follow-up either. Odd.'

'That's one thing the Weasel's always been good at. Wiggling out of tight spots. Getting away with it. Maybe that's why the Wolf wanted him for this job.'

'No,' said Monnie and she turned and stared into my eyes. 'The Wolf wanted him because Geoffrey Shafer has gotten under your skin. And because you're close to the Director of the FBI.'

Chapter Forty-Three

At two that same afternoon, I was on my way to Cuba, Guantánamo Bay. Gitmo, as it's called. I was on a mission from the Director, and also the President of the United States. Lately, our base at Guantánamo Bay has been much in the news on account of over seven hundred 'detainees' being held there in connection with the war on terror. It's an interesting place, to say the least. An historical one, for better or worse.

Once I landed, I was escorted to Camp Delta, the site of most of the cellblocks. All around the prison area were several guard-towers and razor wire. According to a rumor I'd heard on the ride down, one US corporation was receiving in excess of a hundred million dollars a year for services provided at Guantánamo Bay.

The man I was here for was originally from Saudi

Arabia. He was being kept in the small psych ward, which was in a separate building from the cellblocks. I wasn't given his name. Nor was I told very much about him, except that he had important information about the Wolf.

I met with the prisoner inside a 'quiet room', an isolation cell with mattresses on the walls and no windows. Two small chairs had been brought into the room for the purpose of the interview.

'I've told the others everything I know,' he said to me in very good English. 'I thought that we made a deal for my release. I was promised as much two days ago. Everybody here lies. *So who are you?'*

'I was sent down here from Washington to listen to your story. Just tell me everything again. This can only help you. It can't hurt.'

The prisoner nodded wearily. 'No, nothing can hurt me any more. It's true. You know, I have been here two hundred and twenty-seven days. I did not do anything wrong. Not a single thing. I was teaching high school in Newark, New Jersey. I have never been charged with anything. What do you think of that?'

'I think you have a way out of here now. Just tell me what you know about the Russian who goes by the name Wolf.'

'And *why* do I talk to you? I think I may have missed that part. Who are you, again?'

I shrugged. I'd been told not to reveal who I was to

the prisoner. 'You have everything to gain, nothing to lose. You want to get out of here and I can help you achieve your goal.'

'But will you, sir?'

'I will help you if I can.'

So the man talked to me. In fact, he went on for over an hour and a half. His life had been interesting, to say the least. He had worked in security for the Royal Family in Saudi Arabia, and sometimes traveled with them in the United States. He liked what he saw here and decided to stay, but he still had friends back home who worked in security.

'They told me about a Russian who had talks with dissident Royal Family members, of whom there are many. This Russian was looking for capital to finance a big operation that would seriously hurt the United States as well as certain countries in Western Europe. A Doomsday scenario was discussed, though I don't have specifics.'

'Do you have a name for the Russian? Where was the man from? What country, what city?'

'This is the most interesting thing,' said the prisoner. 'The Russian — it is my impression it was a woman, not a man. I am confident about my information. The code-name or whatever, was definitely Wolf.

'Now what?' the prisoner asked when he was finished talking. 'Will you help me?'

'No, now you *repeat* your story,' I said. 'From the top.'

'It will be the same,' he said. *'Because it is the truth.'*

Late that night I left Gitmo for Washington. Although it was very late I had to report on my interview with the prisoner. I met with Director Burns and Tony Woods in the Director's small conference room. Burns wanted to know my bottom line on the Saudi's credibility. Had we learned something useful about the Wolf? Was he negotiating in the Middle East?

'I think we should let the prisoner go,' I told Burns.

'So you believe him?'

I shook my head. 'I think he was given information, for whatever reason. I don't know if the information is accurate. Neither does he. I think that either we charge him, or we let him free.'

'Alex, was the Wolf in Saudi Arabia? Is it possible the Wolf *is a woman*?'

I repeated myself. 'I think he told us what *he* was told. Let the schoolteacher go home to Newark.'

And Burns snapped at me, 'I heard you the first time.' He let out a long sigh. 'I was with the President today, his advisors. They don't see how we can make a deal with these bastards. It's their position that we won't.' Burns stared at me. 'Somehow, we have to find the Wolf. *In the next two days.*'

Chapter Forty-Four

It's extraordinarily bad to be waiting for something devastating to happen, and not be able to do a damn thing to prevent it. I was up at five the next morning, and I had breakfast with Nana. 'We have to talk about you and the kids,' I said as I sat at the kitchen table with coffee and a slice of unbuttered cinnamon toast. 'You awake for this?'

'I'm fully awake, Alex. How about you?' she said. 'You ready to match wits with me?'

I nodded, and bit my tongue. Nana had something to say to me, and I was supposed to listen. I've learned that no matter how old you get, to some extent you always remain a child in the eyes of your parents and grandparents. That was certainly true with Nana Mama.

'Go ahead, I'm listening,' I said.

'You better be. The *reason* that I'm not going to

move out of Washington,' Nana began, 'is twofold. Are you with me so far? *Good.*

'First of all, this has been my home for eighty-three years. This is where Regina Hope was born, and where I plan to die. That may be a little foolish, I know, but it is what it is. I love the city of Washington, love our neighborhood, and I especially love this old house where so much has happened to me. It goes, I go with it. And second, I know it's sad, really sad, but the situation here in Washington is a part of life now. This is the way of the world now, Alex.'

I had to smile a little at my grandmother. 'You know, you just jumped right back into your old schoolteacher tone of voice. You realize that?'

'Maybe I did, and if so, then so what? It's a serious subject,' Nana said. 'I didn't sleep most of the night. I was lying there in the dark, thinking about what I wanted to say to you. Now, what do *you* have to say on the subject? You want us to move, don't you?'

'Nana, if the kids got hurt, I'd never be able to forgive myself.'

'Neither would I,' she said. 'Goes without saying.' Her eyes remained steely. *God, she is tough.*

Nana stared deeply into my eyes, but she was thinking, reconsidering, I hoped. 'This is where I live, Alex. I have to stay. If you think it's the right thing to do, the kids should go with Aunt Tia for a while.

Now – is that all you're going to eat? A measly slice of toast? Let me make you a decent breakfast. I'm sure you have a long day in front of you, a terrible day.'

Chapter Forty-Five

The Wolf was in the Middle East, so at least *some* of the rumors about him appeared to be true.

The meeting, which the Wolf called 'a little fund-raiser', took place in a city of tents in the desert about seventy miles south-west of Riyadh in Saudi Arabia. Those present were split between the Arab world and Asia. And then there was the Wolf, who called himself 'a world traveler, a citizen of no particular country'.

But was this person really the Wolf? Or merely a representative? A stand-in? No one knew for certain. Wasn't the Wolf supposed to be a female? That was one of the current rumors.

But this *man* was tall, with long, dark-brown hair and a full beard, and the other participants couldn't help thinking he would be hard to disguise, and presumably easy to find, but that didn't seem to be the case; it only enhanced his reputation as a person of mystery, and possibly a true mastermind.

So did his behavior during the half-hour or so before the meeting began. While some sipped whisky and others mint tea, and chatted amicably, the Wolf stood off to the side, talking to no one and impatiently waving off the few who approached him. He seemed so *above it all*.

The weather was balmy, so it was decided to hold the meeting outside in the open air. The participants left the tent and were seated according to country of origin.

The business meeting was then called to order and the Wolf took center stage. He addressed the gathering in English. He knew all of them spoke the language, or at least understood it well enough.

'I am here to report that everything is going very well so far, very much according to plan. We should all rejoice, give thanks.'

'How do we know this, other than your word?' asked one of the principals at the meeting. The Wolf knew the man was a mujahid – a fighter, a warrior for Islam.

The Wolf smiled genially. 'As you said, you have my word. And perhaps not in this country, but in most of the world there are televisions, newspapers, and radios to verify that we've created problems for the Americans, the English, the Germans. Actually, CNN is available here – *inside the tent* – if you'd like some validation other than my word.'

The Wolf's dark eyes shifted away from the mujahid, who was now red-faced with embarrassment, but also clearly angry.

'The plan is working, but now it's time for another donation to keep all our important *pieces* in motion. I'll go around the table and you can signal if you are in agreement with me. You have to spend money to make money. A Western idea perhaps, but a true one.'

The Wolf went from face to face, receiving nods or raised hands as he proceeded – except from the one Arab troublemaker, who sat with his arms folded defiantly and said, 'I need to hear more. Your word is not enough.'

'Understood,' said the Wolf. 'I have gotten your message, and now I have one for you, *warrior*.'

In a split second the Wolf raised his hand – and a pistol shot rang out. The bearded Saudi fell from his chair, dead on the spot, lifeless eyes staring up at the heavens.

'Does anyone else need to hear more? Or is my word good enough?' the Wolf asked. 'Do we move on to the next important phase of our war against the West?'

No one said a word.

'Good. Then we move on to the next phase,' said the Wolf. 'This is exciting, no? Trust me, we are winning. Allahu Akhbar.' *God is great. And so am I.*

Chapter Forty-Six

I was feeling relatively peaceful at six-fifteen in the morning, driving to work along Independence Avenue, coffee cup in hand, Jill Scott singing on the radio. Suddenly my cell phone went off and I knew that all was lost.

Kurt Crawford was on the line and he sounded excited, wouldn't give me a chance to get in a word. 'Alex, Geoffrey Shafer was just spotted on a surveillance tape in New York City. He visited an apartment that we were watching before this mess even began. We think we've found the cell that might be ready to strike in Manhattan.

'They're *al Qaeda*, Alex. What the hell does that mean? We want you in New York this morning. We're holding a seat for you so get on your horse out to Andrews.'

I grabbed the 'bubble' off the passenger seat and

slapped it on the roof of the car. It felt a little like my old policing days.

I headed out to Andrews Air Force Base, and less than half an hour later, I was on board a jet-black Bell helicopter bound for the Downtown Manhattan Heliport on the East River. As we flew over the city, I imagined New York in full panic. So far, word of the Wolf's threat had not leaked to the media, but the strikes in Nevada, England, and Germany had the whole world on edge.

As soon as I arrived at the Heliport on the East River I was rushed to the FBI offices in Lower Manhattan. Tense, high-level meetings had been going on there since early that morning when some-one looking at surveillance tapes recognized Shafer. What was he doing in New York now? And visiting with al Qaeda? Suddenly the rumors about the Wolf's travels in the Middle East made some sense. But what was going on?

Inside Federal Plaza I got a quick, thorough briefing about a terrorist cell that was staying in a small brick building near the Holland Tunnel. It wasn't clear whether Shafer was still inside, though. He had entered at nine last night and no one saw him leave.

'The others are clearly members of al-Jihad,' I was told by Angela Bell, the information analyst assigned to the counterterrorism squad in New York. She said that the decrepit, three-story structure where the cell was holed up was shared by a Korean import-export business and a Spanish-translation business. The terrorist cell was posing as a relief charity called *Afghan Children Assistance.*

Based on the surveillance reports we had in hand, there were several indicators of terrorist planning and activity around New York. Chemicals and mixing apparatuses had turned up in self-storage space in Long Island City. The place had been rented by an occupant of the property near the Holland Tunnel; a pickup truck owned by a cell member had been modified with heavy-duty springs to handle a very heavy load. *A possible bomb? What kind of bomb?*

That morning plans were being coordinated for raids on the Long Island storage facility and the walk-up near the Holland Tunnel.

Finally, around four in the afternoon, I was driven to TriBeCa to join the strike team.

Chapter Forty-Seven

We had been warned not to do this. *But how could we obey?* What's more, how could anyone expect us to obey when so many lives were in danger? And maybe we could argue that the raid was solely a hit on al Qaeda and had nothing to do with the Wolf. Hell, maybe it didn't.

The apartment where the terrorists were staying, and where Geoffrey Shafer still might be, was a fairly easy one to monitor. The front of the red-brick building had only a single entrance. The rear fire escapes emptied into a narrow alley where we had already put closed-circuit wireless cameras. One side of the building abutted a textbook printer; the other opened onto a small parking lot.

Was the Weasel still inside?

A Hostage Rescue Team and a SWAT team from the NYPD had taken over the top floor of a TriBeCa meat-packing plant a couple of blocks from the Holland Tunnel. We assembled there, fine-tuning the assault, waiting for word to come about whether the attack would happen or not.

HRT wanted a *go*, and they were pushing hard for an assault between two and three in the morning. I didn't know what I would do if it was my call. We had a cell of known terrorists, and possibly Shafer, in our sights. But we'd been warned about the consequences. Also, it could be a set-up, some kind of test for us.

At a little before midnight word began to circulate that HRT surveillance had turned up something else. Around one in the morning I was called into a small bookkeeping room that was serving as headquarters. It was getting close to put-up or shut-up time.

Michael Ainslie from our New York Office was the Senior Agent in Charge. He was a tall, reed-thin, good-looking man with loads of experience in the field – but I had the distinct impression he would have been more comfortable on a tennis court than in the middle of a dangerous mess like this one.

'Here's what we have so far from surveillance,' Ainslie told the group. 'One of HRT's snipers picked up a couple of images and then we shot some more. We think it's all pretty good news. Take a look for yourselves.'

The visual images had been downloaded to a laptop and Ainslie played them for us. The video stream was a series of wide and tight shots showing half a dozen windows on the east side of the building.

'We were concerned that these windows haven't been covered up,'Ainslie pointed out.'These little shits are supposed to be smart and careful, right? Anyway, we've identified five males and two females inside the building. I'm sorry to say that Colonel Shafer hasn't shown up on any of the surveillance tapes. Not so far anyway.

'We don't have anything on him leaving the building either, just going inside. We're using thermal imaging to see if we might have missed him or any others.'The Washington PD hadn't been able to afford thermal, but I'd seen it work since coming to the Bureau. It picked up heat variances, hot spots, which allowed surveillance to see right through walls.

Ainslie pointed to the close-up shot that was on the laptop screen now.'Here's where it gets interesting,'he said and froze a shot showing two men seated at a small table in the kitchen.

'On the left is Karim al-Lilyas. He's number fourteen on Homeland Security's hit list; he's definitely al Qaeda. Suspected of involvement in the ninety-eight bombings of our embassies in Dar Es Salaam, Tanzania and Nairobi. We don't know when he arrived, or why, but he sure as hell is here now.

'The man beside al-Lilyas, Ahmed el-Masry, is big – number eight on the list. He's hot. Also, he's an engineer. Neither of these bastards was on earlier surveillance tapes. Both must have just snuck into town. *For what reason?* Under ordinary circumstances we'd be in that kitchen with them right now, making mint tea for everybody, getting ready for a nice long chat.

'They have these same pictures downtown and in Washington right now. We ought to hear something soon, one way or the other.'

Ainslie looked around the room and finally cracked a smile. 'For the record, I recommended that we go in, make some tea, have that chat.'

The small room broke into loud applause. For a brief moment there, it was almost fun.

Chapter Forty-Eight

S ome of the more devil-may-care, gung-ho guys from the HRT – which is just about all of them – call this kind of dangerous operation 'five minutes of panic and thrill. *Their* panic, *our* thrill'. The very personal thrill for me would be bringing down Geoffrey Shafer.

HRT and SWAT desperately wanted to go into the building and they were at the ready. Two dozen heavily armed, state-of-the-art warriors were strutting around the wooden floor of the meat-packing plant; they were pumped up and supremely confident in their ability to do the job right, and very quickly. Watching them, it was hard not to agree, and even harder not to ask to be included in the raid.

The real problem was that if they succeeded, *we all might lose*. We had been warned, and also given dramatic lessons about what would happen if we disregarded the orders handed down by the Wolf. And yet – the men under our surveillance might be his attack team in New York. So what did we do?

I knew every detail about the job. Taking down the building would involve full-team deployment of the group including both HRT and NYPD SWAT. There were six assault teams, and six sniper teams, which HRT believed was *two* too many. They didn't *want* help from SWAT. The HRT sniper teams were called X-ray, Whiskey Yankee, and Zulu; each included seven members. One FBI team was assigned to each side of the building; SWAT would assist on the front and rear only.

The interesting thing for me personally was the certainty that HRT was the superior assault team, the opposite of what I'd felt when I was with the D.C. police. The HRT snipers were disguised in 'urban hide' kits, individualized bunches of black muslin, rope, dark PVC tubing, and the like. Each sniper had a specific target, and every window and door in the building was covered.

The question remained – *were we going in now?*

And – *was Shafer still there? Was the Weasel in that building right now?*

At two-thirty in the morning, I joined a two-man sniper team in the brownstone directly across the street from the targeted one. This was starting to get very intense and very hairy.

The snipers were holed up inside a ten-by-ten room. They had made a tent out of black muslin and it sat back about three feet from the window. The window itself was kept closed, and I was given an explanation by one of them. 'If we get the signal to *go*, we'll use a lead pipe to knock out the windowpane. Seems kind of crude, but nobody's come up with a better option.'

There wasn't too much small talk in the cramped, hot room, but for the next half hour I got to watch the targeted building through a sniper scope from a back-up rifle. My heart was starting to race pretty good now. I was searching for Shafer in the scope. What if I saw him? How could I stay up here?

The seconds were ticking away and I could just about measure them with my own heartbeats. The assault team was the 'eyes and ears' for Command, and all we could do was wait for our official orders to come down.

Go.

No go.

I finally broke the silence in the small room. 'I'm going down on the street. I need to be down there for this.'

Chapter Forty-Nine

This was more like it.

I set up with an HRT assault team just around the corner from the terrorist hideout. Technically I wasn't supposed to be there – so I officially *wasn't* – but I'd called Ned Mahoney, their head, and he smoothed the way for me.

Three o'clock in the a.m. The minutes passed very slowly, without more news or clarification from Command in New York, or FBI headquarters in the Hoover Building in Washington. What were they thinking? How could anybody make an impossible decision like this one?

Go?

No go?

Obey the Wolf?

Disobey and take the consequences?

Three-thirty came and went. Then four o'clock. Still

no word from the higher-ups back at headquarters.

I got strapped up in a black flight suit with full armor, and was given an MP-5. The HRT guys all knew about Shafer and my personal stake in this.

The Senior Agent in Charge sat down beside me on the ground. 'You okay? Everything all right?'

'I was D.C. Homicide. I've gone into a lot of places, lot of hot spots.'

'I know you have. If Shafer's in there, we'll get him. Maybe you'll get him.' *Yeah, maybe I would blow that creep away after all.*

And then, amazingly, we got the order to *go*. Green light! *Five minutes of panic and thrill.*

First thing – I heard the snipers breaking windows across the street. Then we were running toward the hideout building. Everybody was strapped-up for war, all in black flight suits and armed to the teeth.

Two eight-passenger Bell helicopters suddenly appeared and veered in toward the roof of the brick building. They hovered and assault specialists began to 'fast-rope' down.

One team of four was climbing *up* the side of the building, an amazing sight in itself.

Another of HRT's 'go to war' slogans flashed through my head – *speed, suspense, and violence of action*. It was happening just like that.

I heard explosive entry charges blasting out doors, three or four different blasts within seconds. There would be no negotiating as part of this assault.

We were *in*. This was good – *I* was in.

Gunshots echoed through the dark halls of the building. Then machine-gun bursts came from somewhere above me.

I made it up to the second floor. A male with wild, bushy hair came out of a doorway. He had a rifle.

'Hands in the air!' I yelled at him. *'In the air. High.'*

He understood English – put his hands up and let the rifle drop.

'Where's Colonel Shafer? Where's Shafer?' I screamed.

The man just shook his head back and forth, back and forth, looking dazed and confused.

I left the prisoner with a couple of HRT guys, then hurried upstairs to the third floor. I wanted the Weasel so badly now. Was he in here somewhere?

A waif of a woman in black suddenly ran across a large living-room area at the head of the stairs.

'Stop!' I bellowed. *'You* – stop!'

But she didn't – she went right out of an open window in the living room. I heard her scream, then nothing after that. Sickening to watch.

And finally I heard – *'Secure.* The building is secure! All floors secure!'

But nothing about Geoffrey Shafer, nothing about the Weasel.

Chapter Fifty

HRT and NYPD SWAT teams were swarming around the building. All the doors had been blown off their hinges, and several windows were shattered. So much for 'knock and announce' protocol, but the plan seemed to have worked well, from what I could see so far. *Except for finding Shafer. Where was that son of a bitch? I'd missed him like this a couple of times before.*

The woman who'd gone out the top-floor window was dead, which is what happens when you plunge head-first three stories down onto a sidewalk. I congratulated a few HRT guys as I made my way up to the top floor; they did the same for me.

I met Michael Ainslie on the stairs. 'Washington wants you involved with the interrogations,' he told me, and didn't seem too pleased. 'There are six of them. How do you want to handle it?'

'Shafer?' I asked Ainslie. 'Anything on him?'

'They say he isn't here. We don't know for sure. We're still looking for him.'

I couldn't help feeling a letdown about the Weasel, but I sucked it up. I walked inside a workspace that had been turned into a quasi-apartment. Sleeping bags and a few stained mattresses were strewn across the bare wooden floor. Five males and a woman sat together handcuffed like prisoners of war – which I suppose they were.

I stared at them without saying a word at first.

Then I pointed to the youngest-looking male: small, thin, wire-rim glasses, scruffy beard of course. '*Him,*' I said and started to walk out of the room. 'I want that one. Bring him now!'

After the young male was taken from the main living area to a smaller, adjoining bedroom, I looked around the main room again.

I pointed to another youngish male with long curly black hair and a full beard. 'That one,' I said, and he also was escorted out. No explanation.

Next, I was introduced to an FBI interpreter, a man named Wasid who spoke Arabic, Farsi, Pashto. We entered an adjoining bedroom together.

'He's probably Saudi, possibly all of them are,' the interpreter told me on the way in. Wherever he was from, the small, thin young man seemed extremely nervous. Sometimes, Islamic terrorists are more comfortable with the idea of dying than being captured and questioned by the Devil. That was my leverage here: *I was the Devil.*

I encouraged the translator to engage the terrorist suspect in small talk about his hometown and then his difficult transition to life in New York, *the Devil's den.* I asked that he slip in that I was a fairly good man, and one of the few FBI agents who wasn't inherently evil. 'Tell him I read the Koran. Beautiful book.'

In the meantime, I sat and tried to model the terrorist's behavior, to mimic it, without being too obvious. He sat forward in his chair. So did I. If I could become the first American he would learn to trust, even a little, he might let something slip.

It didn't work too well at first, but he did answer a few questions about his city of origin; he maintained that he came to America on a student visa, but I knew he didn't have a passport. He also didn't know the locations of any universities in New York, not even NYU.

Finally, I got up and stomped angrily out of the room. I went to see the second suspect and repeated the same process with him.

Then I returned to the skinny youth. I carried in a stack of reports and threw them on the floor. There was a loud whack and he actually jumped.

'Tell him he lied to me!' I yelled at the translator. 'Tell

him I trusted him. Tell him the FBI and CIA aren't filled with fools, whatever he's been told in his country. Just keep talking to him. Yelling is even better. Don't let him talk until he has something to tell us. Then yell over whatever he has to say. Tell him he's going to die and then we'll track down his entire family in Saudi Arabia!'

For the next couple of hours, I kept going back and forth between the two rooms. My years as a therapist made me fairly good at reading people, especially in a disturbed state. I picked out a third terrorist, the remaining woman, and added her to the mix. CIA officers were questioning the subjects every time I left a room. No torture, but it was a constant barrage.

In the FBI training sessions at Quantico, they talk about their principles of interrogation as the RPMs: Rationalization, Projection, and Minimization. I *rationalized* like crazy: 'You're a good person, Ahmed. Your beliefs are true ones. I wish I had your strong faith.' I *projected* blame: 'It isn't your fault. You're just a young guy. The United States government *can* be evil at times. Sometimes I think we need to be punished myself.' I *minimized* consequences: 'So far, you've committed no actual crimes here in America. Our weak laws and judicial system can protect you.' And I *got down to business*: 'Tell me about the Englishman. We know that his name is Geoffrey Shafer. He's called the Weasel. *He was here yesterday*. We have videotapes, photographs, audiotapes. We know he was here. Where is he now? He's the one we really want.'

I kept at it, repeating my pitch again and again. 'What did the Englishman want you to do? He's the guilty one, not you or your friends. We already know this. Just fill in a few blanks for us. You'll be able to go home.'

Then I repeated the same questions – about the Wolf.

Nothing worked with any of the terrorists, though, not even the young ones. They were tough; more disciplined and more experienced than they looked; smart, and clearly very motivated.

Why not? They *believed* in something. Maybe there's something to be learned from that too.

Chapter Fifty-One

The next terrorist I chose was older, ruddily good-looking, with a thick mustache and white, nearly perfect teeth. He spoke English and told me, with some pride, that he had studied at Berkeley and also at Oxford.

'Biochemistry and Electrical Engineering. Does that surprise you?' His name was Ahmed el-Masry, and he was number eight on Homeland Security's hit list.

He was very willing to talk about Geoffrey Shafer.

'Yes, the Englishman came here. You are right about this, of course. Video and audiotapes don't usually lie. He claimed to have something important he wanted to talk to us about.'

'And did he?'

El-Masry frowned deeply. 'No, not really. We thought he might be one of *your* agents.'

'So why did he come here?' I asked. 'Why did you consent to see him?'

El-Masry shrugged off my question. 'Curiosity. He said that he had access to tactical nuclear explosive devices.'

I winced, and my heart started to beat a whole lot faster. Nuclear devices in the metropolitan New York area? 'Did he have the weapons?'

'We agreed to talk with him. We believed he meant suitcase nuclear bombs. "Suitcase nukes". Difficult to obtain, but not impossible. As you may know, the Soviet Union built them during the Cold War. No one knows how many, or what happened to them. The Russian Mafiya has tried to sell them in recent years, or so it's rumored. I wouldn't actually know. I came here to be a Professor, you see. To look for employment.'

A shudder had just passed through me. Unlike conventional warheads, suitcase nukes were designed to go off at ground level. They were about the size of a large valise, and could easily be operated by an infantryman. They could also be concealed just about anywhere, or even carried on foot around New York, Washington, London, Frankfurt.

'So, did he have access to suitcase nukes?' I asked el-Masry.

He shrugged. 'We are just students and teachers. In truth, why should we care about nuclear weapons?'

I thought that I understood what he was doing now

– bargaining for himself and his people.

'Why did one of your *students* kill herself diving from a window?' I asked.

El-Masry's eyes narrowed in pain. 'She was afraid, all the time she was in New York. She was an orphan, her parents killed in an unjust war by Americans.'

I nodded slowly as if I understood and sympathized with what he was telling me. 'All right, you haven't committed any crimes here. We've been watching you for weeks. *But did Colonel Shafer have access to nuclear weapons?*' I asked again. 'That's the question I need answered. It's important for you, and for your people. *Are you following me?*'

'I believe so. Are you suggesting that we would be *deported* if we cooperate? Sent home? Since we've committed no actual crimes?' el-Masry asked. He was trying to pin down the deal.

I came right back at him. 'Some of you have committed serious crimes in the past. Murders. The others will be questioned, and then, they will be sent home.'

He nodded. 'All right then. I did *not* get the impression that Mr Shafer had tactical nuclear weapons in his possession. You say that you've been watching us. Maybe he knew that also? Does that make sense to you? *That you were set up?* I don't pretend to understand this myself. But these are the thoughts that pass through my mind as I sit and talk to you.'

Unfortunately, what he was telling me made sense.

I was afraid that might be what had happened. *A trap; a test.* It was the Wolf's pattern so far.

'How did Shafer get out of here without our seeing him leave?' I asked.

'The basement in the building connects to a building to the south. Colonel Shafer knew that. He seemed to know a lot about us.'

It was nine in the morning by the time I left the building. I felt exhausted, like I could lay down and sleep in an alleyway. The suspects would be transported soon, and the whole area was still shut down, even the Holland Tunnel because of our fear that it might be a primary target, that it might suddenly be blown up.

Had everything been a test – a trap?

Chapter Fifty-Two

The day's weirdness wasn't over.

A crowd had gathered outside the building and as I pushed a way out toward my ride, someone called to me. 'Dr Cross!'

Dr Cross? Who was calling to me?

A kid in a tan-and-crimson wind-cheater waved so that I'd see him.

'Dr Cross, over here! *Dr Alex Cross!* I need to talk to you, man.'

I walked over to the young man, who was probably in his late teens. I stopped and leaned in close to him. 'How do you know my name?' I asked.

He shook his head and backed up a step. 'You were *warned*, man,' he said. 'You were warned by the Wolf!'

As soon as the words were out of his mouth I was all over him, grabbing at his hair, his jacket. I took him down on the ground in a headlock. I fell on top of him with all my weight.

Red-faced, his lean body torquing powerfully, he started screaming at me. '*Hey, hey!* I was *paid* to give you a message. Get the fuck off me. Guy gave me a hundred bucks. I'm just a messenger, man. English guy told me you were Dr Alex Cross.'

The youth, the *messenger*, looked into my eyes. '*You don't seem like no doctor to me.*'

Chapter Fifty-Three

The Wolf was in New York. He couldn't miss the big deadline, not for all the money in the world. This was going to be too good, too delicious not to savor.

The negotiation was really heating up now. The US President, the British Prime Minister, the German Chancellor – of course none of them wanted to make a deal, to be exposed for the incredible weaklings they were. *One couldn't deal with terrorists, could one. What kind of precedent would it set?* They needed even more pressure, more stress, more convincing before they collapsed.

Hell, he could do that. He would be only too happy to oblige, to torture these fools. The whole thing was so predictable – to him anyway.

He went for a long walk on the East Side of Manhattan. A constitutional. He was feeling at the top of his game. How could the governments of the world compete with him? He had every advantage. No politics, no media pundits, bureaucracies, laws or ethics to get in his way. Who could beat that?

He returned to one of several apartments he owned around the world, this one a stunning penthouse overlooking the East River, and he made a phone call. Lightly squeezing his black rubber ball, he spoke to a Senior Agent from the New York FBI office, one of their top people, a woman.

The agent told him everything the Bureau knew so far, and what they were doing to find him – which was basically nothing of consequence. They had a far better chance of suddenly finding bin Laden than of finding him.

The Wolf yelled into the telephone receiver. 'I'm supposed to pay you for this shit? For telling me what I already know? I should kill you instead.' But then the Russian laughed. 'Just a nasty joke, my friend. You bring me good news. And I have news for you: there is going to be an incident in New York very soon. Stay away from the bridges. Bridges are very dangerous places. I know this from past experience.'

Chapter Fifty-Four

Bill Capistran was the man with the plan, and also a very bad and dangerous attitude, serious anger-management problems to put it mildly. But soon, he'd also be the man with two hundred and fifty thousand in his bank account in the Caymans. All he had to do was his particular job, and that wasn't going to be too hard. *I can do this, no problemo.*

Capistran was twenty-nine years old, slim and sinewy, originally from Raleigh, North Carolina. He had played lacrosse for a year at North Carolina State, then left for the Marines. After a three-year stint he'd been recruited to do merc work for a company out of Washington. Then two weeks ago, he'd been approached by a guy he knew from D.C., Geoffrey Shafer, and he'd agreed to do the biggest job of his career. Two hundred and fifty thousand worth.

He was on the job now.

At seven in the morning, he drove a black Ford van east across Fifty-Seventh Street in Manhattan, then turned north at First Avenue. Finally, he parked near the Fifty-Ninth Street Bridge, also called the Queensboro.

He and two men in white painter's overalls climbed out of the van, then gathered up equipment from the back. *Not* paint and dropcloths and aluminum ladders. Explosives. A combination of C4 and nitrate to be packed into the bridge's lowest trusses at a strategic point near the Manhattan side of the East River.

Capistran knew the Queensboro inside and out by now. He stared up at the sturdy, ninety-five-year-old bridge, and what he saw was an open, flexible structure, a cantilever-truss design, the only one of the four East River bridges that wasn't a suspension bridge. Which meant that it required a special kind of bomb, one that he just happened to have in the back of the van.

This is something else, Capistran couldn't help thinking as he and his compadres hauled their gear toward the bridge. New York City. The East Side. All these fancy-assed big-business dicks, these blonde princesses, walking around like the world was theirs for the taking. Nerves aside, he was almost enjoying himself now, and he found himself whistling a song that struck him as pretty funny.'The 59th Street Bridge

Song (Feelin' Groovy)' by Simon and Garfunkel – whom he considered to be typical New York City assholes too. *Both* of them – Curly and the Midget.

For the past couple of days, Capistran had been working into the wee hours with a couple of sympathetic engineering students at Stony Brook University out on Long Island. One whizkid was from Iran, the other from Afghanistan. They got a kick and a half out of the irony, too – *New York-trained college students helping to blow up New York. Land of the fucking free, right?* They called their team 'the Manhattan Project'. Another insider joke.

At first they had considered an ANFO, a type of bomb that would blow a crater in a road for sure, but was unlikely to topple a large bridge like the Queensboro. The college whizzes told Capistran he could see what an ANFO would accomplish just by setting off a firecracker on a city street. Or imagining it. The explosion would be characterized by 'coward forces which always seek the path of least resistance'. In other words, the bomb would make a nasty little burn on the road, but the real destructive power would escape up and sideways into the air.

Not good enough for today. Too benign. Not even close to what was needed.

Then the clever-as-hell college students came upon a much better way to blow up the bridge. They instructed Capistran on how and where to attach several small charges at different points in the foundation. This was similar to the way demolition companies toppled old buildings, and it would work like a charm.

Since he had absolutely no interest in being caught, Capistran had considered sending divers into the East River to set the charges on the structured supports. He had approached the bridge several times himself. And to his surprise, he found security to be virtually non-existent.

That's exactly the way it was early that morning. He and his two associates walked out on the lower supports of the Fifty-Ninth Street Bridge and nobody said 'boo' to them.

From a distance, the ornate silver-painted ironwork and finials had made the old bridge look rather delicate. Up close, the real power of the structure was revealed: the massive trusses; rivets as large as a man's kneecaps.

This sounded crazy, but it would work – his *piece* would work.

Sometimes he wondered how he'd gotten so sour on everything, so bitter and full of rage. Hell, years ago in the Marines he'd been part of the rescue team that had extracted downed pilots like Scott O'Grady in Bosnia. Well, he wasn't a war hero any more. He was just another capitalist, working in the system, right? And that was a lot truer statement than most people could let themselves believe.

As he continued to walk out on the support structure, Capistran couldn't help humming, then singing the words, 'Groovy. Feeling very groovy.'

Chapter Fifty-Five

The strangest, most puzzling thing happened next. *The deadline passed* – and nothing happened. There was no message from the Wolf, no immediate attacks. Nothing. *Silence*. It was eerie, but also incredibly scary.

The Wolf was the only one who knew what was going on now – or maybe, the Wolf, the President, and a few other world leaders. Rumor had it that the President, Vice President and the Cabinet had already been moved out of Washington.

This thing wouldn't stop, would it? The news stories certainly wouldn't. The *Post*, the *New York Times*, *USA Today*, CNN, the networks – they had all got hold of some version of the threats against major cities. No one knew *which* cities, or who was doing the threatening. But after years of yellow and orange alerts from Homeland Security, no one seemed to take the threats and rumors too seriously.

The uncertainty, the war of nerves had to be part of the Wolf's plan too. I was in Washington for the Memorial Day weekend, and was asleep when I got a call to get over to the Hoover Building right away.

I looked at the alarm clock, squinting to focus, saw that it was three in the morning. *Now what? Had there been reprisals? If so, they weren't telling me over the phone.*

'I'll be right there,' I said, pushing myself out of bed, cursing under my breath. I showered under hot, then cold water for a minute or two, toweled off, threw on clothes, then got in the car and drove through Washington in a horrible daze. *All I knew was that the Wolf was going to call in thirty minutes.*

Three-thirty in the morning, after a long weekend, with the expired deadline hanging over our heads. He wasn't just controlling, he was a sadist.

When I arrived at the crisis room on five, there were at least a dozen others already there. We greeted one another like old friends at somebody's wake. For the next couple of minutes, bleary-eyed agents kept filing into the conference room, nobody seeming completely awake. A ragged line formed at the coffee table as a couple of pots finally arrived. Everybody looked nervous and on edge.

'No Danish?' said one of the other agents. 'Where's the love?' But nobody even smiled at his joke.

Director Burns came in a few minutes past three-thirty. He was wearing a dark suit and tie, formal for him, but especially at this time of the morning. I had the sense that he didn't have any idea what was happening either. *The Wolf was in charge, not any of us.*

'And you thought I was a tough boss,' Director Burns cracked after a couple of minutes of silence in the room. Finally, there was a sprinkling of laughter. 'Thank you for coming,' Burns added.

The Wolf came on the line at three-forty-three. The filtered voice. The characteristic smugness and disdain.

'You're probably wondering why I scheduled a meeting in the middle of the night?' he began. 'Because I can. How do you like that? *Because I can.*

'In case you haven't been able to tell, I don't like you people very much. Not at all, actually. I have my reasons, good ones. I hate everything America stands for. So maybe this is partly about revenge. Maybe you've wronged me somewhere, at some place in the past. Maybe you wronged my family. That's a part of the puzzle. Revenge is a sweet bonus for me.

'But let me get to the present. Correct me if I'm wrong, but I think I instructed you not to conduct any more investigations into my whereabouts.

'So what do you do? You bust six poor bastards in downtown Manhattan because you suspect they're working with me. Why, one poor girl was so distraught that she went out of a third-floor window. *I saw her fall!* I suppose that your thinking – such as it is – was that if you took out my operatives there, then New York City would be safe.

'Oh, I'm sorry, I almost *forgot*. There's also a little matter of a *deadline* you missed.

'Did you think I had forgotten about that? Well, I didn't forget about the deadline. Or the insult in your missing it. Now – *watch* what I can do.'

Chapter Fifty-Six

At three-forty in the morning, following his instructions, the Weasel took up a position on a bench in the riverfront park on Sutton Place and Fifty-Seventh Street. There was a great deal that bothered him about this job, but the problems were balanced by two large positives: he was being paid a lot of money and he was in the middle of the action again. *Jesus, was he ever in the middle of the shit.*

He stared down on the East River with its dark, swift-moving currents. A red tugboat marked *McAllister Brothers* was assisting a container ship on its way. *The city that never sleeps, right?* Hell, the bars on First and Second Avenues were just getting down to their 'last call'. A little earlier he'd passed an Animal Medical Center that was still open for late-night pet emergencies. *Pet emergencies?* Jesus, what a city, what a messed-up country America had become.

A lot of New Yorkers would be wide awake soon, and they would find it exceedingly difficult to get back to sleep. There would be weeping and the gnashing of teeth. The Wolf was going to make certain of that in a minute or so.

Shafer watched the seconds on his watch tick down to 3:43, but he was also keeping an eye on the river, and the Queensboro Bridge.

Cars and cabs and quite a few trucks were whizzing along up there, even at this hour. Easily a hundred vehicles were crossing the bridge right now, probably more than that. The poor wankers!

At three-forty-three Shafer pressed a button on his cell phone. This transmitted a simple coded squirt to a small antenna on the Manhattan side of the bridge. A circuit began to close . . .

A primer fired . . .

Microseconds later, a message straight from hell was delivered to the people of New York City, and the rest of the world.

A symbolic message.

Another wake-up call.

A massive explosion ripped into the girders and trusses of the Fifty-Ninth Street Bridge. Joints were severed instantly. The old steel structures snapped like peanut brittle. Huge rivets popped out and plummeted toward the East River. Tarmac crumbled. Reinforced concrete fractured like paper being shredded.

The upper roadbed cracked in two, then enormous sections dropped like bombs onto the lower deck, which was breaking up as well, peeling away, twisting and twirling toward the river below.

Cars were falling into the water. A delivery truck carrying a full load of newspapers from a plant in Queens rolled backwards down the inverted roadway and then pirouetted into the East River. It was followed by more cars and trucks, dropping like lead weights. Electric lines drooped and sparked along the entire length of the bridge. More cars, dozens of them, plummeted from the bridge, fell into the river, then disappeared beneath the surface.

Some people were exiting their cars, then jumping to their deaths in the river. Shafer could hear their terrified screams all the way across the river.

And in every apartment building lights began to blink on, then TVs and computers, as the people of New York heard the first reports about a terrible disaster that was impossible to believe, and that would have been unthinkable until a few years ago.

His work for the night done, Geoffrey Shafer finally rose from his park bench and went to get some sleep. If he *could* sleep. He understood this much: things were just getting started. He was on his way to London.

London Bridge, he thought. *All the bridges of the world, falling, crashing down. Modern society coming*

apart at the seams. The sodding Wolf might be a madman, but he was a brilliant bugger at being bad. A bloody brilliant madman!

PART THREE

WOLF TRACKS

Chapter Fifty-Seven

The Wolf slowed his powerful black Lotus to just over a hundred miles an hour, while he talked on his mobile phone, one of six he had with him in the car. He was headed toward Montauk on the tip of Long Island, but he had important business to attend to on the way, even at one in the morning. He had the American President, the German Chancellor and the British Prime Minister on the line. *Top to top.* What could beat that?

'This call can't be traced, so don't waste your time trying. My tech people are better than your people,' he informed them. 'Now what's on everybody's mind? We're eight hours past the deadline. *And?*'

'We need more time.' The British Prime Minister spoke up for the group. Good for him. Was he the real leader of the three? That would be a surprise. The Wolf had thought of him more as a follower.

'You have no idea—' the American President started to say, but he was interrupted by the Wolf, smiling to himself, relishing the show of disrespect toward the powerful world leader.

'Stop! I don't want to hear any more lies!' he yelled into the phone.

'You have to listen to what we have to say,' the German Chancellor interjected. 'Give us the opportunity—'

The Wolf ended the conversation then and there. He lit up a victory cigar, took a couple of satisfied puffs, then set the cigar down in the ashtray. He re-connected the call, using a second cell phone.

They were still there, waiting for him to call back. He didn't actually underestimate any of these powerful men, not really, but what choice did they have but to wait on his call?

'Do you want me to attack all four cities? Is that what I have to do to prove how serious I am? I'll do it in a flash. I'll do it now, give the order right now. But don't tell me you need more time. You don't! The countries holding the prisoners are your puppets, for Christ's sake.

'The *real* problem is that you can't be seen for who you really are. You can't be viewed around the world as weak and powerless. But you are! How did it happen? How did you allow it to happen? Who put people like you into these positions of great power? Who elected you? Remember: the money *and* the political prisoners. Goodbye.'

The Prime Minister spoke before the Wolf could disconnect again. 'You have it all wrong! It is *you* who have a choice to make, not us. We take your point about the strength of your position versus ours. It's a given. But we cannot put this package together quickly. It can't physically be done and I think you know that. Of course we don't want to make a deal with you, but we will. We have to. We just need more time to get it done. We will get it done. You have our promise on it.'

The Wolf shrugged. The British Prime Minister definitely surprised him: he was succinct, and he at least had some balls.

'I'll think about it,' said the Wolf, then he disconnected. He picked up his cigar, and savored this idea: he was the most powerful person in the world right now. And unlike any of them, he was the right man for the job.

Chapter Fifty-Eight

A business-class passenger who called himself Randolph Wohler deplaned the British Airways flight from New York at 6:05 in the morning. His passport and other pieces of ID backed up his identity. *It is good to be home again*, thought Wohler, who was actually Geoffrey Shafer. *And it was going to be even better if he got to blow London off the map.*

The seventyish-looking gentleman passed through Customs without a problem. He was already thinking about the next move: he was to visit his children. That was his *piece*. Curious and strange. But he was past questioning orders from the Wolf. Besides, he wanted to see his progeny. Daddy had been away for far too long.

He had a part to play, another mission, another 'piece' of the puzzle. The brat pack lived with his deceased wife's sister in a small house near Hyde Park.

He remembered the house as he pulled up in a rented Jaguar S-type. He had a most unpleasant memory of his wife now, Lucy Rhys-Cousins, a brittle, small-minded woman. He'd murdered her in a Safeway in Chelsea, right in front of the twins. That truly merciful act had orphaned his twin daughters, Tricia and Erica, who were six or seven now, and Robert, who must be fifteen. Shafer believed they were far better off without their whining, sniveling mother.

He knocked on the front door of the house and found that it was unlocked, so he barged in unannounced.

He discovered his wife's younger sister, Judi, playing with the twins on the living-room floor, bent over a game of Monopoly, which he believed they were all capable of *losing* – there wasn't a winner in the group.

'Daddy's home!' he exclaimed and beamed a smile that was perfectly horrible. He then pointed a Beretta at dear Aunt Judi's chest.

'Don't make a sound, Judi, not one. Don't give me the slightest excuse to pull this trigger. It would be so easy, and such a great pleasure. And yes, I sincerely hate you too. You remind me of a fat version of your beloved sister.

'Hello, children! Say hello to your dear old dad. I've come a long ways to see you. All the way from America.'

His twin girls, his sweet daughters, started to cry, so

Shafer did the only thing he could think of to restore order: he pointed his gun straight at Judi's tear-stained face and walked closer to her. 'Make them stop whining and screeching. Now! Show me you deserve to be their *keeper*.'

The aunt bent low and pressed the girls to her chest, and while they didn't actually stop crying, the sound was at least muffled and subdued.

'Judi, now listen to me,' Shafer said as he moved behind her and pressed the barrel of the Beretta to the back of her head. 'As much as I would like to, I'm not here to fuck and murder you. Actually, I have a message for you to be passed on to the Home Secretary. In a strange, ironic twist, your absurd, pitiful life actually matters for now. Can you believe it? I can't.'

Aunt Judi seemed confused, her natural state as far as Shafer could tell. 'How would I do that?' she blubbered.

'*Just call the sodding police!* Now shut up and listen. You're to tell the police that I came to visit, and I told you that no one is safe any more. Not the police, *not their families*. We can go to their houses, just like I came to your house today.'

Just to make sure she got it, Shafer repeated the message twice more. Then he turned his attention back to Tricia and Erica, who interested him about as much as the ridiculous porcelain dolls covering the mantelpiece. He hated those silly, frilly porcelain creatures that had once belonged to his wife, and on which she doted as if they were real.

'How is Robert?' he asked the twins and received no reaction.

What was this? The girls had already mastered the hopelessly lost and confused look of their mother and their blubbering auntie. They said not a word.

'Robert is your *brother*!' Shafer yelled, and the girls started to sob loudly again. 'How is he? How is my son? Tell me something about your brother! Has he grown two heads? Anything!'

'He's all right.' Tricia finally gulped.

'Yes, he's all right.' Erica followed her sister's lead.

'He's *all right*, is he? Well, that's *all right* then,' Shafer said with utter disdain for these two clones of their mother.

He found that he was actually missing Robert though. He rather enjoyed the mildly twisted lad at times. 'All right, give your father a kiss,' he finally demanded. 'I am your father, you pitiful twits,' he added for good measure, 'in case you've *forgotten*.'

The girls wouldn't kiss him, and he wasn't permitted to kill them, so Shafer finally had to leave the dreadful house. On the way out, he swept the porcelain dolls off the mantel, sending them crashing to the floor.

'In memory of your mother!' he called back over his shoulder.

Chapter Fifty-Nine

The most common complaint from soldiers serving in Iraq is that they feel that everything around them is absurd and makes no sense. More and more, this is the way of modern-day warfare. I felt it now myself.

We were past the deadline and living on borrowed time. That's how it seemed to me. Feeling like I hadn't been able to catch my breath in days, I was on my way to London with two agents from our International Terrorism Section.

Geoffrey Shafer was in England. Even more insane, *he wanted us to know he was there*. Or someone did.

The flight into Heathrow Airport arrived at a little before six in the morning and I went straight to a hotel just off Victoria Street and slept until ten. After that short rest, I made my way to New Scotland Yard, just round the corner, in Broadway. It was great to be so near to Buckingham Palace, Westminster Abbey, and the Houses of Parliament.

Upon arrival, I was taken to the office of Detective Superintendent Martin Lodge of the Met. Lodge told me, modestly enough, that he kept the Anti-Terrorist Branch called SO13 running smoothly. On our way to the morning's briefing he gave me a thumbnail sketch of himself.

'Like you, I came up through the police ranks. Eleven years with the Met after a stint with SIS in Europe. Before that I trained at Hendon, became a constable on the beat. Chose the detective track and was moved into SO13 because I have a few languages.'

He paused, and I spoke at the first break. 'I know about your AT squad – the best in Europe, I've heard. Years of practice with the IRA.'

Lodge gave me a thin smile – a veteran trouper's smile. 'Sometimes the best way to learn is through mistakes, or so they say. We've made plenty in Ireland. Anyway, here we are, Alex. They're all waiting inside, eager to meet you. Get ready for some incredible bullshit though. MI5 and MI6 will both be here. They fight over everything. Don't let it get to you. We manage to sort it all out in the end. Most of the time, anyway.'

I nodded. 'Like the Bureau and the CIA back home. I'm sure I've seen it before.'

As it turned out, Detective Superintendent Lodge

was right on about the turf wars, and I figured that the feud was probably hurting progress in London, even under the present-crisis circumstances. Also in the room were a few Special Branch men and women. The Prime Minister's Chief of Staff. Plus the usual crowd from London's emergency services.

As I took a seat I groaned inside – another god-damn meeting. Just what I didn't need. *'We're past the deadline – they're blowing things up!'* I wanted to yell.

Chapter Sixty

The large beach-house outside Montauk on Long Island didn't belong to the Wolf. It was a rental, forty thousand a week, even in the off-season. *A complete rip-off,* the Wolf knew, but he didn't mind so much. Not today anyway.

It was quite an impressive place though – Georgian-style, three stories rising above the beach, immense swimming pool shielded from the wind by the house itself, pebbled driveway lined with cars – mostly limousines, muscular drivers in dark suits congregating around them.

Everything here, he thought with some bitterness, *paid for with my money, my sweat, my ideas!*

They were waiting for him, several of his associates in the Red Mafiya. They were gathered inside a library-sitting room with panoramic views of the deserted beach and the Atlantic.

They pretended to be his dearest, closest friends as he entered the room, shaking his hand, patting his broad back and shoulders, muttering easy lies about how good it was to see him. *The very few who know what I look like. The inner circle, the ones I trust more than anyone else.*

Lunch had been served before he arrived and then the entire household staff had been removed from the house. He had parked at the back, then came in through the kitchen. No one had seen him, except the men in this room, nine of them.

He stood before them and lit up a cigar. *To victory.*

'They have asked for an extension of the deadline. Can you believe it?' the Wolf said between satisfying puffs.

The Russian men around the table began to laugh. They shared the Wolf's disdain for the current governments and world leaders. Politicians were weak by nature, and the few strong ones who snuck into office somehow were soon weakened by the processes of government. It had always been that way.

'Drop the hammer!' one of the men shouted.

The Wolf smiled. 'You know, I should. But they have a point – if we act now, we lose too. Let me get them on the line. They're expecting an answer. This is interesting, no? We *negotiate* with the United States, Britain and Germany. As if we were a world power.'

The Wolf raised his index finger as the call went

through. 'They're expecting to hear from me . . . You're all on the line?' He spoke into the phone.

They were.

'No small talk, the time for that has passed. Here is my decision. You have another two days, till seven o'clock, eastern standard time, but – the price has just doubled!'

He disconnected. Then he looked around at his people.

'What? You approve, or what? Do you know how much money I just made for you?'

They all began to clap, then to cheer.

The Wolf stayed with them for the remainder of the afternoon. He endured their false compliments, their requests thinly disguised as suggestions. But then he had other business to do in New York City, so he left them to enjoy the house by the sea, and whatever.

'The ladies will arrive soon,' he promised. 'Models and beauty queens from New York. They say, the most beautiful pussy in the world. Have fun.' *On my money, my sweat, my brilliance.*

He was back in the Lotus then, heading toward the Long Island Expressway. He was squeezing the black rubber ball, but finally he set it down and took out his cell phone again. Pressed a few numbers. A code was transmitted. A circuit closed. A primer fired.

Even from that far away, he heard the beach house explode. He didn't need them any more; he didn't need anyone.

Zamochit! The bombs had broken every bone in all of their worthless, useless bodies.

Payback, revenge.

It was a beautiful thing.

Chapter Sixty-One

We received word in London that the deadline had been extended by forty-eight hours, and the relief, though temporary, was still extraordinary for all of us. Within the hour, we got word of a bombing on Long Island – several Red Mafiya bosses reported dead. What did it mean? Had the Wolf struck again? At his own people?

There was nothing useful for me to do after the long series of meetings at Scotland Yard. Around ten at night, I met with a friend from Interpol at a London restaurant, the Cinnamon Club, which was on the site of what had once been the Old Westminster Library in Great Smith Street.

I was past being exhausted and, in fact, I had my second wind. Besides, I always looked forward to spending time with Sandy Greenberg, who was probably the smartest police officer I had ever worked with. Maybe she had a new idea about the Wolf. Or the Weasel. At any rate, no one knew the European underworld better than she did.

Sandy is *Sondra* to all but her closest friends and I am fortunate enough to be one of those. She's tall, attractive, chic, a little gawky, witty and very funny. She gave me a big hug and kisses on both cheeks.

'Is this the only way I get to see you, Alex? Some kind of terrifying international emergency? Where's the love?'

'You could always come to Washington to see *me*,' I said as we pulled apart. 'You look absolutely great, by the way.'

'I do, don't I,' said Sandy. 'Come on, we have a table in the back. I've missed you terribly. God, it's good to see you. You look wonderful yourself, even with all of this going on. How do you do it?'

The dinner was a fusion of Indian and European that couldn't be found in the States, at least not anywhere around Washington. Sandy and I talked for well over an hour about the case. But over coffee we lightened up and let things get a little more personal. I noticed a gold signet ring and a trinity band she wore on her pinkie finger.

'Beautiful,' I told her.

'From Katherine,' she said and smiled. Sandy and Katherine Grant had been living together for about ten years and were one of the happiest couples I had ever met. Lessons to be learned, but who can ever figure it all out? Not me. I couldn't even master my own life.

'I see *you're* still not married,' she said.

'You noticed.'

Sandy smirked. 'Detective, you know. Investigator par excellence. So tell me everything, Alex.'

'Not a lot to tell,' I said and found my choice of words interesting. 'I'm seeing someone who I like a lot—'

Sandy interrupted. 'Oh hell, you like *everyone* a lot. That's the way you are, Alex. You even liked Kyle Craig. Found some good in the creepy, psychopathic bastard.'

'You could be right, generally speaking. But I'm over Kyle. And I don't like anything about Colonel Geoffrey Shafer. Or the Russian who calls himself Wolf.'

'I *am* right, dear boy. So who is this incredible woman whom you *like* a lot, and whose heart you'll break, or she'll break yours – one or the other, I'm certain of it already. Why do you keep torturing yourself?'

I grinned, couldn't help it. 'Another detective – well, actually her title is Inspector. She lives in San Francisco.'

'How convenient. That's brilliant, Alex. What is it, two thousand miles away from Washington? So you have a date, what, every other month?'

I laughed again. 'I see your tongue is as sharp as ever.'

'Practice, practice. So you *still* haven't found the right woman. Pity. A real shame. I have a couple of friends . . . Well, hell, let's not even go there. Let me ask you a personal question, though. Do you think you're truly over Maria?'

The thing about Sandy, as an investigator, is that she has thoughts that others don't; she explores areas that are often ignored. My wife, Maria, had been murdered over ten years ago in a drive-by shooting. I'd never been able to solve it – and maybe I *wasn't* over Maria. Maybe, just maybe, I couldn't find closure until I solved her murder. The case was still open. That thought had been tugging at me for years and still caused some pain whenever it entered my head.

'I am totally smitten with Jamilla Hughes,' I said. 'That's all I know for now. We enjoy each other. Why is that a bad thing?'

Sandy smiled. 'I heard you the first time, Alex. You like her a lot. But you haven't told me that you're madly in love, and you're not the kind of person who settles for *smitten*. Right? Of course I'm right. I'm always right.'

'I love *you*,' I said.

Sandy laughed. 'Well then, it's settled. You're staying at *my* place tonight.'

'All right. Fine,' I agreed.

We both laughed, but half an hour later Sandy dropped me at my hotel off Victoria Street.

'You think of anything,' I said as I climbed out of the taxi.

'I'm on it,' said Sandy, and I knew she was as good as her word. I needed all the help I could possibly get in Europe.

Chapter Sixty-Two

Henry Seymour lived not too far from the Weasel's hideout on Edgware Road, in the area between Marble Arch and Paddington that is sometimes known as 'Little Lebanon'. Colonel Shafer walked to the former SAS member's flat that morning, and as he trudged along, he was wondering what had happened to the city, *his* city, and to his bloody country as well? What a dismal scene.

The streets were filled with Middle Eastern coffee shops and restaurants and grocers. The aromas of ethnic cuisine were thick in the air that morning– tabbouleh, strong coffee and lentil soup, mixed with the fragrance of pastilla. In front of a newsagent's two elderly men smoked tobacco through a water-filtered hookah. *Bloody hell! What the fuck has happened to my country?*

Henry Seymour's apartment was located above a

men's clothing shop and the Weasel went straight away to the third floor. He knocked once and Seymour opened up for him.

As soon as he saw Henry, though, Shafer was concerned. The man had lost thirty or forty pounds since he'd seen him last, and that was only a few months ago. His full head of curly black hair was almost gone, replaced by a few scraggly tufts of grey and white frizz.

Indeed, it was a struggle for Shafer to connect this man with his former Army mate, and one of the best demolition experts he'd ever known. The two had fought side by side in Desert Storm and then again as mercenaries in Sierra Leone. In Desert Storm, Shafer and Seymour had been part of the SAS's 22nd Regiment 'Mobility Troop'. Mobility's primary mission was to go behind enemy lines and cause 'havoc'. Nobody was better at it than Shafer and Henry.

Poor Henry didn't look capable of causing too much havoc now, but looks could be deceiving. Hopefully, anyway.

'So, are you ready for a job, an important mission?' Shafer asked.

Henry Seymour smiled, and he was missing a couple of front teeth. 'Suicide, I hope,' he said.

'As a matter of fact,' said the Weasel, 'that's rather a nice idea.'

He sat down across from Henry and gave him his

'piece', and his old friend actually applauded once he'd heard the plan.

'I've always wanted to blow up London,' he said. 'I'm just the man for the job.'

'I know,' said the Weasel.

Chapter Sixty-Three

Dr Stanley S. Bergen of Scotland Yard addressed several hundred of us in a conference room that was filled to the rafters with police and other government officials. Dr Bergen was a little over five feet and had to be close to two hundred pounds, and at least sixty years of age. But he was still a commanding presence.

He spoke without notes and not once during his talk did any of us look away. We were definitely operating on borrowed time, and everyone in the room knew it all too well.

'We are at a critical point where we have to implement our contingency plans for London,' Dr Bergen said. 'Responsibility is under the London Resilience Forum. I have every confidence in them. You should too.

'All right, this is how we will respond in London. If

we have *any* warning that a disaster is coming it will be required that all broadcasters turn over their airtime to us. Text-messaging alerts to mobile phones and pagers will also be available. Other less-effective methods include loud-hailers, mobile public address systems, et cetera.

'Suffice it to say that the people *will* know if *we* know ahead of time that an attack is coming. The Met's Police Commissioner or the Home Secretary will go on TV with the message.

'If there is a bomb, or a chemical attack, the police and fire services will set up immediately in the area. Once it is clear exactly what has happened, the affected area will be isolated as best we can. The fire brigade and police will then define three zones at the scene – *hot, warm* and *cold.*

'Those in the *hot* zone – if they are alive – will be kept there until they are decontaminated, if that is possible.

'Fire and ambulance services will be set up in the *warm* zone. So will decontamination shower units.

'The *cold* zone will be used for investigation, command-and-control vehicles, and also for loading ambulances.'

Dr Bergen stopped talking and looked out at us. His face was set in a worried look, but also revealed the compassion he was feeling for his city and its people. 'Some of you may have noticed that I have *not* actually made mention of the word "evacuation". This is because the evacuation of London is not a possibility, not unless we begin now, and the repugnant and villainous Wolf has promised to strike immediately, should we do so.'

Maps and other emergency materials were then distributed around the room. It seemed to me that the mood was as low as it could possibly go.

As I sat there looking at the paperwork, Martin Lodge came up to me. 'We got a call from the Wolf,' he said in a whisper. 'You'll appreciate this. He says he likes our plan very much. And he agrees, it's hopeless to try and evacuate London—'

Suddenly, there was a terrible explosion in the building.

Chapter Sixty-Four

W hen I finally made it downstairs to the site of
the bombing, I was stunned by the unbelievable scene of chaos and confusion. The world-famous
Scotland Yard sign in front had been completely blown
away. There was a smoking hole and rubble where the
Broadway road entrance had been. The remains of a
black van were embedded in the pavement outside.

A decision had already been made not to abandon
the Yard, to hold our ground. I thought that was smart,
or at least, courageous. A couple of dozen men and
women were already viewing a videotape in semi-
darkness when I arrived at the crisis center. One of
them was Martin Lodge.

I took a seat in back and began to watch. I looked
down, and my hands were trembling.

The film segment showed Broadway that morning,
the usual armed policemen on duty outside the huge,

imposing building. A black van appeared, driven at reckless speed the wrong way along Caxton Street, opposite the main entrance to Scotland Yard. It roared straight over Broadway and crashed into the barrier erected at the entrance. Almost instantly, there was a fiery explosion. It was silent on the film. The whole building was illuminated.

I heard someone speak from near the front of the room. Martin Lodge had taken the floor. 'Our enemy is truly a terrorist, and obviously single-minded. He wants us to know that we are vulnerable. I think we've got the message by now, don't you? It's interesting that no one was killed this morning, other than the driver of the vehicle. Maybe the Wolf has a heart after all.'

A voice came from the back of the room. 'He *doesn't* have a heart. He just has a plan.' The voice, which I almost didn't recognize, was my own.

Chapter Sixty-Five

I worked at Scotland Yard for the rest of the day and I slept there that night. At three in the morning I awoke and went right back to work. The second deadline ran out at midnight. No one could begin to imagine what would happen then.

At seven that morning I was in cramped quarters, inside an unmarked police van headed to an estate in Feltham, out near Heathrow Airport. I rode with Martin Lodge and three of his detectives from the Met. We had recently been granted special permission to carry guns on this assignment. That was better.

Lodge explained the situation during the ride. 'Our men, along with Special Branch, are all over Heathrow and the surrounding areas. We're working closely with the airport police too. One of our people spotted a suspect with a missile launcher on the rooftop of a private home. We have surveillance there now. We don't want to go in, for obvious reasons, made only too clear yesterday. He's bound to be watching the neighborhood.'

One of the other detectives asked, 'Do we have any idea who it is, sir? Have we sussed out anything at all?'

'The house is rented. It belongs to a property developer. Pakistani, if that means anything. We don't know who the tenants are yet. The house is a few hundred yards from the runways at Heathrow. Need I say more?'

I looked over at Lodge, who had his arms wrapped tightly around his chest. 'Very nasty stuff,' he said. 'Understatement of the year – right, Alex?'

'I've had that feeling for a while. Ever since I first encountered the Wolf. He enjoys hurting people.'

'You have no idea who he is, Alex? What makes him this way?'

'He seems to change his identity on a regular basis. He – or she. We got close a couple of times. Maybe we'll get lucky now.'

'It'd better happen soon.'

We arrived at our destination in Feltham a few minutes later. Lodge and I met up with SO19, British Specialist Operations, who would execute the raid. Police surveillance had video monitors set up inside several nearby buildings. Tape was being shot from half a dozen different cameras.

'It's like watching a movie. There's nothing we can do to influence the action,' Lodge said after we'd studied the videos for a few minutes. What an impossible mess. We weren't supposed to be there. We'd been warned against it. But how could we stay away?

Lodge had a list of all the flights scheduled into Heathrow that morning. In the next few hours, over thirty flights would be arriving. The first one was from Eindhoven, then three from Edinburgh, two from Aberdeen, then a British Airways flight from New York. Serious discussions were being held about halting all flights into both Heathrow and Gatwick, but no decision had yet been made. The jet from New York was due in nineteen minutes.

One of the detectives pointed. 'There's someone else on the roof! *Look – there he is!*'

Two monitors showed the house rooftop from opposite angles. A man in dark clothing had appeared. Then a second man, this one carrying a small surface-to-air missile launcher, emerged from a hatchway.

'Fucking hell,' somebody hissed. Tempers were running very high now. Mine too.

'Reroute all the flights now! We have no choice,' Lodge barked. 'Do our snipers have these two bastards covered?'

Word came back that SO19 were ready to fire. Meanwhile, we watched the two men get into position. There could be little doubt now that they were there to bring down a plane. And we were watching the frightening scene, without being able to lift a finger to stop it.

'Arseholes!' Lodge swore at the monitors. 'There's not going to be anything for you bastards to shoot at. How do you like that?'

'They look Middle Eastern to me,' said one of the other detectives. 'They certainly don't look *Russian!*'

'We *don't* have the go-ahead to shoot,' a man wearing headphones announced. 'We're still on hold.'

'What the bloody hell is going on?' Lodge complained in a high-pitched voice. 'We have to take them out. Come on!'

Suddenly there were gunshots! We could hear them on the video. The man with the launcher on his shoulder went down. He didn't get up, didn't move at all. Then the second suspect was hit. Two clean headshots.

'What the hell?' someone shouted. Then everyone was cursing and yelling.

'Who gave the order to shoot? What's going on here?' screamed Lodge.

Word finally came back, but nobody could believe it.

Our snipers hadn't made the hit. Somebody else had shot the two men on the roof.

Madness.

It was total madness.

Chapter Sixty-Six

E verything was a wild ride like nothing anyone could imagine, like nothing anyone ever *had* imagined. The latest deadline was hours away and nobody in the rank and file knew what was happening. Maybe the Prime Minister knew something? The President? The Chancellor of Germany?

Every passing hour just rubbed it in for us. Then it was the passing minutes that hurt. There was nothing we could do, except pray that the ransom would be paid. Soldiers in Iraq, I kept thinking to myself. That's what we are like. Observers of absurdity.

Back in London, at one point in the late afternoon I took a brief walk down near Westminster Abbey. There was so much powerful history on display in this part of the city. The streets weren't deserted, but traffic was very light around Parliament Square, with few tourists and pedestrians. The people of London didn't know what was happening, but whatever it was, it wasn't good.

I called my house in Washington several times. Nobody answered. Had Nana moved? Then I talked to the kids at their Aunt Tia's in Maryland. No one knew where Nana Mama was. Another thing to worry about – just what I needed.

There really was nothing to do but wait; the waiting was frustrating and nerve-racking. Still, no one had a clue what was going on. And not just here in London – in New York, Washington and Frankfurt. No announcement had been made, but the rumor was that none of the ransoms would be paid. In the end, the governments weren't willing to negotiate, were they? They couldn't give in to terrorists, not without a fight. Was that what came next? The fight?

Once again, the deadline passed, and I felt as if we were playing Russian roulette.

There were no attacks in London, New York, Washington or Frankfurt that night. The Wolf didn't retaliate right away. He just let us stew.

I talked to the kids at my aunt's house, and then, *finally*, to Nana. Nothing had happened in D.C. so far. Nana had gone for a walk in the neighborhood with Kayla, she told me. Everything was fine there. *Walk in the park – right, Nana?*

Finally, at 5:00 a.m. in London most of us went home to get some much-needed rest, if we *could* sleep.

I dozed for a few hours, then the phone rang. Martin Lodge was on the line.

'What's happened?' I asked as I sat upright in my hotel bed. 'What has he done?'

Chapter Sixty-Seven

'**N**othing's happened, Alex. Calm down. I'm downstairs in the hotel lobby. I repeat: *nothing's happened.*' Maybe he was bluffing. Let's hope so. 'Get dressed and come for breakfast at my house,' Lodge went on. 'I want you to meet my family. My wife wants to meet you. You need a break, Alex. *We all do.*'

How could I say no, after all that we'd been through in the last few days? Half an hour later, I was in Martin's Volvo headed out to Battersea, just over the river from Westminster. Along the way, Martin tried to prepare me for breakfast, and for his family. We both wore our beepers, but neither of us wanted to talk about the Wolf or his threats. Not for an hour or so anyway.

'The wife is Czech – Klára Cernohosska, born in Prague, but she's a real Brit now. Listens to Virgin and

226

XFM, and all the talk shows on BBC radio. She insisted on a Czech breakfast this morning, though. She's showing off for you. You'll love it – I hope. No, I think you will, Alex.'

I thought so too. Martin was actually smiling as he drove and talked about his family. 'The eldest of my brood is Hana. Guess who chooses the names in our family? Hint – the kids are called Hana, Daniela and Jozef. What's in a name, though? Hana is obsessed with Trinny and Susannah on the TV show *What Not to Wear*. She's fourteen, Alex. The middle child, Dany, plays hockey at Battersea Park – and she's also crazy about ballet. Joe is mad about football, skateboarding and PlayStation. That just about covers it, don't you think? Did I mention that we're eating Czech for breakfast?'

A few minutes later we arrived in Battersea. The Lodge house was a Victorian red-brick with a slate roof, and largish garden. Very neat and nice, appropriate for the neighborhood. The garden was colorful and well-tended and showed that somebody had their priorities in order.

The whole family was waiting in the dining room, where the food was just being laid out. I was formally introduced to everyone, including a cat named Tigger, and I immediately felt pretty much at home, as well as missing my own family, feeling a sharp pang that stayed with me for a while.

Martin's wife, Klára, identified the food as it was laid out on the sideboard. 'Alex, these are *koláče*, pastries with a cream-cheese center. *Rohlíky* – rolls. *Turka*, which is coffee Turkish-style. *Párek*, two kinds of sausage, very good, a specialty of the house.'

She looked at the eldest daughter, Hana, who was a neat blend of her mother and dad. Tall, slim, a pretty face but with Martin's hooked nose. 'Hana?'

Hana grinned at me. 'What kind of eggs would you like, sir? You can have *vejce na měkko*. Or *míchaná vejce*. *Smažená vejce*, if you like. *Omeleta*?'

I shrugged, then said, '*Míchaná vejce*.'

'Excellent choice,' said Klára. 'Perfect pronunciation. Our guest is a born linguist.'

'Good. Now what is it?' I asked. 'The food I ordered?'

Hana giggled. 'Just scrambled eggs. Perfect with the *rohlíky* and *párek*.'

'Yes, the rolls and sausage,' I said and the girls clapped for my show-off performance.

It went that way for the next hour or so, most pleasantly, with Klára asking a lot of informal questions about my life in America, while telling me about the American mystery novels she enjoyed, as well as the latest Booker Prize winner *Vernon God Little*, which she said, 'Is very funny, and captures the craziness of your country much like Günter Grass did with Germany in *The Tin Drum*. You should read it, Alex.'

'I live it,' I told Klára.

It was only at the end of the meal that the kids admitted that the names for the breakfast foods were just about the only Czech words they knew. Then they began to clear away the food and started in on the dishes.

'Oh, and there's *ty vejce jsou hnusný,*' said Jozef, or Joe, the eight-year-old.

'I'm almost afraid to ask – what does that mean?'

'Oh, that the eggs were gross,' said Joe, who laughed with little-boy delight at his joke.

Chapter Sixty-Eight

There was nothing to do once I left Martin and Klára's, except worry about the Wolf and where he might strike, *if* he was going to retaliate. Back at the hotel, I caught a few more hours of sleep, then I decided to take a walk. I felt that this might be a long walk. I needed it.

Something strange, though. I was strolling along Broadway and I had the feeling somebody was following me. I didn't think I was being paranoid. I tried to see who it was, but either they were very good, or I wasn't that skilled at spy games. Maybe if this had been Washington instead of London... But it was difficult for me to spot who or what was out of place here – *except me, of course*.

I stopped in at Scotland Yard and there was still no word from the Wolf. And so far, no reprisals in any of the targeted cities. Was this the calm before the storm?

An hour or so later, having walked up Whitehall, past Number Ten Downing Street, to Trafalgar Square and back, and feeling much better for the exercise, I made my way to the hotel, and had that same creepy feeling again – as if someone was watching me. Who? I didn't actually see anyone.

Back in my room, I called the kids at Aunt Tia's. Then I talked to Nana who was on Fifth Street by herself. 'Oddly peaceful,' she joked. 'But I wouldn't mind a full house again. I miss everybody.'

'So do I, Nana.'

I fell off to sleep again, in my clothes, and didn't wake until the phone rang. I hadn't bothered to pull the drapes and it was dark outside. I looked at the clock – Jesus, it was *four in the morning*. I guess I was finally catching up on some of the sleep I'd lost.

'Alex Cross,' I said into the phone.

'It's Martin, Alex. I'm on my way from home. He wants us to go to the Houses of Parliament, to meet him on the pavement outside the Strangers' Entrance. Shall I pick you up?'

'No. It's faster if I walk. I'll meet you there.' Parliament at this time of the morning? It didn't sound good.

Maybe five minutes later I was back outside again, hurrying along Victoria Street, heading towards Westminster Abbey. I was certain the Wolf was going to pull something, and that it would hurt like hell.

Did that mean all four cities were about to be hit? That wouldn't surprise me. Nothing would at this point.

'Hello, Alex. Fancy meeting you here.'

A man stepped out of the shadows. I hadn't even noticed him standing there. I'd been preoccupied, maybe only half-awake, a little careless.

He stepped all the way out of the shadows and I saw his gun. It was pointed at my heart.

'I'm supposed to be out of the country by now. But there was this one thing I had to do. *Kill you.* I wanted you to see it coming, too. Just like this. I've had dreams about this moment. Maybe you have, too.'

The speaker was Geoffrey Shafer. He was so cocky and confident; and he clearly had the upper hand. Maybe that's why I didn't even think about what I should do now. Without hesitating, I barreled into Shafer, waited for the thundering gunshot to follow.

It came, too. Only he didn't hit me. The shot must have been deflected to the side. Didn't matter. I blocked Shafer hard into the building behind him. I saw surprise and pain in his eyes and that was the motivation I needed. Also – his gun had gone flying in the scuffle.

I hit him hard with an uppercut into his stomach, probably below the belt, maybe a nut cruncher. I hoped so. He grunted and I knew I'd hurt him. But I wanted to hurt Shafer more, for all kinds of reasons. I wanted to kill him right there in the street. I crunched another shot to his stomach and I could feel it go weak under my fist. Then I went for the bastard's head. I slammed a hard right hand into his temple. Then a left to his jaw. He was hurt badly, but he wouldn't go down.

'That all you got, Cross? Here's something for you,' he snarled.

He had a switchblade and I started to step away – but then I realized that he was hurt now, and this was my best chance. I hit Shafer again, on the tip of his nose. Broke it! He still wouldn't go down and he swiped out viciously with the knife. He sliced my arm, and I realized how crazy I was now; how lucky not to be hurt, or killed.

I had a chance to reach for my own gun and I pulled it out of the holster on the back of my belt.

Shafer charged at me and I'm not sure if he saw the gun. Maybe he thought I wouldn't be armed in London.

'No!' I yelled. It was all I had time to say.

I fired point blank into his chest. He fell back against the wall and slowly slid to the ground.

His ruined face was nothing but shock, as maybe he realized that he was mortal after all. 'Fucker, Cross,' he muttered. 'Bastard.'

I bent down over him. 'Who is the Wolf? Where is he?'

'Go to hell,' he said, and then he died, and went there instead.

Chapter Sixty-Nine

London Bridge is falling down,
Falling down, falling down.

Minutes after the Weasel died on the streets of London, his old Army mate, Henry Seymour, drove an eleven-year-old white van through the night – and he was thinking that he had no fear of death. None at all. He welcomed it, actually.

At a little past four-thirty, traffic was already heavy on Westminster Bridge. Seymour parked as close to it as he could, then walked back and rested his arms on the parapet. He loved the sight of Big Ben and the Houses of Parliament from the grand old bridge, always had since he was a small boy visiting London on day trips from Manchester, where he'd been raised.

He was noticing everything this morning. On the opposite bank of the Thames he saw the London Eye, which he thoroughly despised. The Thames was as dark as the early-morning sky and fast-flowing. The smell in the air was slightly salty and fishy. Rows of plum-colored tourist buses sat idle near the bridge, waiting for the day's first passengers.

Wasn't going to happen, though. Not on this day of days. Not if old Henry had his way.

Wordsworth had written of the view from Westminster Bridge (he thought it was Wordsworth): 'Earth has not anything to show more fair.' Henry Seymour always remembered that one, though he wasn't much for poets, or what they had to say.

Write a poem about this shit. Somebody write a poem about me. The Bridge and poor Henry Seymour and all these other poor bastards out here with him this morning.

He went to fetch the van.

At 5:34 a.m., the bridge seemed to ignite at its center. Actually, Henry Seymour's van was what blew up. The strip of roadway beneath it rose up and then split apart; the bridge's teal supports toppled; triple-globed lampposts flew into the air like uprooted flowers blowing in the fiercest wind anyone could imagine. For a moment everything was quiet, deadly quiet, as Seymour's spirit floated away. Then police sirens began to scream all over London.

And the Wolf called Scotland Yard to take credit for his handiwork. 'Unlike you people, I keep my promises,' he said. 'I tried to build bridges between us, but you keep tearing them down. Do you understand? Do you finally understand what I'm saying? This London bridge is gone . . . and it's only the beginning. This is too good to end – I want it to go on and on.'

Payback.

PART FOUR

PARIS, SCENE OF THE CRIME

Chapter Seventy

The test track was a familiar one, located sixty kilometers south of Paris. The Wolf was there to drive a prototype race car, and he had some company for the ride.

Walking beside him was a former KGB man, who had handled his business in France and Spain for many years. His name was Ilya Frolov, and Ilya knew the Wolf by sight. He was one of the few men still alive who did and that filled him with some dread today, though he thought of himself as one of the Wolf's few friends.

'What a beauty!' the Wolf said as the men walked up beside a red Porsche-powered prototype Fabcar. This very model had run in the Rolex Sports Car Series.

'You love your cars,' Ilya said. 'Always have.'

'Growing up outside Moscow, I never thought I would own a car, any car. Now I own so many that I lose count sometimes. I want you to take a ride with me. Get in, my friend.'

Ilya Frolov shook his head and raised both his hands in protest. 'Not me. I don't like the noise, the speed, anything about it.'

'I insist,' said the Wolf. He raised the gull wing on the passenger side first. 'Go ahead, it won't bite you. You'll never forget the ride, Ilya.'

Ilya forced a laugh, then started to cough. 'That's what I'm afraid of.'

'After we finish, I want to talk to you about next steps. We're very close to getting our money. They're weakening day by day, and I have a plan. You're going to be a rich man, Ilya.'

The Wolf climbed in the driver's seat, which was on the right side. He flipped a switch, the dashboard lit, and the car roared and shook. He watched Ilya's face go pale and the Wolf laughed merrily. In his own strange way he loved Ilya Frolov.

'We're sitting right on the engine. It's going to get very hot in here now. Maybe a hundred and thirty degrees. That's why we wear a cool suit. It's going to get noisy too. Put on your helmet, Ilya. Last warning.'

And then they were off!

The Wolf lived for this – the exhilaration – the raw power of the world's finest race cars. Also that at this speed he had to concentrate on the driving. Nothing else mattered – there *was* nothing else while he spun around the test track. Everything about the ride was about power: the *noise*, since there was no sound-dampening material inside; the *vibration* – the stiffer the suspension, the faster the car could change direction; the *g-force*, resulting in as much as six hundred pounds of pressure on some turns.

God, what a glorious machine, so perfect. Whoever made it was a genius.

There are still some of us in the world, he thought to himself. *I should know.*

Finally, he slowed and steered the highly temperamental car off the track. He climbed out, pulled off his helmet, shook out his hair, and shouted to the skies.

'That was so great! My God, what an experience. Better than sex! I've ridden women and cars – I prefer the racing car!'

He looked over at Ilya Frolov and saw that the man was still pale and he was shaking a bit. Poor Ilya.

'I'm sorry, my friend,' the Wolf spoke softly. 'I'm afraid you don't have the balls for the next ride. Besides, you *know* what happened in Paris.'

He shot his friend dead on the test track. Then the Wolf just walked away, never looked back. He had no interest in the dead.

Chapter Seventy-One

That same afternoon the Wolf visited a farmhouse about fifty kilometers south-east of the test track. He was the first to arrive and settled in the kitchen, which he kept dark as a crypt. Artur Nikitin had been ordered to come alone and he did as he was told. Nikitin was former KGB and had always been a loyal soldier. He had worked for Ilya Frolov, mostly as an arms dealer.

The Wolf heard Artur approaching on the back steps. 'No lights,' he called. 'Just come inside.'

Artur Nikitin opened the door and stepped inside. He was tall, with a thick white beard, a big Russian bear of a man, physically not unlike the Wolf himself.

'There's a chair. Sit, please. You are my guest,' said the Wolf.

Nikitin obeyed. He showed no fear. Actually, he had no fear of death.

'You have always done good work for me in the past. This will be our last job together. You'll make enough to walk away from the life, to do as you wish. Does that sound all right?'

'It sounds very good. Whatever you wish, I do. It's the secret of my success.'

'Paris is very special to me,' the Wolf continued. 'In another life, I lived here for two years. And now, here I am again. It's no coincidence, Artur. I need your help here. More than that, I need your loyalty. Can I depend on you?'

'Of course. Without a doubt. I'm *here*, aren't I?'

'I plan to blow a big hole in Paris, cause lots more trouble, then get filthy rich. I can still depend on you?'

Nikitin found himself smiling. 'Absolutely. I don't like the French anyway. Who does? It will be a pleasure. I especially like the "filthy rich" part.'

The Wolf had found his man for the job. Now he gave him his 'piece' of the puzzle.

Chapter Seventy-Two

Two days after the bombing of Westminster Bridge, I traveled back to Washington. During the long flight, I forced myself to make extensive notes about what the Wolf might do next. What *could* he do? Would he strike again, keep on bombing cities until he got his money? And what was the significance of *bridges* to him?

Only one thing seemed obvious to me: *the Wolf wasn't going to disappear and leave things as they had been before. He wasn't going away.*

Even before my plane had landed I got a message from Ron Burns's office. I was to go to headquarters as soon as I arrived in Washington.

But I didn't go to the Hoover Building; I went home instead. Like Bartleby the Scrivener, in Herman Melville's book, I 'respectfully declined my employer's request'. I didn't think twice about it. The Wolf would still be there in the morning.

The kids had come into the city with their Aunt Tia. Nana was there on Fifth Street, too. We spent the night together at our house, the one Nana had been born in. In the morning, the kids would return to Maryland with Tia. Nana would stay on Fifth Street – and so would I. Maybe the two of us were more alike than I wanted to admit.

Around eleven that night, someone was at the front door. I had been playing the piano on the sun porch and it was only a few steps to the door. I opened up and saw Ron Burns standing there with a couple of his agents. He ordered his men to go wait by the car. Then he invited himself in.

'I need to talk to you. Everything has changed,' the Director said as he walked past me at the door.

And so, I sat out on our small sun porch with the Director of the FBI. I didn't play the piano for Burns; I just listened to what he had to say.

The first thing had to do with Thomas Weir. 'We have no doubt that Tom had some connection with the Wolf back when he came out of Russia. He may have known who the Russian was. We're on it, Alex, and so is the CIA. But of course this puzzle refuses to unravel easily.'

'Everybody's *cooperating* with everybody else though,' I said and frowned. 'How nice.'

Burns stared at me. 'I know that this has been tough

for you. I know the job isn't the perfect fit so far. You want to be in the middle of the action. And you want to be with your family.'

I couldn't deny it, not any of what Burns had said. 'Go ahead, Director. I'm still listening.'

'Something happened in France, Alex. It involved Tom Weir, and the Wolf. It happened a long time ago. A mistake was made – a big one.'

'What mistake?' I asked. Were we finally getting close to some answers? 'You have to stop playing games with me! Do you ever wonder why I'm having second thoughts about my job?'

'Believe me, we don't know what happened back then. We're getting closer to an answer. A *lot* has occurred in the last few hours. The Wolf made contact again, Alex.'

I sighed heavily, but I listened, because I had promised that I would.

'You said it before – that he wants to hurt us, to break our back if he can. He says that he *can*. He said that the rules are changing, and that he's the one changing them. He's the only one with the answers to this puzzle. *You're* the only one with a clue about him.'

I had to stop Burns. 'Ron, what are you trying to say? Just tell me. I'm either in this thing – all the way – or I'm all the way out.'

'He gave us ninety-six hours. Then he promised a Doomsday scenario. He changed some of the target cities – it's still Washington and London, but also *Tel Aviv* now, and *Paris*. He won't explain the change. He wants four billion dollars, and he wants the political prisoners released. He won't explain a goddamn thing to us.'

'That's all?' I said.'Four doomed cities? A few billion in ransom? Free some murderers?'

Burns shook his head.'No, that's not all. He's given everything to the press this time. There's going to be panic around the world. But especially in the four cities: London, Paris, Tel Aviv and here in Washington. He's gone public.'

Chapter Seventy-Three

On Sunday morning, after breakfast with Nana, I left for Paris. Ron Burns wanted me in France. End of discussion.

Exhausted and probably depressed, I slept for a good part of the flight. Then I read a lot of CIA files about a KGB agent who had lived in Paris eleven years ago, and might have worked with Thomas Weir: that agent supposedly was the Wolf. And something had happened. A 'mistake'. A big one, apparently.

I'm not sure what kind of reception I was expecting from the French, especially given the recent history between our countries, but things went fairly smoothly once I arrived. In fact, it seemed to me that the command center in Paris worked better than the similar command centers I'd seen in either London or Washington. The reason for this was clear immediately.

The infrastructure in Paris was simpler, the organization much smaller. One official told me, 'It's easy to share here, because the file you need is next door, or right down the hall.'

I received a quick briefing, and then I was thrown into a high-level meeting. A general in the Army looked at me and addressed me in English. 'Dr Cross, to be honest with you, we haven't ruled out the possibility that this violence is part of the jihad, that is to say, Islamic terrorist attacks. Please believe me, they are clever enough to dream up something bizarre like this. They are duplicitous enough to have even *dreamed up the Wolf.* This would explain the demand to release the hostages – would it not?'

I didn't say a word. How could I? *Al Qaeda? Behind everything so far? Behind the Wolf?* This was what the French believed? That was why I was here?

'As you know, our two countries don't share the same perspective about the connection between the Islamic terror networks and the current situation in the Middle East. We believe that jihad *isn't* actually a war against Western values. It is a complex reaction against the leaders of Muslim nations who haven't adopted radical Islam.'

'And yet, the four main targets of radical Islam are the US, Israel, France and England,' I spoke from my seat. 'I agree that the current targets of the so-called Wolf are *Washington, Tel Aviv, Paris, London*. But I have to tell you, I've seen no real evidence that Islamic terrorists are behind this threat.'

'Please keep an open mind on the matter. In addition, you should know that former KGB officers were involved and very influential with Saddam Hussein in Iraq. As I say, keep an open mind.'

I nodded. 'I have an open mind. But I've dealt with the Wolf before. Believe me, he doesn't embrace the values of Islam. He isn't a religious man.'

Chapter Seventy-Four

That night I had dinner by myself in Paris. Actually, I walked around just to see the situation in the city first-hand. There were heavily armed French soldiers everywhere. Tanks and jeeps in the streets. Not too many people out walking. Worried looks on the faces of those who ventured out for whatever reason.

I ate at one of the few places open for business – *Les Olivades* on Avenue De Ségur. The restaurant and clientèle were extremely laid back, and that was what I needed, given the jet-lag and confusion, not to mention the state of the siege in Paris.

After the meal I walked some more, thinking about the Wolf and also Thomas Weir. *The Wolf had murdered Weir on purpose, hadn't he? He'd targeted Paris for a reason, too. Why? What was his thing with bridges? A possible clue for us? Were bridges symbolic for him? What was the symbolism?*

It was sad and strange to walk around Paris knowing that a deadly attack could come at any time. I was here to find some way to stop it – but honestly, no one knew where to start; no one had turned up one clue as to the identity of the Wolf or where he might be staying, not even a country. *The Wolf had lived here, eleven years ago. Something bad had happened. What was it?*

This section of Paris was gorgeous, broad avenues and wide sidewalks cutting a swath between the well-kept stone buildings. Wavering trails of a few car lights streamed up and down the avenues. People leaving Paris? And then – when we would least expect it – *boom! Kiss your ass goodbye.*

The scary thing was that a really bad end almost seemed inevitable now. And not just another bridge this time.

That's how well he has us set up. He's in full control – but we have to turn that around somehow.

When I got back to my hotel, I called the kids. It was six at night in Maryland; their Aunt Tia would just be getting dinner ready, the kids complaining they were too busy to help. Jannie answered the phone. *'Bonjour, Monsieur Cross.'* Was she psychic?

Then Jannie launched into a half-dozen questions she'd been saving up for me. In the meantime, Damon had picked up the extension. Both of them began to rattle off questions. I think that they wanted to lessen

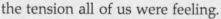

the tension all of us were feeling.

Had I visited Notre Dame Cathedral? Did I meet the Hunchback (ha, ha)? Did I see the famous gargoyles, like the one they remembered who was *eating* another?

'I didn't have time to climb the towers to the Gallery of Fabulous Beasts today. I'm working here.' I got in a couple of sentences.

'We know that, Dad,' Jannie said. 'We're just trying to keep everything light. We miss you,' she whispered.

'Miss you, Dad,' Damon said.

'Je t'aime,' said Jannie.

Minutes later, I was alone in a faraway hotel room – in a city under a death threat.

Je t'aime aussi.

Chapter Seventy-Five

The clock was ticking . . . *loudly*. Or was that just my heart getting ready to explode?

Early the next morning it was arranged for me to have a partner. His name was Etienne Marteau, a detective with the French National Police. Marteau was a small and wiry man, cooperative and competent, on the face of it. But I had the sense that he'd been assigned to watch me more than to work with me. That was so messed up, so counter-productive, it started to drive me crazy.

In the late afternoon, I spoke to Ron Burns's office about my going home. My request was denied. By Tony Woods! Tony never even bothered to take it to the Director. He reminded me that Thomas Weir and the Wolf had probably met in Paris.

'I didn't *forget*, Tony,' I told him and hung up.

So I began to wade through the records and data

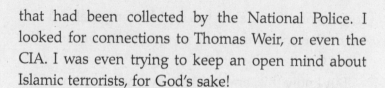

that had been collected by the National Police. I looked for connections to Thomas Weir, or even the CIA. I was even trying to keep an open mind about Islamic terrorists, for God's sake!

Detective Marteau was slightly helpful, but the process was slow and the Frenchman needed frequent breaks for cigarettes and coffee. This wasn't going anywhere, and again I had the feeling that whatever help I could bring to the situation was being wasted here. I was getting a really bad headache, too.

Around six o'clock we gathered in the crisis center. The goddamn clock was ticking! The Wolf would be calling again, I finally learned. The mood in the room was charged, but clearly very negative: we all knew we were being manipulated, and insulted. I was sure the atmosphere was the same in Washington, London, Tel Aviv.

Suddenly, we heard his voice on the speaker phone. *Heavily filtered. Familiar. Obscene.*

'Sorry to keep everybody waiting,' he said, and although he didn't laugh, there was nothing but derision in his tone. I wanted to scream at the bastard.

'But then, of course, *I have been kept waiting, haven't I?* I know, I know, it's because the precedent is unacceptable to all the governments, the loss of face. I *understand.* I get it.

'And now, I need you to *understand* something, too. This deadline is the final one. I will even make a concession. If it makes you feel better, go ahead and try to find me. Bring your investigations out into the open. Catch me if you can.

'But know this, and know it well, you bastards. This time, the money must be paid on time. All of it. The prisoners of war must be released. All of them. The deadline will not be extended, and believe me, it is a *dead*line. If you miss it, even by minutes, there will be tens of thousands of murders in each of the four cities. You heard me right – I said *murders*. Believe me, I will push the button. I will kill in a way the world has rarely seen. Especially in Paris. *Au revoir, mes amis.*'

Chapter Seventy-Six

L ater that night, Etienne Marteau and I thought that we might have stumbled onto something useful and maybe even important. At this point every clue was being looked at as vital.

The French National Police had intercepted several messages dialed on the phone of a known arms dealer working out of Marseilles. The dealer specialized in hardware from the Red Army, contraband which was floating all over Europe, but especially in Germany, France, and Italy. In the past, he'd sold contraband to radical Islamic groups.

Marteau and I read and reread the transcript of a phone conversation between the arms dealer and a suspected terrorist with ties to al Qaeda. The conversation was coded, but the French police had broken most of it down:

Arms Dealer: Cousin, how is your business these days? (ARE YOU READY TO DO THE JOB?) Are you coming to see me soon? (CAN YOU TRAVEL?)

Suspected Terrorist: Oh, you know I have a wife and too many children. These things are sometimes complicated. (HE HAS A LARGE TEAM.)

Dealer: For God's sake, I have told you before – bring your woman and the children with you. You should come right now. (BRING YOUR WHOLE TEAM NOW.)

Suspected Terrorist: We are all very tired. (BEING WATCHED.)

Dealer: Everyone is tired. But you will love it here. (IT'S SAFE FOR YOU.) I guarantee it.

Suspected Terrorist: All right, then. I will start loading up my family.

Dealer: I have my stamp collection ready for you. (PROBABLY SPECIAL TACTICAL WEAPONS.)

Etienne Marteau and I read the transcript again and again.

'What does he mean – *my stamp collection*?' I asked. 'That's a key phrase, isn't it?'

'They're not sure, Alex. They believe it's weapons. What kind – who knows for certain? Something serious.'

'Will they stop the terrorist team now? Or let them into France and watch them?'

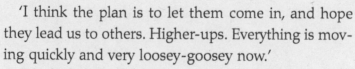

'I think the plan is to let them come in, and hope they lead us to others. Higher-ups. Everything is moving quickly and very loosey-goosey now.'

'Maybe a little too loosey-goosey,' I said. *Where did this guy learn English?*

'We do things differently here. Please try to respect that, to understand it if you can.'

I nodded. 'Etienne, I don't think there will be any contact with higher-ups on the ground here. That isn't how the Wolf works. Every player has a part to play – but no clue about the larger plan.'

The detective looked me in the eye. 'I'll pass that on,' he said.

But I doubted very much that he would. An idea struck me and it was hard to handle. *I was all alone over here, wasn't I? I was the Ugly American.*

Chapter Seventy-Seven

I finally went back to the Relais at two in the morning. I was up again at six-thirty. No rest for the righteous, or the ridiculous. *But the Wolf didn't want us rested, did he? He wanted us stressed and afraid and capable of making mistakes.*

I walked to the Préfecture de Police, obsessing about the twisted mind behind all of this. Why was he twisted? The Wolf had supposedly been a KGB agent before he came to America, where he became a powerful force in the Red Mafiya. He'd spent time in England, and here in France. He was clever enough that we still didn't know his identity, not even a name, and we definitely didn't have a complete history for him.

He thought big. But why would he align himself with Islamic terrorist groups – unless he'd been involved with al Qaeda from the start. Was that really a possibility? If it was, then it scared the hell out of me, because it was so incredibly unthinkable, so preposterous in a way. But so much that was happening in the world seemed preposterous these days.

Out of the corner of my eye – a flash!

Suddenly I was aware of a silver-and-black motorcycle coming at me *on the sidewalk*! My heart clutched and I jumped out into the street. I spread my arms and balanced myself to move quickly, left or right, depending on the motorcycle's path.

But then I noticed that none of the other pedestrians around me seemed concerned. A smile finally crossed my lips. I remembered Etienne mentioning that over-sized motorcycles were popular in Paris and that their riders acted as if they were on much smaller mopeds or scooters, sometimes circumnavigating traffic by going up onto sidewalks.

The bike rider, decked out in his blue blazer and tan slacks, was a Paris businessman. Not an assassin. He passed by without so much as a nod. *I was losing it, wasn't I?* But that was understandable. Who wouldn't begin to lose it under this pressure?

At eight-thirty that morning, I walked to the front of a room full of important French police and Army officials. We were inside the Ministère de l'Interieur which was located in L'Hôtel Beauvau.

We had just over thirty-three hours left to *Doomsday*. The room was a strange mix of expensive-looking eighteenth-century-style furniture and genuinely expensive modern technology. In sharp contrast, scenes from London, Paris, Washington and Tel Aviv played on TV monitors on the walls. Mostly empty streets. Heavily armed soldiers and police everywhere.

We are at war, I thought to myself. *With a madman.*

I'd been told that I could speak in English to the group, but it would be best if I went slowly and enunciated my words clearly. I figured they were afraid I was going to deliver my talk in street slang that no one in the room would understand.

'My name is Dr Alex Cross. I'm a forensic psychologist,' I began. 'I was a homicide detective in Washington, D.C. before I became an agent with the FBI. Less than a year ago, I worked on a case that put me in touch with the Red Mafiya. In particular, I was involved with a former KGB man known only as the Wolf. The Wolf is my subject this morning.'

I could do the rest in my sleep. For the next twenty minutes I talked about the Russian. But even as I was finishing up, and the question-and-answer period had begun, it was clear to me that although the French were willing to listen to what I had to say, they were steadfast in their belief that Islamic terrorists were the real source of the threat to the four targeted cities. *Either the Wolf was part of al Qaeda – or he was working with them.*

I was trying to keep my mind open, but if their

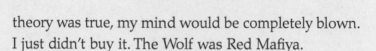

theory was true, my mind would be completely blown. I just didn't buy it. The Wolf was Red Mafiya.

Around eleven o'clock, I went back to my cubicle office, and found that I had a new partner.

Chapter Seventy-Eight

A new partner? Now?

Everything was going so fast; it was all a blur to me, often incomprehensible. I had to assume that the FBI had contacted someone and pulled some strings. Someone had. The new partner was an 'agent de police', a woman named Maud Boulard, who immediately informed me that we would be working in the 'French Police way', whatever the hell that was supposed to mean.

Physically, she was very much like Etienne Marteau: thin, with an aquiline nose and sharp features – but shiny red hair. She went out of her way to tell me she had visited New York and Los Angeles, and didn't care for either city at all.

'Our deadline is close,' I told her.

'I know the deadline, Dr Cross. Everyone does. To work fast does not mean to work intelligently.'

What she called 'our surveillance of the Red Mafiya' began along the Parc Monceau in the eighth arrondissement. Unlike in the US, where the Russians seemed to hang out in working-class neighborhoods like Brighton Beach in New York, the Mafiya was apparently situated in pricier digs here.

'Maybe because they know Paris better, and have operated here longer,' Maud suggested. 'I think so. I have known the Russian thugs for many years. *They* don't believe in your Wolf, by the way. I've asked around.'

And that's what we did for the next hour or so. Spoke to Russian thugs about the Wolf. If nothing else, the morning was beautiful, with bright blue skies, which made it excruciating for me. What was I doing here?

At one-thirty, Maud said very cheerfully, 'Let's have lunch – with the Russians, of course. I know just the place.'

She took me into what she called 'one of the oldest Russian restaurants in Paris', Le Daru, with its *Specialités Russes*. The front room was paneled with warm pine as if we were inside the dacha of a wealthy Muscovite.

I was angry, but trying not to show it. We simply didn't have time for a sitdown lunch.

Nevertheless, Maud and I ate. I wanted to strangle her, the obsequious waiter, anybody I could get my hands on. I'm certain she had no idea how angry I was. *Some detective!*

As we finished, I noticed that two men at a nearby table were watching us, or maybe they were eyeing Maud, with her lustrous red hair.

I told her about the men, and she shrugged it off as, The way men are in Paris. Pigs.

'Let's see if they follow,' she said as we got up and left the restaurant. 'I doubt that they will. I don't know them. I know *everybody* here. Not your Wolf though.'

'They're leaving right behind us,' I told her.

'Good for them. It is the *exit*, after all.'

The short rue Daru ended at rue du Faubourg St-Honoré, which Maud now told me was a window-shopping experience that continued all the way to the Place Vendôme. We had only walked a block when a white Lincoln limousine pulled up alongside us.

A dark bearded man opened the rear door and looked out. 'Please get in the car. Don't make a scene,' he said in English with a Russian accent. 'Get in, now. I'm not fooling around.'

'No,' said Maud. 'We won't get in your car. You come out here and talk to us. Who the hell are you? Who do you *think* you are?'

The bearded man pulled a gun and he fired twice. I couldn't believe what had just happened right in the middle of a Paris street.

Maud Boulard was down on the sidewalk, and I was

certain she was dead. Blood seeped from a horrible, jagged wound near the center of her forehead. Her red hair was splayed in a hundred directions. Her eyes were open wide, staring up into the blue skies. In the fall, one of her shoes had been thrown off and lay out in the middle of the street.

'Get in the car, Dr Cross. I won't ask you again. I'm tired of being *polite*,' said the Russian, whose gun was pointed at my face. 'Get in, or I'll shoot you in the head too. With pleasure.'

Chapter Seventy-Nine

'Now comes show-and-tell time,' the black-bearded Russian man said once I was inside the limousine with him.'Isn't that how they say it in American schools?You have two children in school, don't you? So – I'm *showing* you things that are important, and I'm *telling* you what they mean. I told the detective to get in the car and she didn't do it. Maud Boulard was her name, no? Maud Boulard wanted to act like the tough cop. Now she's the dead cop, not so tough after all.'

The car sped away from the murder scene, leaving the French detective dead in the street. We changed cars a few blocks from the shooting, getting into a much less obtrusive gray Peugeot. For what it was worth, I memorized both license plates.

'Now we go for a little ride in the country,' said the Russian man, who seemed to be having a good time so far.

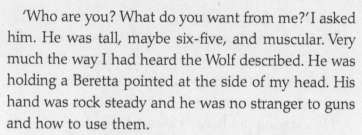

'Who are you? What do you want from me?' I asked him. He was tall, maybe six-five, and muscular. Very much the way I had heard the Wolf described. He was holding a Beretta pointed at the side of my head. His hand was rock steady and he was no stranger to guns and how to use them.

'It doesn't matter who I am, not in the least. You're looking for the Wolf, aren't you? I'm taking you to meet him now.'

He threw me a dark look, then handed me a cloth sack. 'Put this over your head. And do exactly as I say from now on. Remember, *show* and *tell*.'

'I remember.' I put on the hood. I would never forget the cold-blooded murder of Detective Boulard. The Wolf and his people killed easily, didn't they? What did that mean for the four cities under threat? Would they kill thousands and thousands so easily? Was that their plan to demonstrate power and control? To get revenge for some mysterious crime in the past?

I don't know how long we rode around in the Peugeot, but it was well over an hour: slow city driving at first, then an hour or so on the open highway.

Then we were slowing again, possibly traveling on a dirt road. Hard bounces and bumps shocked and twisted my spine.

'You can take off the hood now,' Black Beard spoke to me again. 'We're almost there, Dr Cross. Nothing much to see out here anyway.'

I took off the hood, and saw that we were in the French countryside somewhere, riding down an unpaved road with tall grass waving on either side. No markers or signs anywhere that I could see.

'He's staying out here?' I asked. I wondered if I was really being taken to the Wolf. For what possible reason?

'For the moment, Dr Cross. But then he'll be gone again. As you know, he moves around a lot. He is like a ghost, an apparition. You'll see what I mean in a moment.'

The Peugeot pulled up in front of a small, stone farmhouse. Two armed men immediately came out the front door to meet us. Both held automatic weapons aimed at my upper body and face.

'Inside,' said one of them. He had a white beard, but he was nearly as large and muscular as the man who had accompanied me thus far.

It was obvious that he had seniority over Black Beard, who had seemed in control until now. '*Inside!*' he repeated to me. 'Hurry up! Can't you hear, Dr Cross?'

'He is an animal,' White Beard then said to me. 'He shouldn't have killed the woman. I am the Wolf, Dr Cross. It's good to meet you at last.'

Chapter Eighty

'**D**on't try to do anything heroic, by the way. Because then I'll have to kill you, and find a new messenger,' he said as we walked inside the farmhouse.

'I'm a messenger now? For what?' I asked.

The Russian waved off my question like it was a pesky fly buzzing around his hairy face.

'Time is flying. Weren't you thinking that with the French detective? They were just keeping you out of the way, the French. Didn't you think as much?'

'The thought crossed my mind,' I said. Meanwhile – I couldn't believe that this was the Wolf. I *didn't* believe it. But who was he? Why had I been brought here?

'Of course it did. You're not a stupid man,' he said.

We had entered a small, dark room with a fieldstone fireplace, but no fire. The room was cluttered with heavy wooden furniture, old magazines, yellowing newspapers. The windows were tightly shuttered. The place was airless. The only light came from a single standing lamp.

'Why am I here? Why show yourself to me now?' I finally asked him.

'Sit down,' said the Russian.

'All right. I'm a messenger,' I said and lowered myself into a chair.

He nodded. 'Yes. A messenger. It's important that everyone fully understands the seriousness of the situation. This *is* your last chance.'

'We understand,' I said.

Almost before I had finished speaking, he lunged forward and hit me in the jaw. My chair went over backwards, I was in free fall, then my head struck the stone floor. I might have been out for a couple of seconds.

But then I felt myself being dragged back up by a couple of the other men in the room. My head was spinning and there was blood in my mouth.

'I want to be clear about this,' the Russian continued. It was as if hitting me had been a necessary pause in his speech. 'You *are* a messenger. And none of you fools understand the seriousness now. Just as no one seems to understand, really understand, that they are going to die, and what that means, *until the moment that it happens* . . . The stupid woman in Paris today?

Do you think she understood before a speeding bullet blew open her brain? The money must be paid this time, Dr Cross. *In full. In all four cities.* The prisoners must be released.'

'Why the prisoners?' I asked.

He hit me again, but this time I didn't go down. Then he turned and left the room. 'Because I say so!'

He came back a moment later, and he had a heavy black valise. He set it on the floor right in front of me.

'This is the dark side of the moon,' he said. Then he opened it for me to see inside.

'It's called a Tactical Nuclear Explosive Device. More simply, a *suitcase nuke*. Produces a horrific explosion. Unlike conventional warheads, it operates at ground level. Easy to conceal, easy to transport. No mess, no fuss. You've seen pictures of Hiroshima, of course. Everyone has.'

'What about Hiroshima?'

'This suitcase has approximately the same yield. Devastating. We, the old Soviet Union, used to manufacture these bombs by the truckload. Want to know where some of the others are right now? Well, there is one or more in Washington, D.C., Tel Aviv, Paris, London. So, as you see, there is a new member of the exclusive nuclear community. *We* are that new member.'

I was starting to feel cold all over. Was there really a nuclear bomb in the suitcase?

'That's the message you want me to deliver?'

'The *other* reactors are in place. And to show my good faith, you can take *this* reactor back with you. Let the boys in the shop look it over. But tell them to look very quickly.

'Now, maybe – *maybe* – you understand. Get out of here. To me, you are a gnat, but at least you are a gnat. Take the nuclear weapon with you. Consider it a gift. Don't say I didn't warn you about what was going to happen. Now, go. *Hurry*, Dr Cross.'

Chapter Eighty-One

E verything was a blur from here on that afternoon. The dark cloth hood had just been for show, I figured, since I wore nothing over my eyes on the ride back to Paris, which seemed a lot shorter than the ride out.

I kept asking my captors where I was being brought – with the suitcase bomb – but neither man in the car would give me an answer. Not a word. They spoke nothing but Russian on the ride.

To me, you are a gnat . . . Take the nuclear weapon with you . . .

Soon after we entered Paris, the Peugeot stopped in the crowded parking lot of a shopping center. A gun was held in my face, and then I was handcuffed to the suitcase. 'What's this about?' I asked my captors but received no answer.

Moments later the Peugeot stopped again, at Place

Igor Stravinsky, one of the more populated areas of Paris, though mostly deserted now.

'Get out!' I was told – the first English words I'd heard in close to an hour.

Slowly, carefully, I emerged from the sedan with the bomb. I felt a little dizzy. The Peugeot roared off.

I was aware of a certain liquidity in the air, particles, a real sense of atoms. I stood motionless near the huge plaza of the Centre National d'Art et de Culture Georges Pompidou, handcuffed to a black valise that weighed at least fifty pounds, probably more.

Supposedly, it carried a nuclear bomb, the full equivalent of the ones Harry Truman had ordered to be dropped on Japan. My body was already covered with cold sweat, and I felt as if I were watching myself in a dream. Could it all end like this? Of course it could. All bets were off, but especially any bets on my life. Was I about to be blown up? Would I suffer radiation sickness if I wasn't?

I spotted two policemen near a Virgin record store and made my way up to them. I explained who I was, and then told them to please call the Directeur de la Securité Publique.

I didn't say what was in the black valise to the cop, but I quickly revealed the contents to the Directeur when he came on the line. 'Is the threat real, Dr Cross?' he wanted to know. 'Is the bomb live?'

'I don't know. How could I? Please respond as if it

is. That's what I'm doing.' *Get your bomb squad over here. Now! Get off the phone!*

Within a few minutes, the whole of the Beaubourg district had been evacuated, except for a dozen or so patrolmen, the military police, and several bomb-squad experts. At least I hoped they were experts, the best France had to offer.

I was told to sit on the ground, which I did. Right alongside the black valise, of course. I did everything I was told to do, because I had no choice in the matter. I was feeling sick to my stomach and sitting made it a little better, though not much. At least the initial dizziness I'd felt was starting to pass.

First, a bomb-sniffing dog was brought in to smell me and the suitcase. A beautiful young German shepherd bitch, the *chien explo*, approached very cautiously, eyeing the suitcase as if it were a rival dog, an enemy.

When the dog got within five yards of me, she completely froze. A low growl rumbled up from her chest. The hair on her neck rose. *Oh shit. Oh God,* I thought.

The dog continued to growl until she was certain of radioactive contents, then she quickly retreated to her handlers. Very wise. I was left alone again. I'd never been more frightened in my life; nothing even came close to this. The thought of being blown apart, possibly vaporized, isn't a pleasant one, tough to wrap your mind around.

After what seemed like an eternity, though it was only a few minutes, two bomb-squad technicians in moonsuits cautiously headed my way. I saw that one of them was clutching bolt cutters. God bless him! This was such an incredibly surreal moment.

The man with the cutters knelt down beside me. 'It's okay, you're okay,' he whispered. Then he carefully sliced through the handcuffs.

'You can leave. Get up slowly,' he said. I rose cautiously, rubbing my wrist, but already backing away from the suitcase.

My alien-looking escorts and I hurried out of the designated 'hot zone' to where two black bomb-squad vans were parked. Of course, the van was still in the 'hot zone' as well. If a nuclear bomb went off, at least a square mile of Paris would be vaporized instantly.

From inside one of the vans I watched the team of technicians work to deactivate the bomb. If they could. I never considered leaving the scene, and the next few minutes were the longest of my life. No one in the van spoke and we were all holding our breaths. The idea of dying like this, so suddenly, was almost impossible to conceive.

Word came back from the French bomb technicians –'*the suitcase is open.*'

Then, less than a minute later, '*The fissile material is there. It's real. It seems to be in working order, unfortunately.*'

The bomb was real. It wasn't a fake threat. The Wolf was still keeping his promises, wasn't he? The sadistic bastard was everything that he said he was.

Then I saw one of the technicians pump his arm in the air. A cheer went up around the console in the van. I didn't understand exactly what had happened at first, but it seemed like good news. No one explained anything to me.

'What just happened?' I finally asked in French.

One of the techs turned to me. 'There's no trigger! It couldn't blow up. They didn't want it to explode, thank God. They only wanted to scare the shit out of us.'

'It worked,' I told him. 'I shit you not.'

Chapter Eighty-Two

O ver the next couple of hours it was revealed that the suitcase bomb had everything necessary for a nuclear explosion except a single part, a pulsed neutron emitter, a trigger. All of the difficult elements were there. I couldn't eat that night, couldn't keep anything down, couldn't concentrate at all. I'd been tested – but I couldn't get the idea of radiation poisoning to leave my brain.

I also couldn't get Maud Boulard out of my mind: her face, the tenor of her voice, our absurd lunch together, the detective's stubbornness and naiveté, her red hair splayed out on the sidewalk. The casual brutality of the Wolf and his people.

I kept flashing back to the Russian who had struck me in the farmhouse. Had it been the Wolf? Why would he let me see him? And then – why not?

I went back to the Relais and suddenly wished that

I hadn't asked for a room facing the street. My body felt numb all over, exhausted, but my mind wouldn't stop racing at warp speed. The noise rising from the street was a disturbance that I couldn't handle right now. *They have nuclear weapons. This isn't a bluff. It's going to happen. A holocaust.*

I decided to call the kids at around six o'clock their time. I talked to them about all of the things in Paris that I *didn't* see that day – everything except what had really happened to me. So far, the media had none of it, but that wouldn't last.

Then I called Nana. I told her the truth about how it had felt sitting on the pavement with a bomb attached to my wrist. She was the one I had always told about my worst days, and this was probably the worst of them all.

Chapter Eighty-Three

When I arrived at my small office at the Préfecture I got another surprise. Martin Lodge was waiting there for me. It was seven-fifteen: ten hours and forty-five minutes to Doomsday.

I shook Martin's hand, and told him how glad I was that he was here. 'Not much time left. Why are you here?'

'Last words, I suppose. I have to give the final update on the situation in London. As well as Tel Aviv. From our vantage point anyway.'

'And?'

Martin shook his head. 'You don't want to hear the same rotten story twice.'

'Yeah. I do.'

'Not this story, you don't. Oh hell, it's all cocked up, Alex. I think he might have to blow up a city to get them to act – that's how bad it is. The worst is Tel Aviv.

I think it's basically hopeless there. They don't make deals with terrorists. You asked.'

The morning briefing started at eight sharp and it included a quick summary on the briefcase bomb from the technicians who had taken it apart. They reported that the bomb was authentic in design, but there was no neutron emitter, no trigger, and possibly not enough radioactive material inside.

An Army general spoke about the current situation in Paris: the people were frightened, and staying off the streets, but only a small percentage had actually fled the city. The Army was prepared to move in and declare martial law at around the time of the deadline, which was 6:00 p.m.

Then it was time for Martin. He strode to the front of the room and spoke in French. 'Good morning. Isn't it incredible what can happen once we adapt ourselves to a new reality? The people of London have been splendid for the most part. There has been some rioting, but not too much. I suspect that those who might have given us the most trouble got out of London early. As for Tel Aviv, they're so accustomed to crises and living under threatening scenarios – let's just say that they're handling this very well.

'Anyway, that's the good news. The bad is that we've raised most of the money, but not all of it. That's in London. And Tel Aviv? As best we can tell, they're not going to make a deal. The Israelis hold their cards very close to their chest, so we're not sure what's transpired there.

'We're putting on pressure, of course. And so is Washington. I know that private individuals have been approached to put up the entire ransom. That could still happen. But it isn't clear whether the Israeli government will take the money. They simply don't want to meet terrorist demands.

'There are less than ten hours,' Martin went on. 'To be blunt, we don't have time for a lot of bullshit. We must come down heavily on anyone who's resisting paying the ransoms.'

A policeman had come up to me and was whispering against my ear. 'Sorry. You're needed, Dr Cross.'

'What is it?' I whispered back. I wanted to hear everything that was being said in this meeting.

'Just come. It's an emergency. Right now, please.'

Chapter Eighty-Four

I knew that, ironically, an 'emergency' had to be considered good news at this point in the countdown. At eight-thirty that morning I was inside a speeding police cruiser, the blare of its siren disturbing the peace all along our route across Paris.

My God, the streets were bleak and deserted – except for soldiers and the police, anyway. My part in an ongoing interrogation was explained to me during the ride. 'We have an arms dealer in custody, Dr Cross. We have reason to believe that he helped supply the bombs. Maybe he's one of the men you saw out in the country. He's a Russian – with a white beard.'

Minutes later we arrived in front of the Brigade Criminelle, a dark, nineteenth-century building in a quiet neighborhood along the Seine. Actually, this was the infamous 'La Crim' from countless French movies and police stories, including several about Inspector

Maigret that Nana and I had read together when I was a kid. *Life imitates art*, or something like that.

Once inside La Crim I was led up a rickety staircase, all the way to the top floor, the fourth. The interrogation was being conducted up there.

I was brought down a narrow hallway to Room 414. The brigadier who escorted me knocked once, and then we stepped inside.

I recognized the Russian arms dealer instantly.

They had caught *White Beard*, the one who'd told me he was the Wolf.

Chapter Eighty-Five

The room was small and cramped, as it was situated right under the eaves. It had a low, rain-stained, sloping ceiling and a tiny Velux – a skylight. I looked at my watch – fifteen minutes to nine. Tick, tick, tick.

I was hurriedly introduced to the interrogation team of Captain Coridon and Lieutenant Leroux – and their prisoner, a Russian arms dealer, Artur Nikitin. I already knew Nikitin, of course. He wore no shirt or shoes and was cuffed, hands behind his back. He was also sweating profusely. He was definitely the white-bearded Russian from the farmhouse.

I had been told during the ride over that the Russian hoodlum did business with al Qaeda and that it had made him millions. It was believed that he was involved with suitcase nukes, that he knew how many had been sold, and that he knew who had bought them.

'Cowards!' he was shouting at the French police as I entered the room. 'Fucking goddamn cowards. You can't do this to me. I've done nothing wrong. You French claim to be such liberals, but you are not!'

He looked at me – and pretended he had no idea who I was. His bad acting made me smile.

Captain Coridon told him, 'You may have noticed that you have been brought to the Préfecture de Police rather than the offices of the DST. That's because you're *not* being charged as an illegal trafficker in arms. The charge is murder. We are homicide detectives. Trust me, there are no liberals in this room, unless it's you.'

Nikitin's brown eyes remained wide with anger, but I also detected traces of confusion, especially now that I was here. 'This is bullshit! I can't believe it. I've done nothing wrong. I am a businessman – a French citizen. I want my lawyer!'

Coridon looked at me. 'You try.'

I stepped forward and threw a hard uppercut into the Russian's jaw. His head snapped back. 'We're not even *close* to being even,' I told him. 'No one knows that you're here! You *will* be tried as a terrorist, and you will be executed. No one will care, not after tomorrow. Not after your bombs help to destroy Paris, and kill thousands.'

The Russian yelled at me. 'I tell you again – I've done nothing! You can't do anything to me. What weapons? What bombs? Who am I, *Saddam Hussein*? You can't do this.'

'We can, and we will execute you,' shouted Captain Coridon from off to the side. 'You are a dead man as soon as you leave this room, Nikitin. We have other scum to talk to. Whoever helps us first, we help them.

'Get him out of here,' Coridon finally said. 'We're wasting time with this bastard!'

The brigadier grabbed Nikitin by his hair, and also the band of his pants. He threw him halfway across the room. The Russian's head smacked against the wall, but he scrambled to his bare feet. His eyes were large and fearful now. Maybe he was beginning to understand that the rules of interrogation had changed, everything had changed now.

'Last chance to talk,' I said. 'Remember, you're just a *gnat* to us.'

'I didn't sell *anything* to *anyone* here in France! I sell in Angola – for diamonds!' Nikitin said.

'I don't *care*, and I don't *believe* you,' Captain Coridon bellowed at the top of his voice. 'Get him out of here.'

'I know something!' Nikitin suddenly blurted out. 'The suitcase nukes! The number is *four*. It's al Qaeda who's behind it. Al Qaeda made the plan! They call the shots. The prisoners of war – everything.'

I turned to the French policemen and shook my head. 'The Wolf gave him up to us. And he's not going to be pleased with his performance. He'll kill him for us. I don't believe a word he just said.'

Nikitin looked at the three of us, then he spat. '*Al Qaeda!* Fuck you if you don't like it, or believe it.'

I stared back at him. 'Prove what you're saying. Make us believe you. Make *me* believe you, because I don't.'

'All right,' Nikitin said then. 'I can do that. I'll make all of you believers.'

Chapter Eighty-Six

As soon as I arrived back at the Préfecture, Martin Lodge caught up with me. 'Let's go!' He started to pull me along.

'What? Go where?' I looked at my watch – something I seemed to be doing every couple of minutes now. It was twenty-five past ten.

'A raid is going down in a few minutes. The hideout that the Russian gave you – it's real.'

Martin and I hurried upstairs to the crisis room at police headquarters. My old pal Etienne Marteau met us and guided us to a row of monitors set up to view the raid. Everything was happening incredibly fast for a change. Too fast maybe, but what choice did we have?

Marteau said, 'They're confident, Alex. They coordinated with the power authority, EDF–GDF. The power grid in the area goes down and then they go in.'

I nodded at what he was saying and watched the screens in front of us. It was strange to be once-removed from the action. Then it was happening! French soldiers appeared out of nowhere, dozens of them. They wore RAID jackets: *Recherche, Assistance, Intervention, Dissuasion.* They carried assault rifles.

The soldiers rushed toward a small townhouse that looked harmless enough. They broke down the front door. It happened in seconds.

A UBL, a French version of the Hummer, an off-road vehicle, appeared and crashed through a wooden gate in the rear. Soldiers jumped from the UBL.

'We'll see soon enough,' I said to Martin. 'RAID is good at what they do?'

'Yes, they are skillful at destruction and death.'

A couple of the French police were miked and they carried cameras, so we got to see and hear much of the raid as it happened. A door was thrown open – a gun fired from inside – then a blaze of return fire.

Someone's shrill scream; the sound of a body thumping against the floorboards.

Two gunmen ran out into a narrow hallway. Both in their underwear. Shot down before they knew what hit them.

A half-naked female with a handgun – shot in the throat.

'Don't kill them all,' I muttered at the monitor.

A Cougar helicopter swooped down and more

commandos appeared. Inside the house, soldiers swarmed into a bedroom, then fell on a man lying in a cot. They took him alive, thank God.

Others terrorists were surrendering, their hands held high.

Then more rapid gunshots – off-camera this time.

A suspect was marched down the hall with a gun held to his head. An older man. The Wolf? Was it possible they had captured him? The policeman with the gun was smiling as if he had scored something big. The raid was certainly fast and efficient. At least four of the terrorists had been captured alive.

Then we waited impatiently for news. The cameras at the raid site were shut down. We waited some more.

Finally, at around three in the afternoon, an Army colonel stood at the front of the room in the crisis center. Every seat was taken; there was no more standing room, the tension was almost unbearable.

The Colonel began, 'We have identified the prisoners, those who are alive. One from Iran, a Saudi, a Moroccan, two Egyptians. A cell. Al Qaeda. We know who they are. It is doubtful that we caught the Wolf. It is also doubtful that these terrorists were involved in the threat to Paris. I am sorry to give you bad news at this late hour. We did our best. But he remains a step ahead of us. I'm sorry.'

Chapter Eighty-Seven

The terrible 'final' deadline was so close now, and no one had any more information on what could happen next. We seemed to have run out of options to try and stop the Wolf.

At a quarter to six, I was one of several nervous men and women climbing out of dark Renaults and then hurrying toward the tall ironwork gates of the Ministère de l'Interieur building for a meeting with the DGSE (General Directorate for External Security), which is the French equivalent of our CIA. The front gates were immense. Like supplicants entering a cathedral, we seemed small and insignificant as we passed through them. I *felt* small and insignificant, as well as at the mercy of higher powers, and not just God.

The gates opened onto a grand courtyard, a vast expanse of cobblestones, and I was reminded of the horse-drawn carriages that had once rolled through these very gates. Had there been progress in the world since then? It didn't seem like it on this particular day.

I walked with other police officers, government ministers and directors into a magnificent entry hall with a marbled pink-and-white tile floor. Armed guards lined the staircase. Hardly anyone spoke on the way up. There was only the dull sound of our plodding footsteps, the occasional nervous cough. It was very possible that within the hour, Paris, London, Washington and Tel Aviv would be bombed and thousands might die. There could be a much higher number of casualties. A hundred thousand or more was a possibility.

A Russian gangster was doing this? One with mysterious ties to al Qaeda? We were at his mercy now, weren't we? How incredibly strange.

The meeting was in the Salle des Fêtes, and once again I couldn't help wondering what I was doing here. I was the American representative in Paris because the FBI wanted me here, because there was a chance that I could make a difference with my experience as a psychologist and homicide detective, because something tragic might have happened to the Wolf in Paris a long time ago. We still hadn't figured out what.

Inside the main hall, tables had been arranged in a U-shape and covered with plain white fabric. Propped on easels were laminated maps of Europe, the Middle

East and the United States. The target areas were circled in thick red crayon. Crude, but effective.

A dozen or more TV monitors were up and running. So was a state-of-the-art teleconferencing system. There were more gray and blue suits than usual, more important people, more obvious power on display. For some reason, I noticed several pairs of rimless titanium eyeglasses – the ever-fashionable French.

Live feed scenes from London, Washington, Paris and Tel Aviv played on the TV monitors mounted on the walls. The cities were quiet. At this hour, most of the Army and police were inside as well. Etienne Marteau came and sat beside me. Martin Lodge had already returned to London.

'What do you think our realistic chances are here in Paris, Alex?' Etienne asked.

'Etienne, I don't know what's happening. No one does. Maybe we stopped the main cell of terrorists earlier. My guess is that everything has been leading up to today's deadline. I think the Wolf knew how difficult it would be to pull this together. Something happened to him here in Paris. We still don't know what it is. What can I say? We're out of time. We're fucked.'

Suddenly, Etienne sat up straight in his chair. 'My God, it's President Debauney.'

Chapter Eighty-Eight

A ramis Debauney, the French President, looked to be in his mid-fifties, and was very well dressed for the occasion, very formal. He was a compact man with slicked-back silver-gray hair, a pencil-thin mustache, and wire-rim eyeglasses. He looked calm and in control of his emotions as he strode quickly to the front of the room, and began to talk. You could hear a pin drop.

'As you know, I have worked in the trenches and on the front lines of law enforcement for many years myself. So I wanted you to hear from me now. I also wanted to be with you for these final minutes before the deadline runs out.

'I have news. The money has been raised. In Paris. In London. Washington. And in Tel Aviv, with help from many friends of Israel around the world. The entire sum will be transferred in three and a half minutes, approximately five minutes *before* the deadline expires.

'I want to thank everyone in this room, and all of those you represent, for countless hours of hard work, for personal sacrifices that no one should ask, for the most heroic effort, incredible bravery by so many. We did the best that we could, and most important, we will survive this crisis. Eventually, we will get these inhuman bastards, all of them! We will get this Wolf, the most inhuman of them all.'

There was a gold Empire clock on the wall behind the President. Everyone watched it intently. How could we not?

At 5:55 p.m. Paris time, President Debauney said, 'The money is being transferred now. It will happen in a matter of seconds . . . All right. *It's done.* This should be over now. We will be all right. Congratulations to all of you. Thank you.'

There was an audible sigh of relief in the cavernous room, smiles and handshakes, some hugs.

Then we waited, almost a reflex action.

For any kind of communication from the Wolf.

For breaking news from the other targeted cities: Washington, London, Tel Aviv.

The final sixty seconds before the deadline were incredibly tense and dramatic, even though the ransom had been delivered. I could do nothing but watch the second hand on the clock. Finally, I said a prayer for my family, for the people in all four cities, for the world we live in.

Then it was five in London and six in Paris; twelve in Washington; seven in Tel Aviv.

The deadline had passed. But what did it mean? Were we truly safe?

There were no significant changes on any of the monitors; no disruptions; no explosions on the live video feeds. Nothing.

And there was no call from the Wolf.

Two more minutes passed.

Ten minutes.

And then, a terrible explosion rocked the room – and the world.

PART FIVE

DELIVER US FROM EVIL

Chapter Eighty-Nine

The bomb or bombs – not nuclear, but powerful enough to cause massive damage – went off in the first arrondissement, near the Louvre. The entire area, a maze of lanes and dead-end streets, was nearly flattened. Close to a thousand people died immediately, or at least in a few seconds. The terrible multiple explosions were heard, and felt, all over Paris.

The Louvre suffered only minor damage from the blasts, but the three-block area covering rue de Marengo, rue de l' Oratoire and rue Bailleul were almost completely destroyed. As was a nearby bridge – a small one – crossing the Seine.

A bridge. Another bridge. In Paris this time.

Not a word of explanation was heard from the Wolf. He didn't take credit for the wanton and despicable act, nor did he deny it.

He didn't need to explain his actions, did he? He thought that he was God.

There are other supremely arrogant people who labor inside our government in Washington, and also some who work in the national media, who believe that they can accurately predict what will happen in the future because they know, or think they know, what happened in the past. I suspect it's the same in Paris, London, Tel Aviv, and everywhere else in the world: all of these basically intelligent, maybe even well-intentioned people who proclaim, *'That couldn't happen,'* or *'Here's how it would happen in the real world.'* As if they really know. But they don't know. Nobody does.

All bets are off nowadays. Anything can happen, and sooner or later, it probably will. We don't seem to be getting any smarter as a species, just crazier and a whole lot more dangerous. Unbelievably, unbearably more dangerous.

Or maybe that was just my mood as I flew back from Paris. A terrible tragedy had occurred there, after all. The Wolf had won, if what he did could be called winning, and it hadn't even been a close contest.

A power-mad Russian gangster had adopted the tactics of terrorism, or so it seemed. He was better than we were – more organized, more cunning, and far more brutal when he needed results. I couldn't even remember the last time we'd had a victory in our battle with the Wolf and his forces. I just prayed that this was over now. Could it be? Or was this another calm before another storm? I couldn't bear to think about that possibility right now.

I arrived home at a little before three on a Thursday afternoon. The kids were back; Nana had never left Fifth Street. When I got there I insisted on cooking dinner, wouldn't take no for an answer. It was what I needed: cook a good meal, talk to Nana and the kids about anything we wanted to talk about, get lots of hugs. Not have a single thought about what had happened in Paris, or the Wolf, or any kind of police work.

So I made my interpretation of a French-style dinner and I even spoke French with Damon and Jannie while the meal was being prepared. Jannie set the dining table with Nana's silver, cloth napkins, a lace tablecloth that we only used for special occasions. The meal? *Langoustines roties brunoises de papaye poivrons et oignons doux* – prawns with papaya, peppers and onions. For a main course, chicken stew in a sweet red wine sauce. We drank small glasses of wine with the meal, a delightful Minervois, and ate with enthusiasm.

But for dessert – brownies and ice cream. I was back in America, after all.

I was home, thank God.

Chapter Ninety

Home again, home again.

The next day I didn't go to work and the kids stayed out of school. It seemed to satisfy everybody's needs, even Nana Mama's who encouraged us all to play hookie. I called Jamilla a couple of times and talking to her helped, as it always did, but something seemed off between us.

For our day of hookie-playing I took the kids on a day trip to St Michaels, Maryland, which is situated on Chesapeake Bay. The village turned out to be a lively snapshot of quaint, coastal charm: a thriving marina, a couple of small inns with rockers set out on the porches, even a lighthouse. And the Chesapeake Bay Maritime Museum, where we got to watch real shipwrights working on a skipjack restoration. It felt as though we were back in the nineteenth century, which didn't seem like such a bad idea right now.

After lunch at the Crab Claw Restaurant we embarked on an actual skipjack charter. Nana Mama had brought her school classes here many times over the years, but she stayed home this trip, protesting that she had too much work to do around the house. I only hoped she was really feeling okay. I still remembered the way she used to teach her students on the field trips, so I took over as the guest lecturer.

'Jannie and Damon, this is the last fleet of working sailing vessels in North America. Can you imagine? These ships have no winches, just manpower, and blocks and tackles. The fishermen are called watermen,' I told them, just as Nana had told her classes years before.

Then off we went on the *Mary Merchant* for a two-and-a-half-hour cruise into the past.

The captain and his mate showed us how to hoist a sail with a block and tackle and soon we had caught a breeze with a loud whoosh and the rhythmic smack of waves against the hull. What an afternoon it was. Gazing up at a sixty-foot mast made from a single log shipped all the way from Oregon. The smells of salt air, linseed oil, residual oyster shells. The closeness of my two oldest children, the look of trust and love in their eyes. Most of the time anyway.

We passed stands of pine trees, and open fields where tenant farmers raised corn and soybean; and great white-columned estates which had once been plantations. It was a good break, much needed R and R. Only a couple of times did I drift into thoughts of police work, but I quickly pulled myself back.

I half-listened as the captain explained that 'only boats under sail can dredge for oysters' – except twice a week when engine-powered yawls were allowed on the Bay. I suspected that it was a clever conservation ploy to make the watermen work hard for their oysters, otherwise the supply might run out.

What a fine day. As the boat heeled to starboard, the boom swung out, the mainsail and jib filled the air with a loud smack, and Jannie, Damon and I squinted into the setting sun. And we understood, for a little while anyway, that this had something to do with the way life was supposed to be lived, and maybe even why moments like this needed to be cherished and remembered.

'Best day of my life,' Jannie told me. 'I'm not even exaggerating too much.'

'Same here,' said I. 'And I'm not exaggerating at all.'

Chapter Ninety-One

When we got home early that evening I saw a scuffed-up white van parked in front of the house. I recognized the bright green logo on the door: *Homecare Health Project*. What was this? Why was Dr Coles here?

Suddenly, I was nervous that something had happened to Nana while I was out with the kids. The fragile state of her health has been on my mind more and more lately; the reality that she's in her middle eighties now, though she won't tell exactly how old she is – or rather, she *lies* about it. I hurried out of the car and up the front steps ahead of the kids by a couple of strides.

'I'm in here with Kayla,' Nana called as I opened the front door and Damon and Jannie slid by me on either side. 'We're just kicking back, Alex. No need for alarm. Take your time.'

'So who's alarmed?' I asked as I slowed and walked into the living room, saw the two of them 'kicking back' on the sofa.

'You were, Mr Worrywart. You saw the *Health* truck outside, and what did you think? *Sickness*,' said Nana.

She and Kayla both laughed merrily, and I had to smile too – at myself. I made a very weak protest. 'Never happened.'

'Then why did you rush up the front steps like your trousers were on fire?' Nana said and laughed some more. Then she waved her hand as if to chase away any unwanted negativity in the room. 'Come. Sit down with us for a minute or two. Can you spare it? Tell me everything. How was St Michaels? Has it changed very much?'

'Oh, I suspect that St Michaels is pretty much the same as it was a hundred years ago.'

'Which is a *good* thing,' Nana said. 'Thank God for small favors.'

I went over and gave Kayla a kiss on the cheek. She had helped Nana when she was sick a while back, and now she stopped in regularly. Actually, I'd known Kayla since we were both growing up in the neighborhood. She was one of us who got out, received an education, and then came back, to give back. The *Homecare Health Project* brought doctors to the homes of the sick in Southeast. Kayla had started it, and she kept it going with incredibly hard work, including fundraising, which she mostly did herself.

'You look good,' I told her. The words just came out.

'Yes, I lost some weight, Alex,' she said and cocked an eyebrow at me. 'It's all this running around that I do. I try my best to keep the weight on, but it just comes off, damn it.'

I *had* noticed. Kayla is close to six feet, but I had never seen her looking so trim and fit, not even when she was a kid. She's always had a sweet, pretty face and a disposition to match.

'It also sets a better example for folks,' she said. 'Too many people in the neighborhood are overweight. Too many are obese, even a lot of the kids. They think it's in their genes.'

Then Kayla laughed. 'Plus, I must admit, it has helped my social life, my outlook on things, whatever. *Whatever.*'

'Well, you always look good to me,' I said, putting my foot in it again.

Kayla rolled her eyes at Nana. 'He lies so *easily*. He's really good at it.' They both laughed again.

'Anyway, thank you for the compliment, Alex,' said Kayla. 'I'll take it for what it's worth. I don't even consider it too condescending. Oh, you know what I mean.'

I decided I'd better change the topic. 'So Nana is fine, and going to live to a hundred?'

'I would expect so,' Kayla said.

But Nana frowned. 'Why do you want to get rid of me so soon?' she asked. 'What did I do to deserve that?'

I laughed. 'Maybe it's because you're a constant pain in my butt. You know that, don't you?'

'Of course I know it,' Nana said. 'That's my job in life: my reason for being is to torment you. Don't you know that yet?'

And as she said those words, I finally felt like I was home again, really home, back from the wars. I took Kayla and Nana out on the sun-porch and played 'An American in Paris' for them on the piano. That's what I had been not too long ago, but no more.

Around eleven, I walked Kayla outside to her *Health* van. We stopped and talked for a moment on the front porch.

'Thanks for coming by to see her,' I said.

'You don't have to thank me,' Kayla said. 'I do it because I want to. It just so happens that I love your grandmother. I love her tremendously. She's one of my guiding lights, my mentor. Has been for years.'

Then Kayla leaned in very quickly, and she kissed me. She held the kiss for a few seconds. When she pulled away she was laughing. 'I've wanted to do that for the longest time.'

'And?' I asked, more than slightly surprised at what had just happened.

'Now I've done it, Alex. Interesting.'

'Interesting?'

'I have to go. I have to run.'

Laughing to herself, Kayla ran out to her van.

Interesting.

Chapter Ninety-Two

After some much needed R and R, I went back to work and found that I was still assigned to the extortion/terrorism case, which apparently now involved chasing down whoever was responsible, whoever had the money. I was told that I was picked – because I'm *relentless*.

In a way, I was glad it wasn't over. I was still in touch with several of my contacts on the case: Martin Lodge in England, Sandy Greenberg with Interpol, Etienne Marteau in Paris, but also police and Intelligence in Tel Aviv and Frankfurt. Everybody I talked to had possible leads, but no one had anything hot, or even what I would consider lukewarm.

The Wolf, or maybe al Qaeda, or some other clever, homicidal bastards were out there with over two billion dollars in their coffers. Among other things, three city blocks in Paris had been destroyed. Political prisoners had been released. There had to be some slip-up, some way to find those responsible, or at least some way to discover who they were.

My second day back, the analyst Monnie Donnelley and I made a paper connection that interested me enough to get me to drive all the way out to Lexington, Virginia. I arrived at a two-story contemporary on a back road called Red Hawk Lane. A Dodge Durango was parked in the driveway. A couple of horses grazed in a nearby paddock.

Joe Cahill met me at the door of the house. The former CIA agent was all smiles, just as I remembered him from past meetings about the Wolf. Joe had told me over the phone that he was eager to help the investigation in any way that he could. He invited me inside and had coffee and a store-bought crumb cake waiting in his den. The room had views of an outlying pasture, a pond, and the Blue Ridge Mountains off in the distance.

'I guess you can tell I miss the job,' Joe said. 'Somedays anyway. You can only do so much hunting and fishing. You fish, Alex? You hunt?'

'I've taken the kids fishing a couple of times,' I said. 'I hunt some, yeah. Right now, I'm hoping to bag the Wolf. I need your help though, Joe. I want to go over some old ground. Something has come up.'

Chapter Ninety-Three

'All right, you want to talk about him again. How we got the Wolf out of Russia? What happened once he arrived in America? How he disappeared after that? It's a sad, but well-known and documented story, Alex. You've seen the files, I know you have. Almost ended my career.'

'Joe, I don't understand why nobody seems to know who he is. What he looks like. His real name. That's the story I've been getting for over a year now, but how can it be? How could we work with Britain to extricate an important KGB guy, and not know who he is? *Something* bad happened in Paris – but nobody knows what. How is it possible? What am I missing? What has everybody missed so far?'

Joe Cahill spread his large, working-man hands palms up. 'Look, I obviously don't have all the pieces either. It's my understanding that he was undercover when he was inside Russia. Supposedly, he was a young, very cagey agent, which would mean he's still only in his early forties. But, I've also read reports that he's in his late fifties or sixties now. That he was actually pretty high up in the KGB when he defected. I've also heard that the Wolf is female. I think he spreads the rumors himself. I'm almost certain that's what he does.'

'Joe, you and your old partner were his controls once he got here.'

'Our boss was Tom Weir, who wasn't the Director yet. Actually the team included three other guys – Maddock, Boykin and Graebner. Maybe you should talk to them.'

Cahill rose from his easy chair. He went and opened the French doors leading out onto a stone patio. A cooling breeze swept into the room.

'I never met him, Alex. Neither did my partner, Corky Hancock. Or the rest of the team – Jay, Sam, Clark. That's the way it was set up from the beginning. It was the deal he brokered when he came out of Russia. He'd help us bring down the old KGB, name names there, and here in the US. But nobody got to see him. Believe me, he delivered names and information that helped bring down the evil empire.'

I nodded. 'Right, he keeps his promises. But now, he's on the loose, and he's established his own crime network, and a whole lot more.'

Cahill took a bite of his coffee cake, then talked with his mouth full. 'Apparently that's exactly what he did. Of course, we had no idea that he would go bad. Neither did the Brits. Maybe Tom Weir did. I don't know.'

I needed some air. I got up and walked to the open doors. A couple of horses were hugging a white wooden fence under the shade of oak trees. I turned to face Joe Cahill.

'Okay, so you can't help me with the Wolf. What *can* you help me with, Joe?'

Cahill frowned and looked confused. 'I'm sorry, Alex, not much. I'm an old plough-horse, not good for much of anything any more. Coffee cake's good, right?'

I shook my head. 'Not really, Joe. Trust me, store-bought's never the same.'

Cahill's face sagged, then he grinned, but his eyes weren't smiling. 'So now we're gonna be honest, I guess. Why the hell are you here? What's this about? Talk to Uncle Joe. What's going on? I'm kind of lost. You're playing way over my head.'

I stepped back into the room. 'Oh, it's all about the Wolf, Joe. See, I think you and your old partner can help us a lot – even if you never met him in person, and I'm not so sure that you didn't.'

Cahill finally threw up his hands in frustration. 'Alex, this is a little crazy, you know. I feel like we're running around in circles. I'm too old and ornery for this shit.'

'Yeah, well it's been a tough couple of weeks for everybody. A lot of craziness going around. You don't know the half of it.' But I'd had enough of 'Uncle' Joe Cahill's crap. I showed him a photograph.

'Take a good look. This is the woman who murdered CIA Director Weir at the Hoover Building.'

Cahill shook his head. 'Okay. So?'

'Her name is Nikki Williams and she's former Army. She operated as a mercenary for a while. A sniper, good one. Lots of private contracts on her resumé. I know what you're going to say, Joe – *so?*'

'Yeah. So?'

'Once upon a time, she worked for you and your partner, Hancock. Your agency shared your files with us, Joe. New era of cooperation. Here's the real twist – *I think you hired her to kill Weir.*

'Maybe you did it through Geoffrey Shafer, but you were involved. I think you worked for the Wolf. Maybe you always did – maybe that was part of his deal too.'

'You're crazy, and you're dead wrong!' Joe Cahill stood up and brushed crumbs from his trousers. 'You know what else? I think you'd better leave now. I'm sorry as hell I invited you into my house. This little talk of ours is over.'

'No, Joe,' I said. 'Actually, it's just getting started.'

Chapter Ninety-Four

I made a call on my cell phone. Minutes later, agents from Langley and Quantico swarmed onto the property and arrested Joe Cahill. They cuffed him and dragged him out of his nice, peaceful house in the country.

We had a lead now, maybe a good one.

Joe Cahill was transported to a CIA safe house somewhere in the Alleghenies. The grounds and the home looked ordinary enough: a two-story fieldstone farmhouse surrounded by grapevines and fruit trees, the entryway thick with wisteria. But this wasn't going to be a *safe* house for Uncle Joe.

The former agent was bound and gagged; then left alone in a small room for several hours.

To think about his future – and his past.

A CIA doctor arrived – a tall, paunchy man who looked to be in his late thirties, horsey, WASPish. His name was Jay O'Connell. We were told by him that an experimental truth serum had been approved for use on Cahill. O'Connell explained that variations of the drug were currently being used on terrorist prisoners at various jails.

'It's a barbiturate, like sodium amytal and brevital,' he said. 'All of a sudden the subject will feel slightly drunk, with diminished senses. After that, he won't be able to defend himself very well against prodding questions. At least we hope not. Subjects can react differently. We'll see with this guy. He's older, so I'm fairly confident we'll nail him.'

'What's the worst we can expect?' I asked O'Connell.

'That'd be cardiac arrest. Oh hell, it's a joke. Well actually, I guess it isn't.'

It was early in the morning when Joe Cahill was moved out of the small holding room and brought into a larger one in the cellar with no windows. His blindfold and gag were removed, but not the binds around his wrists. We sat him in a straight-backed chair.

Cahill blinked his eyes repeatedly before he could tell where he was, and who else was in the room with him.

'Disorientation techniques. Won't work worth a crap on me,' he said. 'This is really dumb. Nonsense. It's horseshit.'

'Yes, we think so too,' said Dr O'Connell. He turned to one of the agents, Larry Ladove. 'Roll up his sleeve for me anyway. There we go. This will pinch. Then it'll sting. Then you'll spill your guts out to us.'

Chapter Ninety-Five

For the next three and a half hours, Cahill continued to slur his words badly and to act like a man who had half a dozen drinks or more in him, and was ready for more.

'I know what you guys are doing,' Uncle Joe said and shook a finger at the three of us in the room with him.

'We know what you're doing too,' said the CIA guy, Ladove. 'And what you've done.'

'Haven't done anything. Innocent until proven guilty. Besides, if you know so much, why are we talking?'

'Joe, where is the Wolf?' I asked him. 'What country? Give us something.'

'Don't know,' Cahill said, then laughed as if something he'd said was funny. 'All these years, I don't know. I *don't*.'

'But you've met him?' I said.

'Never seen him. Not once, not even in the beginning. Very smart, clever. Paranoid maybe. Doesn't miss a trick though. Interpol might have seen him during the transport. Tom Weir? The Brits, maybe. Had him for a while before we got him.' We'd already checked with London, but they had nothing substantial about the defection. And there was nothing about a *mistake* in Paris.

'How long have you been working with him?' I asked Cahill.

He looked for an answer on the ceiling. 'Working *for* him, you mean?'

'Yes. How long?'

'Long time. Sold out early in the game. Jesus, long time ago.' Cahill started to laugh again. 'Lot of us did – CIA, FBI, DEA. So he claims. *I* believe him.'

I said, 'He gave you orders to have Thomas Weir killed. You already told us that.' Which he hadn't.

'Okay,' he said. 'If I did, I did. Whatever the hell you say.'

'Why did he want Thomas Weir killed?' I continued. 'Why Weir? What happened between them?'

'Doesn't work that way. You just get *your* job. You never see the whole plan. But there was something between him and Weir – bad blood.

'Anyway, he sure as hell never contacted me. Always my partner. Always Hancock. He's the one who got the Wolf out of Russia. Corky, the Germans, the Brits. I told you that, right?' Cahill said, then winked at us. 'This stuff is good. Truth serum. Drink the grape juice, boys.' He looked over at O'Connell. *'You too, Dr Mengele.* Drink the fucking grape and the truth will set you free.'

Chapter Ninety-Six

Had we gotten the truth out of Joe Cahill? Was there anything to his drug-induced ramblings? *Corky Hancock? The Germans, the Brits? Thomas Weir?*

Somebody had to know something about the Wolf. Where he was. Who he was. What he might be up to next.

So I was on the road again, tracking down the Wolf. Joe Cahill's partner had moved out to the central Idaho Rockies after he had taken early retirement. He lived on the outskirts of Hailey in the Wood River Valley, about a dozen miles south of Sun Valley. Not a bad life for a former spook.

As we drove from the airport to Hailey we passed through what the Bureau driver described as 'high desert'. Hancock, like his partner Joe Cahill, was a hunter and fisherman, it seemed. Silver Creek Preserve was nearby and it was a world-famous catch-and-release fishing area.

'We're not going to bust in on Hancock. We'll keep him under surveillance, try to see what he's up to. He's off in the mountains hunting right now. We'll run by his place – let you have a look,' said the local Senior Agent, a young Turk named Ned Rust. 'Hancock is an expert shot with a rifle, by the way. Thought I'd mention that.'

We drove up into the hills where several of the larger houses seemed to be on five- to ten-acre lots. Some homes had well-manicured lawns, and they looked unnaturally green in contrast to the ashen hills, which, of course, *were* natural.

'There have been avalanches in the area recently,' Rust said as we drove. He was just chock-full of information. 'Might see some wild horses. Or Bruce Willis. Demi Moore and Ashton Kutcher and the kids. Anyway, there's Hancock's house up ahead. Exterior's river rock. Popular around here. Lot of house for a retired agent with no family.'

'He's probably got some money to spend on himself,' I said.

The house was large all right, and handsome, with spectacular views in three directions. There was a detached barn which was bigger than my house, and a couple of horses grazing nearby. No Corky Hancock, though; he was off hunting.

Well, so was I.

Nothing much happened in Hailey for the next few days. I was briefed by the Senior Agent in Charge, a man named William Koch. The CIA had also sent a heavy from Washington – Bridget Rooney. Hancock returned from his hunting outing and we watched his every move. Static surveillance was set up by an Operations Group which had been flown in from Quantico. There was a Mobile Team whenever Hancock left the house. We were taking him very seriously. After all, the Wolf was out there somewhere, with two billion dollars. In winnings.

But maybe we finally had a way to track him: the CIA agent who brought him out of Russia. And maybe it all was connected to whatever had happened between the Wolf and Thomas Weir.

The mistake in Paris.

Chapter Ninety-Seven

It just wasn't going to happen overnight. Or the next night, or the one after that.

On Friday, I got permission to take a trip out to Seattle to visit with my boy. I called Christine and she said it would be fine, and that Alex would be happy to see me – and so would she. I'd noticed the edge was gone from Christine's voice when we talked these days; sometimes I could even remember how it had been between us. I wasn't sure that was a good thing, though.

I arrived at her house in the late morning and I was struck again by what a warm and charming place it was. The house and the yard were very Christine: cozy and light, with the familiar white picket fence and matching handrails hugging the stone steps leading to the front door; rosemary, thyme and mint filled the herb garden. Everything just so.

Christine answered the bell herself, with Alex in her arms. As much as I tried not to, I couldn't help thinking about the way things might have been if I hadn't been a homicide cop, and my life as a detective hadn't violently derailed the two of us.

I was surprised that she was home and she must have recognized the look in my eyes.

'I won't bite you, Alex, I promise. I brought Alex back from preschool to be with you,' she said. Then she handed over the boy, and he was all I wanted to think about for now.

'Hello, Dada,' he said and laughed shyly, which is his way at first. I smiled back. A woman I know in the D.C. area calls me 'a saint', and she doesn't mean it as a compliment. I'm not – not even close – but I have learned to make the best of things. My guess is that she hasn't.

'You're such a big boy,' I said, expressing my surprise, and I suppose, my pride and delight in my son. 'How old are you now? Six? Eight? Twelve years old?'

'I'm nearly three,' he said, and laughed at my joke. He always *gets* me, at least he seems to.

'He's been talking about seeing you all morning, Alex. He kept saying "Today's Daddy day" ,' Christine said. 'You two have fun together.' Then she did something that surprised me; she leaned in and kissed my cheek. That kind of threw me. I may be cautious, even a little paranoid, but I'm not immune. First Kayla

Coles – and now Christine. Maybe I looked like I needed a little T.L.C. That was probably it.

Well, Alex and I did have some good times together. I acted like Seattle was our hometown, and I went with it. First, we rode over to the Fremont area, where I had visited a retired detective friend a few years back. Fremont was full of older buildings, lots of vintage clothes and furniture shops – character, if such a worthy trait can actually be traced to architecture and style. A lot of people seem to think it can, but I'm not so sure.

When we got there, Little Alex and I shared a scone with butter and blackberry jam from the Touchstone Bakery. We continued on our walking tour, and closely examined the fifty-five-foot-tall Fremont Rocket attached to one of the local stores. Then I bought Alex a tie-dyed kite and we took it for a test flight at Gas Works Park which had a view of Lake Union and downtown Seattle. Seattle has parks galore. It's one of the things I like so much about the city. I wondered if I could ever live out here and imagined that I could, and then I wondered why I was entertaining that line of thought at all. Because Christine had given me a quick little peck on the cheek? Was I *that* starved for affection? Pitiful.

We did some more exploring, and checked out the sculpture garden and 'the Fremont Troll', a large sculpture that reminded me of the singer Joe Cocker, clutching a Volkswagen Bug in one hand. Finally we had a late lunch – organic, of course – a roasted vegetable salad, plus peanut butter and jelly on Ezekiel bread. When in Rome, and all that.

'Life is pretty good out here, huh, buddy?' I said as we munched our food together. 'This is the best, little guy.'

Alex Junior nodded that it was good, but then he stared up at me all wide-eyed and innocent, and asked, 'When are you coming home, Daddy?'

Oh man, oh man. When was I coming home?

Chapter Ninety-Eight

Christine had asked that I have Alex home before six, and I did as I'd promised I would. I am so responsible, so *Alex*, it drives me a little crazy sometimes. She was waiting for us on the porch, in a bright blue dress and heels, and handled everything as well as I could have expected her to. She smiled warmly when she saw us, and hugged Alex against her long legs when he ran up to her squealing, 'Mommy!'

'You two look like you had some fun,' she said as she stroked the top of the Big Boy's head. 'That's nice. I knew you would. Alex, Daddy has to go to his house now. Back to Washington, D.C. You and I have to go to Theo's for dinner.'

Tears filled his eyes. 'I don't want Daddy to go,' he protested.

'I know, but he has to, sweetheart. Daddy has to go to work. Give him a hug. He'll come visit again.'

'I will. Of course I will,' I said, wondering who Theo was. 'I'll always come see you.'

Alex ran into my arms and I loved having him close and didn't want to let him go. I loved the smell of him, his touch, the feeling of his little heart beating. But I also didn't want him to feel the separation that was already making my heart ache.

'I'll be back real soon,' I said. 'Soon as I can. Don't get too big when I'm not looking.'

And Alex whispered, 'Please don't go away, Daddy. Please don't go.'

He kept repeating it over and over until I was inside my rental car and driving away, waving back to my son, who kept getting smaller and smaller, until he disappeared as I turned the corner of his street. I could still feel Alex's little body pressing against mine. I can still feel it now.

Chapter Ninety-Nine

At a little before eight that night I sat alone at the dimly lit bar inside the Kingfish Café on Nineteenth and Mercer in Seattle. I was lost in thoughts about my youngest son – all of my children, really – when Jamilla rolled into the restaurant.

She had on a long, black leather car coat, with a dark blouse and black skirt, and she smiled brilliantly when she saw me sitting there at the bar, maybe looking as good to her as she did to me. Maybe. The thing about Jamilla – she's pretty, but she doesn't seem to know it, at least to believe it. I had mentioned I was coming to Seattle and Jam said she'd fly up to have dinner with me.

At first I hadn't been sure it was a good idea, but that was wrong, all wrong. I was incredibly happy to see her, especially after leaving Alex.

'You look good, Sugar,' she whispered against my cheek. 'But you do seem a little beat-up, darling. You're working too hard. Burning the candle down.'

'I feel a lot better right now,' I told her. 'You look good enough for both of us.'

'I do? Well thank you for saying that. Believe me, I needed to hear it.'

The Kingfish, as it turned out, was a totally democratic restaurant: no reservations, but we were seated quickly at a nice table along the wall. We ordered drinks and food, but mostly, we were there to hold hands and talk about everything that was going on in our lives.

'This thing with Little Alex,' I told Jamilla about midway through dinner, 'it's the worst torture for me. Goes against who I am, everything I learned from Nana. I can't stand to leave him here.'

Jamilla frowned and seemed angry. 'Doesn't she treat him well?'

'Oh no, no, Christine is a good mother. It's the separation that kills me. I love that little boy, and I miss him so much every day I'm away from him. I miss the way he talks, walks, thinks, tells bad jokes, listens to mine. We're pals, Jam.'

'And so,' Jamilla held my eyes with hers, 'you escape into your work.'

'And so,' I nodded, 'I do. But that's another whole story. Hey, let's get out of here.'

'What do you have in mind, Agent Cross?'

'Nothing illegal, Inspector Hughes.'

'Hmmm. Really? Well, that's a shame.'

Chapter One Hundred

You've heard the saying *get a room*, well, I already had one at the Fairmont Olympic on University across from Ranier Square, and I couldn't wait to get there. Neither of us could. Jamilla whistled under her breath as we walked into the impressive lobby. She stared up at the engraved ceiling which must have been forty feet high. There was an actual *hush* inside the large, over-decorated room at a little past ten when we arrived.

'Italian Renaissance décor, big ole antique chandeliers, five stars, five diamonds. I'm wonderfully impressed,' Jam said and grinned. As always, her enthusiasm was exhilarating.

'Every once in a while you just have to build in a treat, you know.'

'This is definitely a treat, Alex,' Jamilla said and gave me a quick kiss in the lobby. 'I'm really happy you're here. And that I'm here too. I like *us* a lot.'

It kept getting better from there. Our room was on the tenth floor and it was everything it needed to be – bright, airy, plush, with a king-size bed. We even had a view of Elliott Bay with Bainbridge Island in the distance, and a ferry just leaving the waterfront in the foreground. The sights and scenes couldn't have been any better if I'd planned them out in elaborate detail, which maybe, just maybe, I had.

About that king-size bed at the Fairmont Olympic. It was covered with a gold-and-green striped comforter – a duvet? – I'm always slightly confused about what distinguishes the two. We didn't bother to remove the comforter/duvet. We just fell onto it, laughing and talking, happy to be here together, realizing how much we'd missed each other.

'Let me make you a little more comfortable, Alex,' Jam whispered as she pulled my shirt out of my pants. 'How's that? Better?'

'And I'll do the same for you. Only fair,' I said to her. 'Tit for tat.'

'Well yes, I do like that tat of yours.'

I began to unbutton Jamilla's blouse and she continued unbuttoning my shirt. Neither of us was in a hurry. We knew better than to rush any of this. The whole idea was to make it last, to pay attention to each detail, each button, the feel of the fabrics, the tiny bumps of anticipation on Jamilla's skin, and on mine, the difficulty catching our breath, the tingle in our bodies, the electricity, sparks, whatever goodness came our way tonight.

'You've been practicing,' she whispered, and she was already a little short of breath. I liked that.

I laughed. 'Uh-uh. Actually, I've been practicing the art of *anticipation*.'

'Like this next button?' she asked.

'Beautiful, isn't it?'

'And the one after that?'

'I don't know how much of this I can take, Jamilla. I'm not kidding.'

'We'll have to see, we'll just have to see. I'm not kidding either.'

When Jamilla's blouse and my shirt were undone we slowly pulled them off. Meanwhile we kept kissing, tickling, scratching, nuzzling, *ever so slowly*. She was wearing perfume and I recognized it as Calèche Eau Délicate. She knew I liked the scent. Jamilla loved a light scratch all over her body so that's what I did next. First the shoulders and back, then her arms, her beautiful face, the long legs, her feet, then back up her legs again.

'You're getting warm . . . warmer,' she sighed and laughed very deep in her throat.

Then we slid back off the bed and stood together, swaying and touching. Finally, I took off her bra and held her breasts in my hands. 'Like I said, I don't know how much more of this I can take.'

I didn't either. I was hard, so hard that it hurt. I slid down and knelt on the Oriental rug. I kissed Jamilla down there. She was strong and confident, and maybe that's why I liked kneeling before her like this. In awe? Out of respect? Something like that.

Finally, I pushed myself up again.'Okay?'I whispered.

'Okay. Whatever you say. I'm your slave. Your master? A little of each?'

I went inside Jamilla while we were still standing, dancing in place, but then we tilted down and dropped onto the bed. I was lost in the moment, lost in Jamilla Hughes, and that was exactly where I needed to be. She was making these tiny sighs and gasps that I loved.

'I missed being with you,' I whispered. 'I missed your smile, the sound of your voice, everything.'

'Ditto,' she said and laughed. 'But especially that tat of yours.'

Moments later, five, maybe ten minutes, the phone on the nightstand began to ring.

For once, I did the right thing – I knocked the damn thing onto the floor, then covered it with a pillow. If it was the Wolf he could call back in the morning.

Chapter One Hundred
and One

The next morning I headed back to the Idaho Rockies. Jamilla and I shared a cab out to the airport together, then we took separate planes going in different directions. 'Big mistake, dumb move,' she told me before we parted. 'You should just fly to San Francisco with me. You need some extended R and R.' I already knew that.

But it wasn't going to be. Corky Hancock was the biggest lead we had, and the surveillance on him had been tightening. There was nowhere Hancock could go in the state of Idaho and not be watched, or at least listened to. There was surveillance on his house, the surrounding acreage, even the stand-alone barn. We had four mobile teams on him, with four more in the wings if needed. Since I'd left, aerial surveillance had been added to the mix.

When I arrived in Idaho, I attended a meeting

which included over two dozen agents assigned to the detail. The meeting was held in a small movie house in Sun Valley. The movie *21 Grams* with Sean Penn and Naomi Watts was playing there in the evenings, but not during the day.

Senior Agent William Koch stood in front of us. Tall and gangly, impressive in his way, he wore a chambray shirt, jeans, scuffed black cowboy boots. He played the local guy to a T, but he was nobody's fool, and he wanted us to know it. The same was true for his CIA counterpart, Bridget Rooney, a confident, dark-haired woman who was smarter than a whip.

'I'll make this pretty simple for everybody. Either Hancock knows we're here, or he's just unbelievably careful by nature,' said Koch. 'He hasn't talked to anybody since we got here. He's been online – eBay for fishing rods, a couple of porn-sites, plays in a fantasy baseball league. He has a girlfriend named Coral Lee, who lives nearby in Ketchum. Asian-American girl. Coral is definitely a good-looker. Corky *isn't*. We figured he probably spends lots of money on her, and it turns out, he *does*. Slightly less than two hundred thousand so far this year. Trips, jewelry, one of those cute little Lexus convertibles the gals like.'

Koch paused and looked around the room. 'That's about it. Except that we know Hancock is connected to the Wolf, and that he's been paid a lot of money for his services. So at 1200 hours, we're going in to take a look for ourselves inside the house. So tired,' Agent Koch said in a sing-song. 'Tired of waiting.'

There were smiles around the room, even from those who didn't get the reference to the Kinks song. Somebody patted me on the shoulder, like I had something to do with the decision that must have come down from Washington.

'Not me.' I turned and shrugged at the agent congratulating me. 'I'm just a soldier here.'

The team going inside Hancock's place was mostly FBI, but there was a handful of CIA agents too, led by Rooney. The CIA was in Idaho as a courtesy, partly because of the new working relationship that existed between the two agencies, but mostly because Hancock was directly involved in the murder of Director Thomas Weir, one of theirs. But I doubted they wanted to take Hancock down any more than I did. I wanted the Wolf, and somehow, somewhere, I was going to get him. At least, that was what I needed to think.

Chapter One Hundred and Two

Koch and Rooney were in charge – and they finally gave us the *go*. At the appointed hour, we swarmed all over the Hancock house. FBI emblazoned shirts and windbreakers were everywhere. Probably scared off a few deer and jackrabbits even though not one shot was fired.

Hancock was in bed with his girlfriend. He was sixty-four years old; Coral was supposed to be twenty-six. Lustrous black hair, good figure, lots and lots of rings and things, slept in the nude, on her back. Hancock at least had the decency to wear a Utah Jazz sweatshirt, and sleep in the fetal position.

He began to shout at us, which was actually kind of ironic and funny. 'What the hell is this shit? Get out of my damn house!'

But he forgot to look surprised, or he just wasn't a good actor. Either way, I got the feeling that he knew we were coming. How? Because he'd spotted us in the past few days? Or had Hancock been warned by someone in one of the cooperating agencies? Did the Wolf know we were onto Hancock?

During the first couple of hours of interviews, we tried Dr O'Connell's truth serum on Hancock. It didn't work as well on him as it had with Joe Cahill. He got happy and high, but he just sat back and went with it. Didn't tell us much, wouldn't even confirm things that Cahill had already confessed.

Meanwhile, a search of the house, barn, and sixty acres of grounds was going on. Hancock owned an Aston Martin convertible, and the Wolf loved fast cars, but nothing else even vaguely suspicious turned up. Not for three whole days during which nearly a hundred agents combed every square inch of the ranch. During that time period, half a dozen computer experts – including loaners from Intel and IBM – tried to break into Hancock's two computers. They finally concluded that he'd had experts put up extra security to protect whatever was inside.

There was nothing to do but wait around some more. I read every magazine and newspaper in Hancock's house, including several back issues of the *Idaho Mountain Express*. I went for long walks and tried to figure out a direction for my life that made some sense to me. I didn't do real well – but the fresh mountain air was a nice treat for my lungs.

When a computer breakthrough finally came, there wasn't much to go on. No direct link to the Wolf, or anyone else who seemed overly suspicious to us, at least not at first.

The next day, though, a hacker from our offices in Austin, Texas, found a file inside an encrypted file. It contained regular communication with a bank in Zürich. Actually, with a couple of banks in Switzerland.

And suddenly we didn't just *suspect*, we *knew* that Hancock had a lot of money. Over six million. At least that much. Which was the best news we'd had in a long while.

So off to Zürich we went. I didn't expect to find the Wolf there, but you never know. And I'd never been to Switzerland. Jannie begged me to bring back chocolate, a suitcase full of the stuff, and I promised I would. *A whole suitcase full of Swiss chocolate, sweetheart. Least I can do for you after missing most of your ninth year.*

Chapter One Hundred and Three

If I was the Wolf, this was a good place to be, to live. Zürich is a beautiful, amazingly clean city on the Lake – the *Zürichsee* – with fragrant, lovely shade trees and wide, winding sidewalks along the water, and fresh mountain air meant to be breathed in deeply. When I arrived, a storm was imminent and the air smelled like brass. The exterior of a majority of the buildings were in light shades, sand and white, and several were adorned with Swiss flags twisting in the blustery wind off the lake.

As I drove into the city I noticed trolley tracks everywhere with heavy-looking wires hanging overhead. The power of the old. Also, several life-size fiberglass cows painted with Alpine scenes, which reminded me of Little Alex's favorite toy, 'Moo'. What was I going to do about Alex? What could I do?

The Zürich Bank was a sixties-looking building,

glass and steel front, situated very close to the Lake. Sandy Greenberg met me outside. She was wearing a gray suit, had a black handbag slung over her shoulder, and looked like maybe she worked inside the bank instead of for Interpol.

'You ever been to Zürich, Alex?' Sandy asked as she gave me a hug and kiss on both cheeks.

'Never. Had one of their multipurpose penknives once when I was ten or eleven.'

'Alex, we have to eat a meal here. Promise me. Let's go inside now. They're waiting on us, and they don't like to wait in Zürich. Especially the bankers.'

The inside of the Zürich Bank was expensive-looking, highly polished, wood paneling everywhere, as spotless as a hospital operating room. The teller area was natural stone, with more wood paneling. The tellers were efficient and professional-looking, and they *whispered* to one another. The bank's branding was understated, but there was a great deal of modern art on the wall. I thought that I understood: the art *was* the bank's branding.

'Zürich has always been a haven for avant-garde intellectuals, cultured types,' Sandy said, and *didn't* whisper.'The Dada movement was born here. Wagner, Strauss, Jung all lived here.'

'James Joyce wrote *Ulysses* in Zürich,' I said and winked at her.

Sandy laughed.'I forgot, you're a closet intellectual.'

We were escorted to the bank president's office, which had a very serious look. Neat as a pin too. Only one transaction on the desk blotter; everything else filed away.

Sandy handed Mr Delmar Pomeroy an envelope. 'A signed warrant,' she said. 'The account number is 616479Q.'

'Everything has been promptly arranged,' Herr Pomeroy said to us. That was all. Then his warrant officer took us to look at the transactions in and out of account number 616479Q. So much for the secrecy and security of Swiss banks. *Everything has been promptly arranged.*

Chapter One Hundred and Four

This was feeling more like an efficient, orderly police investigation now. Even though I knew it really *wasn't*. Sandy, two of her agents from Interpol, and I got to look through all of Corky Hancock's transactions in a small, windowless room somewhere deep in the basement of the Zürich Bank. The former CIA agent's account had grown from two hundred thousand US dollars to slightly over six million. Yowza!

The latest and largest deposits totaled three and a half million and had come in four installments this year.

The source of the payment was an account in the name of *Y. Jikhomirov*. It took us a couple of hours to track down all of the records. There were over a hundred pages and they went all the way back to 1991. The year the Wolf had been brought out of Russia. Coincidence? I didn't believe in them. Not any more.

We carefully examined withdrawals from the Jikhomirov account. They included payments to a company that leased private jets; also regular air travel with British Airways and Air France; hotels – Claridge's, the Bel-Air in LA, the Sherry-Netherland in New York, the Four Seasons in Chicago and Maui. There were wire transfers to America, South Africa, Australia, Paris, Tel Aviv. *The trail of a Wolf?*

And an entry that particularly caught my interest – the purchase of four expensive sports cars in France, all from a dealership in Nice called Riviera Motors. A Lotus, a special edition Jaguar, and two Aston Martins.

'The Wolf is supposed to be a sports car enthusiast,' I said to Sandy. 'Maybe the cars mean something. Maybe we're closer than we suspect. What do you think?'

She nodded agreement. 'Yes, I think we should visit Riviera Motors in Nice. Nice is *nice*. But first, Alex, lunch in Zürich. I made you a promise.'

'No, I think you made *me* promise. After my bad Swiss Army knife joke.'

I was hungry anyway so it seemed a good idea. Sandy chose the Veltliner Keller, one of her favorites and a restaurant she thought I would appreciate.

As we entered, she explained that Veltliner Keller had been a restaurant since 1551, a long time for any business to survive. So, we forgot about police work for an hour and a half. We dined on barley soup –

zuppe engadinèse; a casserole, *veltliner topf*; and very good wine. Everything was just so: crisp white linens and napkins, roses in sterling silver vases, crystal salt and pepper shakers.

'This is one of your better ideas,' I told Sandy near the end of the meal. 'A nice break in the action.'

'It's called lunch, Alex. You have to try it more. You should come to Europe with your *friend*, Jamilla. You're working too hard.'

'It shows, I guess.'

'No, actually you look as good as ever. You're holding up better than Denzel, in his latest movies anyway. Somehow, you persevere. I don't know *how*, but you do. But I can tell that you're twisted up inside. Eat, relax, then we'll go to Nice and check out some sports cars. It will be like a holiday. Maybe we'll even catch a killer. Finish your wine, Alex.'

'Right,' I said, 'and then I have to buy some chocolate for Jannie. A suitcasefull. I made another promise.'

'Didn't you promise to catch the Wolf?' Sandy asked.

'Yeah, that too.'

Chapter One Hundred and Five

Next stop, a luxury-car dealership in Nice. I felt like I was in an Alfred Hitchcock movie.

The owner of *Riviera Motors Nice*, the '*Concessionnaire exclusif Jaguar, Aston Martin, Lotus*' appeared to like drama too, at least in a design sense. To that effect, a long row of gleaming *black* cars were displayed in the showroom. The cars were clearly visible from the street through monumental bay windows. The shiny black machines cut a startling contrast against a spotless white floor.

'What do you think?' Sandy asked as we climbed out of our rented Peugeot, which we had parked across the street from the dealership.

'I think I need a new car,' I said to her. 'And I *know* the Wolf likes fancy sports cars.'

We went inside and stopped at the reception desk in front. Behind it was an elegant reception-person, well-tanned, with a bleached and ironed ponytail. She was checking Sandy and me out: *both over six feet; ebony and ivory. Who are these people?*

'We're here to see Monsieur Garnier,' Sandy spoke to the woman in French.

'You have an appointment with Monsieur, Madame?'

'We do indeed. Interpol and the FBI respectively, and respectfully, I might add. Monsieur Garnier is expecting us, I believe. We're here on important business.'

While we waited, I continued to take in the place. The expensive cars were precisely parked in a herringbone pattern, interspersed with voluminous potted plants. In an adjacent service atelier, mechanics in matching Jaguar green jumpsuits worked with pristine tools.

The manager of the car dealership appeared after a couple of minutes' wait. He was dressed in a fashionable gray suit, but not too flashy, just clearly expensive, and right.

'You've come about a couple of Aston Martins, a Jaguar, a Lotus?' he asked.

'Something like that, Monsieur,' Sandy told him. 'Let's go up to your office. We wouldn't want to hurt business by talking down here in the showroom.'

The manager smiled. 'Oh believe me, Madame, our business is bulletproof.'

'We'll see about that,' I told him in French. 'Or maybe a better way of putting it: let's try and keep it that way. This is a murder investigation.'

Chapter One Hundred
and Six

The manager suddenly became extremely polite and cooperative. The four luxury cars in question had been purchased by an M. Aglionby, who apparently had a home nearby on the beautiful peninsula, Cap Ferrat, just east of Nice. Monsieur Garnier told us it was 'off the Basse Corniche, the main coastal road to Monaco. You can't miss it. And you won't miss the Aglionby estate.'

'*To Catch a Thief*,' Sandy said as we sped along toward Cap Ferrat about two hours later. We had lost a little time calling in backup.

'Actually, the most memorable shots in the Hitchcock movie were filmed up there,' Sandy went on. She pointed toward a parallel road winding along the cliffs; it was at least a hundred yards higher than where we were riding. In other words, very high up, and dangerous-looking.

'Also, we're here to catch a mass murderer without any conscience,' I said, 'not a witty and charming cat burglar like Cary Grant was in the flick.'

'This is true too. Keep me focused, Alex. I could easily get distracted here,' Sandy said. But I knew she was focused – always. That's why we got along so well.

The Aglionby estate was located on the west side of Cap Ferrat, in Villefranche-sur-Mer. There were glimpses of villas and gardens hidden behind high stucco and rock walls as we rode along D125, also known as Boulevard Circulaire. Half a dozen cars and vans followed us, also catching the sights no doubt: *a shiny blue Rolls Royce convertible easing out of one of the estates – a blonde in sunglasses and a kerchief behind the wheel; dark-glassed tourists catching rays on the terrace of the Grand Hôtel du Cap Ferrat; a bathing pool dug into solid rock at Piscine de Sun Beach.*

'You think this is a fool's errand, Alex?' Sandy asked.

'It's what we do. Hit and miss, hunt and peck. I feel good about this one. It has to be something. Monsieur Aglionby has to be connected somehow.'

I was hopeful. We had found an awful lot of money in the account of Corky Hancock, and most of it had come in recently. But how much did he really know about the Wolf? How much did anyone know?

Then we saw the estate we were looking for – and Sandy drove past. '*Got you*, you bastard,' she said. 'Aglionby? The Wolf? Why not?'

'Whoever lives back there is certainly loaded. Jesus – how much is enough?'

'When you have a billion dollars or so, this is rather modest, Alex. It's not a question of a house – it's *houses*. The Riviera, London, Paris, Aspen.'

'If you say so. I've never had a billion myself. Or a villa on the Riviera.'

The place in question was a sun-drenched, Mediterranean-style mansion, creamy yellow with white detailing; it had gleaming balustrades and porticos, shutters that the staff apparently closed to the midday sun. *Or maybe the people inside just didn't want to be seen?* Four stories, thirty-plus rooms – about as cozy as Versailles.

But all we were interested in was a peek for now. As we had planned earlier, we reconnoitered at a small hotel just up the coast. The decision was made by local police officials to use the estate bordering the Aglionby place on the south side. It was vacant now, except for a large staff. We would dress and pose as gardeners and household help, starting tomorrow morning.

Sandy and I listened to the plan as it was laid out, step by step. We looked at each other, shook our heads. *Not this time*.

I spoke. 'We're going in tonight,' I announced. 'With or without your help.'

Chapter One Hundred and Seven

The decision to go now was backed enthusiastically by Interpol, and even by the French in Paris, who were in close contact with Washington, and wanted the murderous Wolf as badly as the rest of the world did, maybe more. For a change, everything happened very quickly that afternoon and through the early evening. I was going to be part of the assault, and so was Sandy.

The attack was planned as if the Wolf was definitely inside the villa. Seven two-person teams of snipers were deployed on all sides of the estate which were designated as north –*'white'*; east –*'red'*; south –*'black'*; west –*'green'*. Every door and window was covered, and each of the snipers had a specific number of targets. They were closest to the estate. Our eyes and ears.

So far they weren't seeing any sign that we'd been spotted.

While the snipers moved into position, the rest of us – Interpol, FBI, the French Army and police – were strapping on war gear: black Nomex flight suits, body armor, handguns, MP-5 submachine guns. Three helicopters were waiting less than a mile away, and would be used during the assault. We were ready for the green light, but some of the more jaded among us expected a last-minute delay for politics, cold feet at the command level, something unforeseen to get in the way.

I lay flat on the ground on my stomach beside Sandy Greenberg. We were less than a hundred yards from the main house. Starting to feel the jitters. At least I was. The Wolf could be inside this house; maybe he was Aglionby.

Some lights were on inside, but we seldom saw anyone at the windows past midnight. Security was modest on the grounds, just a couple of guards.

'Awfully quiet,' said Sandy. 'I don't know if I like this, Alex. Security's light.'

'It's almost two in the morning.'

'You surprised that we're going in?' Sandy asked.

I smiled. '*Are* we going in? No, I'm not surprised. Remember, the French want the Wolf. Maybe even more than we do.'

Then the signal came to *go*! Sandy and I were part of the second assault team, and we ran toward the house about forty-five seconds after the first wave. We entered through the back – *black*. The kitchen, to be exact.

Somebody had switched on the overheads. A guard lay on the floor, his hands cuffed behind his head. Highly polished marble was everywhere; four stoves at the center of the room. I noticed a large glass bowl on a table. I took a peek at what looked like dark noses inside.

Figs, I finally realized, and smiled to myself.

Then Sandy and I were running down a long hallway. No gunshots had been fired inside the house yet. Lots of other noise, though.

We came to the formal living room and it was of diplomatic proportions: chandeliers dangled over our heads, polished-marble floor, half a dozen dark and solemn paintings by French and Dutch masters.

No Wolf so far. No sign of him.

'Is this for entertaining – or signing treaties?' Sandy asked me. 'Alex, why aren't they fighting back? What's going on? *Is he here?*'

We climbed a winding staircase and saw French soldiers leading men and women out of the bedrooms. Most were in underwear; a few were naked. Nobody looked very sexy, but they certainly looked surprised.

I didn't see anybody who might be the Wolf, but how could I tell for certain what the Wolf looked like? How could anybody?

The interrogations began immediately right there in the hallways. *Where was the Wolf? . . . Who was Aglionby?*

The entire house was searched a second time, then a third.

Marcel Aglionby wasn't at the house, we were told by several of the guests. He was on business in New York. One of his daughters was present; this was her party, her guests, her friends – though some of them looked to be twice her age. Her father was a respected banker, she swore to us. No way he was a criminal, no way he was the Wolf.

So was he the Wolf's banker? And where did that lead us?

I hated to think it, but I couldn't help myself – *the Wolf wins again.*

Chapter One Hundred
and Eight

We searched the place one more time, and over the threats of the daughter, started to take it apart, piece by piece.

I had to say the house was amazing, filled with antiques and artwork. Sandy thought that Aglionby might be trying to emulate the nearby La Fiorentina, which had been called the most beautiful house in the world. The banker certainly had expensive tastes, and could afford to indulge them. Hand-painted Louis XVI pieces were everywhere; as were Louis XV chandeliers; antique Turkish carpets; Chinese screens and panels; tapestries; paintings classical and modern, on nearly every wall. Works by Fragonard, Goya, Pieter Breughel. *All of it financed by the Wolf? Why not? He had over two billion to throw around.*

We assembled the 'suspects' in the games room, which had three billiards tables, and nearly as many plush sofas as the living room. The same tailored formality. Did anyone here know anything about the Wolf? It didn't look that way to me. More likely, some of them might know Paris and Nicky Hilton.

'Does anyone want to speak for the group?' the French police commander addressed them.

No one volunteered; no one answered any questions. Either they didn't know, or they had been told not to say.

'All right, then, let's separate them. We'll begin the interviews now. *Someone will talk*,' the commander warned.

Since I hadn't been asked to participate in the interrogations, I wandered out onto the grounds, and walked down toward the water. Had we been given another false lead to follow? The Wolf's game-playing, his strategies and counterstrategies had been relentless from the beginning. Why should it stop now?

There was a large, actually very *long*, wooden boathouse at the water's edge. It stood maybe a hundred yards from the main house. But what was this? Somebody had transformed the old boathouse into a garage – to house a collection of over thirty very expensive sports cars and luxury sedans. Maybe this was something – finally? Evidence that the Wolf might have used this estate? Or was it another ruse, a tease?

I was standing between the boathouse and the water when all hell broke loose!

Chapter One Hundred
and Nine

All he had was his 'piece' of the puzzle, his part in this terrible mission. But it was more than enough. Bari Naffis knew there had been an incursion at the estate-house in Villefranche-sur-Mer, and that within the hour people would die because of it, including friends of his, and one girl he'd slept with, a fashion model from Hamburg. Eye-candy to be sure, but very precious stuff.

The French Army and police had already taken over the mansion. And now, it was Bari's turn to go to work, to do his job. He didn't know why this had to happen – only that it did.

As he turned onto the D125, it seemed to him that he was already too late. But he had his orders. Some-one had obviously foreseen that this would happen.

The Wolf had known it was coming, hadn't he? He had eyes in the back of his head. Eyes everywhere!

What a scary bastard that one was.

That was all that Bari Naffis knew – and all he cared about right now. He had been paid well in advance, even if this made little sense to him, and was highly distasteful. Why kill and maim so many?

Half an hour ago, he'd received a radio signal from the main house; the noise had awakened him from a sound sleep in his hotel room.

He jumped from bed, dressed, then hurried to a prearranged position on an estate to the north. Now, he tried not to think about his friends, and a lover inside the estate-house. Maybe she would survive somehow.

No matter. He wasn't going to cross the Wolf over some girl. Bari ran through the woods and thick brush cover. He was carrying a Man Portable Air Defense System, about as ungainly a weapon as there was. The missile launcher was five feet in length, a little over thirty-five pounds. Still, it was extremely well-balanced and equipped with a rifle-style pistol grip and forestock. It fired an FIM-92A Stinger missile – and there were two other operators in the woods besides himself. Each of them had their little bit of work to do, their *pieces* of the whole.

Three professional killers on the move right now – at this very moment, maybe feeling the same misgivings that he did.

A trap had been set for the police.

A terrible death trap for everybody in that house. Police killed as well. What a mess.

When he was in his final position, only about fifteen hundred feet from the main house, Bari hoisted the ungainly tube up onto his shoulder. He set his right hand on the pistol grip, and sighted the weapon with his left. He held the launcher like a conventional rifle, though it was far from conventional.

He easily found his target in the viewfinder. He could hardly miss hitting a house. Then he waited for a final command in his earphones.

God, he didn't like this! He pictured the astonishingly pretty girl from Hamburg. Jeri was her name. So sweet, and what a perfect body. He waited, half-hoping the signal wouldn't come. For Jeri's sake, for the sake of everyone inside.

But there it was! Electronic. Impersonal as a stranger's funeral. A whistling sound between his ears.

Two short, one long.

He took a deep breath, slowly exhaled. Then, reluctantly, he squeezed the trigger.

Bari felt a very slight recoil, less than a rifle's, actually.

The launch engine inside the weapon ignited. The first-stage engine propelled the missile only about twenty to thirty feet, at which point it was safe for the secondary propulsion system to engage.

His eyes followed a vapor trail of solid rocket-fuel

exhaust. The Stinger was on its way to the target. He heard a low roar as the missile accelerated to 1500 miles per hour.

Be safe, Jeri.

The Stinger struck the estate-house broadside – a near-perfect hit.

He was already reloading for the next shot.

Chapter One Hundred and Ten

There were loud whooshing noises, and then fiery, hellish explosions everywhere I could see. Chaos reigned over all. And death as well.

French police and Army were frantically running for cover. A rocket or missile struck the north roofs of the villa, tossing slate, wood and bricks from a chimney high into the air. Then a second missile struck. A third was only seconds behind.

I had started racing back toward the main house – when I got another surprise out of nowhere.

A side door of the boathouse flew open and a dark blue Mercedes sedan roared up a graveled path toward the main road. I ran to a police sedan parked on the grass, started it up and gave chase.

There wasn't time to tell anybody what I was doing. Not even Sandy. I wondered how a police car was going to keep up with a souped-up Mercedes, though.

Probably not too well. No, probably not at all.

I stayed with the powerful CL55 out of Cap Ferrat, all the way to the Basse Corniche. I nearly killed myself, and maybe a few others on the twisty road, but I didn't lose whoever was speeding in front of me.

Who the hell was in the car? Why was somebody running? *Could it be the Wolf?*

Traffic toward Monaco was moving, but it was heavy. The lights from a vehicle recovery truck up ahead indicated that some poor driver had jack-knifed on this windy road. That was my one long-shot hope. The traffic was slowing the Merc down. But suddenly the Mercedes swung around and headed west.

The sports sedan was moving very fast past an endless array of billboards and restaurant signs. And so was I.

I rounded a curve and the whole of the bay of Villefranche-sur-Mer appeared in all of its inimitable beauty and splendour, the moon large and full-looking in the sky. The city rose above the bay which was filled with sailboats and yachts, like a rich kid's bathtub. The Mercedes spun down a slick, sloping hill, sometimes at a speed of a hundred miles per hour. I thought I remembered from somewhere that the car had close to five hundred horsepower. It sure seemed like it.

Then we were entering the old port of Nice, and I began to close the gap behind the sedan. The narrow streets were surprisingly crowded, especially around the bars and nightclubs, which seemed everywhere now, thank God.

The Mercedes barely avoided a drunken group coming out of the *Étoile Filante* nightclub.

And then, horn blaring, I roared through the same crowd, the pedestrians cursing and shaking fists at me.

The Mercedes made a sharp right – onto the N7, the Moyenne Corniche, a higher road.

I followed as best I could, knowing that I would probably lose him now. Lose who, though? Who was in the blue Mercedes?

The way *up* was incredibly steep and winding. We were headed back toward Monaco, but the traffic was light this way, and the Mercedes was effortlessly picking up speed. The driver had known to go *backward* in order to go forward – much faster – at speeds the police sedan couldn't possibly match.

After about two kilometers I was pretty sure I would lose him. We were back in Villefranche, but the highest part of town. The view down onto Cap Ferrat and Beaulieu was breathtaking and I couldn't avoid looking; even at this speed it filled my eyes like a painting.

I couldn't let him get away, and I pushed the police car up close to a hundred again. How long could I possibly keep up?

There was a tunnel, dimness, then almost total

darkness – and at the end of the tunnel the astonishing sight of a medieval village perched high on a hillside.

Eze read a sign, and I wished I could go *easy*.

Just past the village, the road became even more dangerous. It was as if the Moyenne Corniche were taped onto the side of the cliffs. Down below, the color of the sea seemed to be changing from azure to opal to silver-gray.

I could smell oranges and lemons in the air. My senses were sharp. Fear can do that.

I was losing the Mercedes, though, so I made the only move I could. Instead of slowing around the next curve – I accelerated.

Chapter One Hundred and Eleven

I began to gain on the Mercedes and I kept my foot
pressed to the floor. *Are you suicidal?* I wondered
about myself.

Suddenly the Mercedes skidded all the way across
the opposite lane. It struck the side of the mountain, a
glancing blow, but very damaging to the car at that
speed. Then it swerved back and forth on the road,
using both lanes. It caromed off the rocks again. The
blue sedan suddenly took off into the sky.

It was airborne – falling toward the sea.

I braked to the side of the road and jumped from
my car. I saw the Mercedes hit the side of the cliff
twice, then roll onto the lower highway far below. I
couldn't get down there from where I was. Couldn't
climb down anyway.

I didn't see any movement from the wreck. Whoever
was inside the Mercedes had to be dead. *But who was it?*

I got back in the police car I had commandeered at the estate. It took me close to ten minutes to make my way to the lower highway and the scene of the wreck. French police and an ambulance had already arrived and so had many early-morning onlookers.

As I climbed from my car, I could see that the body hadn't been removed from the wreckage. Medical workers were leaning inside the car and seemed to be working frantically. They were talking to whoever had been driving. Who was it?

One of them shouted, '*He's still alive. One male! He's alive in here!*'

I started to run toward the wreckage to get a look at the driver. Who was he? Could he talk to me? I glanced back up at the Moyenne and wondered how the driver could have survived the long fall and crash. The Wolf was supposed to be a tough guy. *This* tough?

I flashed my creds and the police surrounding the wreck let me move on.

Then I could see. I knew who it was trapped in the wreck. I couldn't believe it, though. I just couldn't believe what I was seeing with my own eyes.

My heart was thumping loudly, racing out of control. So was my mind, what was left of it. I came up to the smoldering, overturned car. I knelt on the rocky ground and leaned forward.

'It's Alex,' I said.

The car's driver looked at me and tried to focus. His

body was trapped inside the crumpled Mercedes. He'd been crushed by the metal everywhere below the shoulders. Just awful to see.

But Martin Lodge was alive, and he was hanging on. He seemed to want to say something and I moved closer.'It's Alex,' I said again. I turned my head so that my ear was near his mouth.

I needed to know the identity of the Wolf. I had so many questions.

Martin whispered,'It's all for nothing.Your manhunt is useless. I'm not the Wolf. I never even saw him.'

Then he died on me, and everyone else who waited for an answer.

Chapter One Hundred and Twelve

The Lodge family had been put into protective custody back in England. We all felt that if the Wolf suspected the wife or any of the children had been told anything incriminating, they would be targets. Maybe he'd kill them just to be safe, or because he felt like killing somebody that day.

The next morning I flew to London and met with the police at Scotland Yard, specifically Lodge's superior, a man named John Mortenson. First, he reported that none of the survivors at Cap Ferrat seemed to know anything about the Wolf, or even who Martin Lodge had been.

'There is a new development, a little wrinkle,' he told me then.

I leaned back in a leather lounger with a view of Buckingham Palace. 'At this point, I'm not surprised about anything, John. Tell me what's going on. This is about the Lodge family?'

He nodded, sighed and then he began. 'It starts with Klára Lodge. Klára Cernohosska, actually. It turns out Martin was on the team that brought a defector named Edward Morozov out of Russia back in ninety-three. Martin worked with the American CIA, with Cahill and Hancock, and also Thomas Weir. Only there was no Edward Morozov. He was an unidentified KGB defector whose name we don't know. We think that it was the Wolf.'

'You started by saying something about Martin's wife, Klára. What about her?'

'For one thing, she's not Czech. She came out of Russia with the man called Morozov. She was an assistant to a KGB chief, and also our main source of information in Moscow. She and Lodge apparently got cozy during the transfer, and then she was relocated to England. He had her identity changed, got rid of the records. Then he married her. How about that?'

'And she knows who the Wolf is, what he looks like? Is that it?'

'We don't know what Klára knows. She won't talk to us. She might talk to *you* though.'

I sat back, shook my head. 'Why me? I only met her once.'

Mortenson shrugged, then he gave a half-smile. 'She says her husband trusted you. You believe that?

What the hell is that supposed to mean? Why would she trust you, if you only met her once?'

Unfortunately, I had no idea.

Chapter One Hundred and Thirteen

What remained of the Lodge family was being kept under wraps in a small town called Shepton Mallet, which is about 120 miles west of London. Rolling valleys, lots of green countryside, perfect for hiding them, at least temporarily.

The Lodges were staying in a converted farmhouse on a No Through road outside of town. The land was fairly flat there and anything approaching could be seen for miles. Besides, this was an armed compound, heavily armed.

I arrived at around six that evening. The inside of the farmhouse was pleasant, with lots of antique furniture, but I had dinner with the family in a cramped bunker that was located below the ground.

Klára didn't cook the meal as she had in London, and I wondered if she approved of the fare. I doubted it. The food was dreadful, worse than airplane fare. 'No *míchaná vejce* on the menu,' I finally tried a joke on her.

'You remember our breakfast in Battersea, even the correct pronunciation. That's good, Alex,' Klára said. 'You're very observant. Martin said you were a good cop.'

When the meal was over, the children, Hana, Daniela, Jozef, were sent to their room to do homework. Klára sat with me and smoked a cigarette. She took long puffs and inhaled deeply.

'Homework?' I asked. 'Here? Tonight?'

'It's good to have discipline, habits to fall back on. So you were with Martin when he died?' she asked. 'What did he say to you? Please tell me.'

I considered my response. What did Klára want to hear? And what should I tell her?

'He said that he wasn't the Wolf. Is that true, Klára?'

'Anything else? What else did he tell you?'

I thought about telling Klára he'd talked about her and the children, but I didn't. I didn't want to lie to her. Probably, I couldn't. 'No, Klára. That's all it was. There wasn't much time. Only a few seconds. He didn't suffer too long. He didn't seem to be in pain. I think he was in shock.'

She nodded. 'Martin thought I could trust you. He said it was your flaw, actually. He would never say anything sentimental, not even with his dying breath.'

I stared into Klára's deep brown eyes, which seemed surprisingly alert.

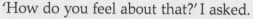

'How do you feel about that?' I asked.

She laughed. 'It's why I loved him.'

She had things to tell me that night in the English countryside. A negotiation was begun between the two of us. Or rather, I got to listen to her demands.

'I want safe passage out of England for myself and the children. New identities and we get to keep some savings to live on. I'll tell you where we want to live, but not right now. That will come a little later.'

'Prague?' I asked. It was a small joke.

'No, definitely not Prague, Alex. And not Russia either. Or anywhere in America for that matter. I'll tell you where, when the time comes. But first, let's decide on what I have to give you to guarantee our safe passage out of England.'

'Oh, that's easy. You have to give us a lot,' I said. 'You have to give up the Wolf. But can you do that, Klára? What do you know? Who is he? *Where is he?* What did Martin tell you?'

Finally, she smiled. 'Oh, he told me everything. Martin adored me.'

Chapter One Hundred and Fourteen

The Wolf flew his own plane into Teterboro Airport in the northern corner of New Jersey. A black Range Rover was waiting there for him and he took it into New York City, a city he'd always despised. The traffic was bad as usual, and it took him as long to get from Teterboro to Manhattan as it had to fly to the metropolitan area from New Hampshire.

The doctor's office was situated in a brownstone on Sixty-Third Street just off Fifth. The Wolf parked the Range Rover and hurried inside.

It was a little past nine in the morning. He didn't bother to check and see if he was being watched. He didn't think so, but if he was, there was nothing to do about it now. Besides, he felt he had this morning sufficiently covered. As usual, there was a plan for every eventuality.

The nurse on duty for the plastic surgery was also

there to act as a receptionist. She and the hotshot surgeon would be the only ones present for the procedures. He had insisted on a staff of two, and also that the office be closed to other patients for the day.

'There are a few legal forms for you to look over and sign,' the nurse told him with a tight smile. She might not know who he was, but she suspected there had to be a very good reason for this much secrecy, not to mention the fact that she was being paid handsomely to work this shift.

'No, I will sign nothing, thank you,' he said, then he pushed past her and went looking for Dr Levine. He found her in a small operating theater that was already brightly lit, and very cold.

'Reminds me of Siberia. A gulag I spent time in one winter,' he spoke.

The doctor turned, and she was mildly attractive, slender, well-preserved, probably in her early forties. He could fuck her, in a pinch, but he wasn't in the mood right now. Maybe later.

'Dr Levine,' he said and shook hands with the surgeon. 'I'm ready, and I don't want to be here more than a few hours. So let's begin. Now.'

'That's not possible,' Dr Levine started to object.

The Wolf raised his hand to silence her, and it almost seemed as if he might actually strike the doctor. She flinched.

'I won't be needing a general anesthetic. As I said, I'm *ready*. So are you.'

'Sir, you have no idea what you're saying. None, I assure you. The procedures we have scheduled include a face, neck, and brow lift. Liposuction. Jaw and cheek implants. And a nose job. The pain will be unbearable. Trust me on that.'

'No, it will be bearable. I've known much worse pain,' said the Wolf. 'I will allow you only to monitor my vital signs. There will be no more stupid discussion about anesthesia. Now, get me ready for the procedures. Or else.'

'Or else *what*?' Dr Levine bristled. The small woman rocked back on her heels.

'Just or *else*,' answered the Wolf. 'That covers a great deal of territory, don't you think? It covers pain beyond what you believe I cannot endure. Can *you*, Dr Levine? Can your two children, Martin and Amy, endure such pain? Or your husband, Jerrold? Let's begin. I have a schedule to keep.'

Always a schedule.

And a plan.

Chapter One Hundred
and Fifteen

He never once screamed, never made a sound during any of the grueling procedures, and neither the surgeon nor the nurse could comprehend what they were witnessing. The patient seemed to have no feeling at all. As males often do, he bled a great deal during the operations, and there was already a lot of deep purple bruising on his face. The pain he endured during the hour and a half rhinoplasty, or nose job, was the worst by far, especially when large chunks of bone and cartilage were removed without even a topical anesthetic.

At the conclusion of the rhinoplasty, the final procedure, he was told by Dr Levine not to stand, but he did anyway.

His neck felt tight and tender, and there was Betadine all over his scalp and throat. 'Not bad,' he rasped. 'I've experienced much worse.'

'*Do not* blow your nose. For at least a week,' the

doctor insisted, seemingly trying to maintain her dignity and a very tenuous sense of control.

The Wolf reached into his trousers and produced a handkerchief, but then he put it back. 'Just kidding,' he said, then frowned. 'Do you have *any* sense of humor, Doctor?'

'You can't drive either,' said the doctor. 'That I will not allow. For the sake of *others*.'

'No, of course not. I wouldn't think of it, putting others in jeopardy. I'll just leave my vehicle here on the street to be carjacked. Let me get your money. It's become boring to be here with you.'

It was at this point, as he walked to fetch his briefcase, that the Russian staggered slightly – and also got a first look at himself in a mirror, his incredibly bruised and swollen face, at least what showed around the bandages.

'You do nice work,' he said and laughed.

He opened the briefcase – and pulled out a Beretta with silencer. He shot the astonished nurse in the face, twice, then turned to Dr Levine, who had hurt him so much.

'Any other things I should or shouldn't do?' he asked. 'Any last bits of advice you wish to impart?'

'My children. Please don't kill me,' the doctor begged. 'You know I have children.'

'They'll be better off without you. I think so, bitch. I bet they would agree.'

He shot her through the heart. A mercy killing, he thought to himself, especially after the way she'd tortured him. Plus – he just didn't like her, humorless bitch.

Finally, the Wolf left the office and walked to his Range Rover. He was thinking that no one knew what he looked like now. Not a single person anywhere.

And that got him laughing, almost uncontrollably. This was his *piece* of the puzzle.

Chapter One Hundred and Sixteen

'There he is – has to be.'

'He's laughing! What's so funny? Look at him. Can you believe it?'

'He looks like he was scalped, then had his skin flayed,' Ned Mahoney said when the heavily band-aged man in a gray overcoat emerged from the brownstone. 'He looks like a goddamn ghoul.'

'Don't underestimate him,' I reminded Ned. 'And don't forget, he *is* a ghoul.'

We were watching the Wolf – at least, the man we believed to be the Wolf, as he left a plastic surgeon's office on the East Side of Manhattan. We had just gotten there, less than sixty seconds ago. Almost missed him again.

'Don't worry, I'm not underestimating him, Alex. That's why we have half a dozen teams getting ready to pounce on him. If we'd gotten here sooner we could have grabbed him inside the doctor's office.'

I nodded. 'At least we're here. It was a complicated negotiation in England. Klára Lodge and her children are somewhere in North Africa now. She did her part.'

'So the Wolf has had a tracking device under his shoulder blade since he came out of Russia? That's the story?'

'We're here, aren't we? According to Klára, Martin Lodge knew where he was all along. *That* kept Lodge alive.'

'We're ready to go then? We take him?' Ned said.

'We're ready. I'm ready.' *Jesus, was I ready. I wanted to take this bastard down so badly.* I couldn't wait to see the look on his face.

Mahoney spoke into the mike attached to his headset. 'Close on him now. And remember, he's extremely dangerous.'

You got that right, Neddo.

Chapter One Hundred and Seventeen

The black Range Rover was stopped at a light on the corner of Fifth Avenue and Fifty-Ninth Street. Dark sedans pulled up on either side. A third car blocked off the intersection. Agents jumped out of the cars. We had him!

Gunfire suddenly erupted from a white Hummer in *front* of the Range Rover. The doors of the Hummer flew open. Three men with automatic weapons came out firing.

'Where the hell did they come from?' Mahoney yelled into his mike. 'Everybody down!'

We were already out of our car and running toward the gunfight. Ned fired and took down one of the Wolf's bodyguards. I hit another, and a third bodyguard opened up on us.

Meanwhile the Wolf was out of the Range Rover and running down Fifth Avenue, staying out in the street with the cars. The condition of his face made him look like he'd already been shot, or maybe badly burned in a fire. People on the sidewalks were hitting the pavement because of the gunshots coming from everywhere. Several were screaming uncontrollably. *How far did the Wolf think he could get, looking the way he did? In New York City – maybe far!*

More gunmen appeared, seemingly out of nowhere. More of his bodyguards. He had certainly brought backup. Had *we* brought enough?

And then the Wolf ducked into a store on Fifth. Mahoney and I followed him. I didn't even notice what store it was. Upscale. Glitzy. *Fifth Avenue, for God's sake!*

The Wolf did the unthinkable then – although nothing he did completely surprised me any more. His right arm shot forward and released a dark object into the air. I watched it start to tumble.

I shouted, 'Grenade! Everybody down! Get down! Grenade!'

A powerful explosion at the front of the store blew out two massive picture windows. Shoppers were hurt. The smoke was very thick, and dark. Everybody inside the store was screaming, including the clerks behind nearly every counter.

I never lost sight of the Wolf, never lost my focus on him. No matter what he did, no matter what the danger, he couldn't be allowed to get away this time. The cost was too high. This was the man who had held the world hostage. He'd already murdered thousands.

Mahoney ran down one aisle and I took another. The Wolf appeared to be headed for an exit onto a side street. I'd lost track of where we were. Fifty-Fifth Street? Fifty-Sixth?

'He doesn't get out!' Ned shouted over to me.

'You've got that right.'

We were getting closer and I could see the Wolf's face. With all the bandages, the bruising and swelling, he looked fiercer than I could have imagined. Worse, he looked desperate, capable of anything. But we already knew that.

He yelled, *'I'll kill everybody in the store!'*

Neither Mahoney nor I answered; we just kept coming. But we didn't doubt what he'd said.

He grabbed a small blond girl away from what looked to be a nanny. 'I'll kill her. I'll kill the little girl. She's *dead*! I'll kill her!'

We kept coming.

He held the toddler against his chest. His blood was dripping all over her. The girl was screaming, squirming wildly in his arms.

'I'll kill—'

Ned and I fired at almost the same time – two shots and the Wolf stumbled backward, letting go of the girl. She fell to the floor then got up screeching, and ran to safety.

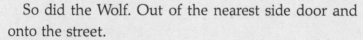

So did the Wolf. Out of the nearest side door and onto the street.

'He's wearing a vest – has to be.'

'We'll shoot him in the head,' I said.

Chapter One Hundred and Eighteen

We chased him east on Fifty-Fifth Street along with a couple of our agents and two fleet-footed New York City policemen. If any of the Wolf's bodyguards had survived the bloody shootout on Fifth Avenue they'd lost track of their boss in the shuffle inside the store. They were nowhere to be seen now.

Still, the Wolf looked like he knew where he was going. Was that possible? How could he have planned ahead for this? He couldn't have – so we'd get him now, right? I couldn't let myself believe otherwise – that all of this could come to nothing.

We had him in our sights. He was right there in front of us.

Suddenly he turned into a building, red-brick, eight to ten stories high. Did he know someone here? More backup? A trap? What?

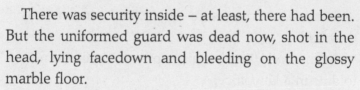
There was security inside – at least, there had been. But the uniformed guard was dead now, shot in the head, lying facedown and bleeding on the glossy marble floor.

The elevators were all busy, red lights flashing the floors – 8 – 4 – 3 – all going *up*.

'He's not getting out of here. That's settled,' Mahoney said.

'We can't know that, Ned.'

'He can't fucking fly, can he?'

'No, but who the hell knows what else he can do. He came in here for a reason.'

Mahoney assigned agents to wait for all of the elevators, then to systematically check the floors from bottom to top. Reinforcements were on the way from the NYPD. There would be dozens of cops here soon. Then hundreds. *The Wolf was in the building.*

Mahoney and I took to the stairs in pursuit.

'Where do we go? How far?'

'The roof. It's the only other way out of here.'

'You really think he's got a plan? How, Alex?'

I shook my head; I had no way of knowing. He was bleeding, had to be weak, maybe he was even delirious. Or maybe he had a plan. Hell, he'd always had a plan before.

So up we went, all the way. The top floor was nine and we didn't see the Wolf as we peeked out of the stairwell. We quickly checked the offices; no one had seen him – and they sure would have remembered if they had.

'In the back there's stairs up to the roof,' someone told us in a law office.

Ned Mahoney and I climbed more stairs, then we stepped outside into bright daylight. We didn't see the Wolf. There was a single-story structure, like a small hat on top of the old building. Water tower? The super's office?

We tried the door – it was locked.

'He has to be here somewhere. Unless he jumped,' Ned said.

Then we saw him coming around from behind the tower. '*I didn't jump*, Mr Mahoney. And I thought I told you not to work on this case. I think I was clear. Put down your guns right now.'

I stepped forward. 'I brought him here.'

'Of course you did. You're indefatigable, don't give up, relentless, Dr Cross. That's why you're so predict-able, and useful.'

Suddenly a New York City policeman stepped out of the same trapdoor opening to the roof that we had used. He saw the Wolf and fired.

He hit the Wolf in the chest, but it didn't stop him. He was wearing a vest, had to be. The Russian growled like a bear and charged the cop, waving both arms over his head.

He grabbed the surprised officer and picked him up.

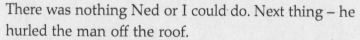

There was nothing Ned or I could do. Next thing – he hurled the man off the roof.

The Wolf started to race toward the other side of the rooftop and he seemed genuinely insane. What was he doing? Suddenly I thought I knew. The building to the south was close enough so that he was going to jump for it. Then, coming in from the west, I saw a helicopter. For him? Was that the escape plan? *Don't let this be happening.*

I ran after him. So did Mahoney. 'Stop! Stop right there!'

He was running in crazy zigzags away from us. We fired, but didn't hit him with the first shots.

Then the Wolf was airborne, both his arms flailing – and he was going to make it to the other rooftop with room to spare.

'*You bastard, no!*' Ned yelled. '*No!*'

I stopped running – aimed carefully – and squeezed the trigger four times.

Chapter One Hundred and Nineteen

The Wolf kept pumping his legs and almost seemed to be running on thin air, but then he started to drop. His arms reached out toward the edge of the other building. His fingers . . . reached for the roof.

Mahoney and I ran up close to the edge of our building. Could the Wolf get out of this one? Somehow, he always found a way. Except this time – I knew I'd hit him in the throat. He had to be drowning in his own blood.

'Fall, you fuck!' Ned screamed at him.

'He's not going to make it,' I said.

And he didn't. The Russian's body fell, and strangely, he didn't fight it, didn't make a sound, never screamed out. Not a sound came from him.

Mahoney yelled down at him. 'Hey, Wolf! Hey, Wolfman! Go to hell!'

The fall looked as if it had been shot in slow

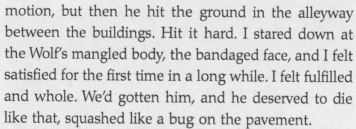

motion, but then he hit the ground in the alleyway between the buildings. Hit it hard. I stared down at the Wolf's mangled body, the bandaged face, and I felt satisfied for the first time in a long while. I felt fulfilled and whole. We'd gotten him, and he deserved to die like that, squashed like a bug on the pavement.

Then Ned Mahoney started to clap and whoop and dance around like a complete madman. I didn't join in, but I knew what he was feeling. The man down there deserved this fate, if anyone ever did. Stone cold dead in an alleyway.

'He didn't scream,' I finally said. 'Couldn't even give us that.'

Mahoney shrugged his wide shoulders. 'I don't care if he did or not. Here we are up here – there he is down with the garbage. Maybe there's some justice after all. Well, and maybe not,' Ned said and laughed, and put his arm around me, and squeezed.

'We won,' I said to him. 'Damn it, we finally won, Neddy.'

Chapter One Hundred and Twenty

We won!

The next morning, I flew back to Quantico in a Bell helicopter with Ned Mahoney and some of his stellar crew. They were celebrating the Wolf's demise at HRT over in Quantico, but I wanted to get home. I'd told Nana to keep the kids away from school because *we* were celebrating today.

We won!

I let myself decompress for some of the car ride from Quantico to Washington. When I finally got to the house, when I could see it up ahead, I started to feel closer to normal, almost myself, or at least somebody that I recognized. No one had come out on the porch yet, so Nana and the kids hadn't seen me arrive. I decided to surprise them.

We won!

The front door wasn't locked and I went inside. A

few lights were on but I didn't see anybody yet. *Maybe they're going to surprise me?*

Keeping very quiet, I made my way back to the kitchen. The lights were on – plates and silverware had been laid out for lunch – but nobody was there either.

Kind of strange. Just a little bit off-kilter. Rosie the cat came meowing from somewhere, rubbing up against me.

Finally I called out, 'I'm home! Your daddy's home! Where is everybody? I'm home from the wars.'

I hurried upstairs but nobody was there either. I checked for notes that might have been left for me. Nothing.

I ran downstairs. I looked out back, then up and down Fifth Street in front of the house. Not a soul in sight anywhere. Where were Nana and the kids? They knew I was coming.

I went back inside and made a few phone calls to places Nana and the kids might be. But Nana almost always left a note when she went out with the kids, even for an hour or so, and they'd been expecting me.

Suddenly, I felt sick. I waited another half-hour before I contacted some people at the Hoover Building, starting with Tony Woods in the Director's office. In the meantime I'd looked around the house again, found no sign of any kind of disturbance.

A team of technical people arrived and shortly

afterward one of them approached me in the kitchen. 'There are footprints out in the yard, probably male. Some dirt was recently tracked into the house. Could have been repairmen, or a delivery service, but it's definitely fresh.'

That was all they found that afternoon, not another clue, not one.

Sampson and Billie came over in the evening and we sat together and waited, at least for a call, something to go on, something to give me hope. But no call came, and some time after two in the morning, Sampson finally went home. Billie had left at around ten.

I stayed up all night – but nothing, no contact. No word at all about Nana and the kids. I talked to Jamilla on my cell phone, and it helped, but not enough. Nothing could have helped that night.

Finally, early in the morning I stood at the front door bleary-eyed, and stared up and down the street. It occurred to me that this had always been my worst fear, maybe everybody's worst fear, to be all alone, with nobody, and to have those you love the most in terrible danger.

We lost.

Chapter One Hundred and Twenty-One

The e-mail came on the fifth day. I almost couldn't bear to read it. I thought that I might throw up as I stared down at the words.

Alex, I read.

Surprise, dear boy.

I am actually not as cruel or heartless a person as you might think I am. The really cruel ones, the truly unreasonable ones, the ones we should all fear, are mostly in your own United States and in Western Europe. The money I have now will help to stop them, help to stop their greed. Do you believe that? You should. Why not? Why the hell not?

I thank you for what you did for me, and for Hana, Daniela and Jozef. We owe you something, and I always pay my debts. To me 'you are a gnat, but at least you are a gnat'. Your family will be returned today, but now we're even. You will never see me again. I don't want to see you either. If I do, you will die. That is a promise.

Klára Cernohosska,
Wolf.

Chapter One Hundred and Twenty-Two

I couldn't let it go; couldn't or wouldn't. The Wolf had invaded my house, taken my family, even though they had been returned unharmed. It could happen again.

Over the next few weeks I tested, then strained, the new cooperative relationship between the Bureau and the CIA. I got Ron Burns to put even more stress on the situation. I traveled out to CIA headquarters in Langley more than a dozen times, talked to everybody from junior analysts to the new Director, James Dowd. I wanted to know about Thomas Weir and the KGB agent he'd helped bring out of Russia. I needed to know everything that they knew. Was that possible? I doubted it, but that didn't stop me from trying.

Then one day I was called up to Burns's office. When I arrived, I found Burns and the new CIA Director waiting for me in his conference room.

Something was up. This was going to be good – or very, very bad.

'Come on in, Alex,' said Burns, cordial as he often was. 'We need to talk.'

I stepped inside and sat across from the two heavies, both in shirt-tails, looking like they had just come out of a long and difficult work session. About what? The Wolf? Something else that I didn't want to hear about?

'Director Dowd wants to say a few things to you,' said Burns.

'I do, Alex,' said Dowd, a New York lawyer who'd been an unexpected choice for CIA Director. He had started in the New York Police Department, then gone into very lucrative private practice for several years. According to rumors, there were things that none of us knew, or wanted to know, about Dowd and his years in private practice.

'I'm just finding my way around out at Langley,' he said, 'and actually, this exercise has helped. We've spent a great deal of time and effort digging into everything about Director Weir.'

Dowd looked over at Burns. 'Just about all of it is good, an excellent record of service. But this kind of digging into old records isn't appreciated by some of the "old warrior" types out in Virginia. Frankly, I don't give a shit what they think.

'A Russian by the name of Anton Christyakov was

recruited and then brought out of Russia in 1990. This man was the Wolf. We're fairly sure about that. He was transported to England, where he met with a few agents including Martin Lodge. Then he was moved to a house outside Washington. His identity was only known to a handful of people. Most of them are dead now, including Weir.

'Finally, he was moved to a city of his choosing – Paris, where he met up with his family: mother and father, wife, two young sons, aged nine and twelve.

'Alex, they lived two blocks from the Louvre, on one of the streets that was destroyed a few weeks ago. His entire family was killed there in ninety-four, but not Christyakov himself. We believe the attack may have been orchestrated by the Russian government. We don't know this for certain, but somebody leaked where he was living to somebody who didn't want him to *continue* living. The attack may have taken place on the bridge across the Seine that was destroyed.'

'He blamed the CIA and Tom Weir,' Burns said. 'And he blamed the governments that were involved. Maybe he went mad after that – who the hell knows. He joined the Mafiya, and rose quickly. Here in America, probably in New York.'

Burns stopped. Dowd didn't add anything more. They were both looking at me.

'So it's not Klára. What else do we know about Christyakov?'

Dowd raised his hands with both palms up. 'There are notes in our records, but precious few. He was known by some Mafiya leaders, but they seem to be dead now, too. Maybe the current Mafiya "big man" in Brooklyn knows something. There's another possible contact in Paris. We're working a couple of angles in Moscow.'

I shook my head. 'I don't care how long it takes. I want him. Tell me everything there is.'

'He was close to his sons – maybe that's why he spared your family, Alex,' said Burns. 'And mine.'

'He spared my family to show how powerful he is, how superior to the rest of us.'

'He squeezes a rubber ball,' said Dowd. 'A handball. Black.'

I didn't follow at first. 'I'm sorry, what?'

'One of his sons gave him a rubber handball before the boy died. A birthday present. In one of the notes we have, it says that Christyakov squeezes the ball when he gets angry. He's also said to favor beards. He's celibate now, according to the rumors anyway. It's all pieces, Alex. That's what we have. I'm sorry.'

So was I, but it didn't matter. I was going to get him.

He squeezes a rubber ball.

He favors beards.

His family was murdered.

Chapter One Hundred and Twenty-Three

Six weeks later I traveled to New York, my fifth out-of-town trip in a row. Tolya Bykov had been at or near the top of the Red Mafiya gangs in New York, specifically the Brighton Beach area, for the last few years. He had been a Mafiya head in Moscow and was the most powerful leader to come to America. I was going to see him.

On a sunny, unseasonably warm day, Ned Mahoney and I made the journey out to Mill Neck on Long Island's Gold Coast. The area we drove through was heavily wooded, served by narrow roads, with no sidewalks anywhere.

We arrived at the Bykov compound with a dozen agents – unannounced. We had a warrant. There were bodyguards posted everywhere and I wondered how Tolya Bykov could live like this – maybe because he had to in order to remain alive.

The house itself was very large, a three-story colonial villa. It had incredible water views across the Sound all the way to Connecticut. There was a Gunite pool with a waterfall, a boathouse and dock. The wages of sin?

Bykov was waiting in his den for our talk. I was surprised at how tired, how old he looked. He had small beady eyes in a pocked face rolling with fat. He was grossly overweight, probably close to three hundred pounds. His breathing was labored and he had a hacking cough.

I'd been told that he spoke no English.

'I want to know about the man called the Wolf,' I said as I sat down across from him at a plain wooden table. One of our agents from the New York office translated, a young Russian-American.

Tolya Bykov scratched the back of his neck, then shook his head back and forth, finally muttering several Russian words between clenched jaws.

The translator listened, then looked at me. 'He says you're wasting his time, and yours. Why don't you leave right now. He knows *Peter and the Wolf*, no other wolves.'

'We're not going to leave. The FBI, the CIA, we're going to be in Mr Bykov's face, in his business, until we find the Wolf. Tell him that.'

The agent spoke in Russian and Bykov laughed in his face. The Russian said something and the sentences mentioned Chris Rock.

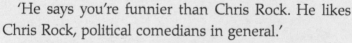

'He says you're funnier than Chris Rock. He likes Chris Rock, political comedians in general.'

I stood up, nodded to Bykov, then I walked out of the room. I didn't expect too much more from the first meeting, just an introduction. I would be back, again and again if necessary. This was the only case I was working now. I was learning to be patient, very patient.

Chapter One Hundred and Twenty-Four

Minutes later, I was leaving the large house, walking side by side with Ned Mahoney. We were laughing about the first interview – what the hell, might as well laugh.

I saw something – and I did a double-take – *saw it again.*

'Ned – Jesus. Look.'

'What?' His head swiveled around, but he didn't see what I saw.

Then I was running ahead on legs that felt unsteady.

'What? Alex, what is it?' Ned yelled behind me. 'Alex?'

'It's him!' I said.

My eyes were pinned on one of the bodyguard-types at the compound. Black suit jacket and shirt, no overcoat. He was standing under a large evergreen, watching us watch him. My eyes dropped to his hand.

In the hand – a black ball, an old one. He was squeezing it and I knew, I just knew, it had to be the handball given to the Wolf by his small son before he died. The man with the ball had a beard. His eyes looked at mine.

Then he started to run.

I yelled back at Ned, 'That's him! He's the Wolf!'

I sprinted across the lawns, moving faster than I had in a while. I trusted that Ned was behind me.

I saw the Russian jump into a bright red convertible – then he started it up. *Oh no, God no!* I thought.

But I tumbled into the front seat before he put it into gear. I hit him with a short, powerful punch to the nose. Blood gushed all over his black shirt and jacket. I knew I'd broken his nose. I hit him again, square on the jaw.

I shoved open the driver's side door. He looked at me, and his eyes were coldly intelligent, like no eyes I'd ever seen, nothing so desolate. *Inhuman.* That was what the French President had called him.

Was he the *real* Tolya Bykov? It didn't matter to me now. He was the Wolf – I could see it in those eyes, the confidence, arrogance, but most of all – the hatred for me, and everyone else.

'The ball,' he said. 'You knew about the ball. My son gave it to me. I congratulate you.'

He gave a strange half-smile – then he bit down hard on something inside his mouth. I thought I knew what had happened. I tried desperately to force open his mouth. His jaw was clamped tightly shut, and suddenly the Russian's eyes were wide, incredibly big and full of pain. Poison. He'd bitten into poison.

Then his mouth opened and he roared full voice. White foam and spit ran over his lips and down his chin. He roared again and his body began to convulse. I couldn't hold him down any longer. I pushed myself up, backed away from his flopping body.

He began to gag, and to claw at his throat. The convulsing, the dying went on for several awful minutes and there was nothing I could do, and nothing I wanted to do, except watch.

And then it happened – the Wolf died in the front seat of the convertible, another of his expensive cars.

When it was over, I bent and picked up the rubber handball. I put it in my pocket. It was what killers I've caught call a trophy.

It was over and I was going home, wasn't I? I had things to think about, and so much to change about my life. I had the uncomfortable thought: *I was taking trophies now too.*

But I had another, much more important thought: Damon, Jannie, Little Alex, Nana.

Home.

The Wolf is dead. I saw him die.

I kept telling myself that – until I finally believed it.

Turn the page for a preview of the next
compelling thriller featuring Alex Cross . . .

JAMES PATTERSON

MARY MARY

Prologue

The Storyteller

Chapter One

A ct One, Scene One, the Storyteller thought to himself, and couldn't hold back a dizzying rush of anticipation. The truth was that ordinary people committed perfect crimes and perfect murders all the time. But you didn't hear about it for the simple reason that the killers never got caught.

And neither would he, of course. That was a given in the story he was about to tell.

Which didn't mean that today wasn't nerve-racking. Actually, this was the most intense moment in the past couple of insane years for him. He was ready to kill somebody, a complete stranger, and he had figured out that New York City was the right place for his first.

It *almost* happened just outside a basement restroom in Bloomingdale's department store, but he didn't feel right about the location.

Too crowded, even at half past ten in the morning.

Too noisy, and yet not noisy enough to provide the proper distraction.

Plus, he didn't like the idea of trying to escape out on to the unfamiliar territory of Lexington Avenue, or especially down into the claustrophobic IRT subway tunnels. When it felt right, he'd know it, and act accordingly.

So the Storyteller moved on and decided to catch a flick at the Sutton Theater on East 57th Street, a funky, rundown place that had obviously seen better days.

Maybe *this* was a good place for a murder. He liked the irony, even if he was the only one who got it. Yes, maybe this was going to work out great, he thought as he sat in one of the two small auditoriums inside.

He began to watch *Kill Bill Volume 2* with seven other Tarantino aficionados.

Which one of these unsuspecting people would be his victim? *You? You? You there?* The Storyteller spun the tale inside his head.

There were two loudmouths in identical New York Yankees baseball caps, worn backwards of course. The irritating morons didn't shut up once through the interminable ads and trailers. They both deserved to die.

So did an atrociously dressed elderly couple, who didn't talk to each other at all, not once in fifteen minutes before the house lights went down. Killing them would be a good deed, almost a public service.

A fragile-looking woman, early forties, seemed to

be having the shakes two rows in front of the moldy oldies. Bothering no one – except him.

And then a big black dude with his sneakered feet up on the seat in front of him. Rude, inconsiderate bastard in his old school Converses that must have been at least size fourteens.

Next, a black-bearded movie nerd who probably had seen the movie a dozen times already and worshipped Quentin Tarantino, of course.

Turned out it was the bearded wonder who got up about halfway through the movie, just after Uma Thurman was buried alive. Jesus, who could walk out on that classic scene?

Duty-bound, he followed, a couple of seconds behind. Out into the dingy hall, then into the men's room, which was located near Theater Two.

He was actually shaking now. Was this it? His moment? His first murder? The beginning of everything he'd dreamed about for months? Make that *years*.

He was pretty much on auto-pilot, trying not to think about anything except doing this right, then getting out of the movie theater without anybody noticing his face or too much else about him.

The bearded guy was standing at the urinal, which was kind of good news actually. The shot was nicely framed and art-directed.

Wrinkled, grungy black T-shirt that said NYU FILM SCHOOL with a clapsticks logo on the back. Reminded him of a character out of a Daniel Clowes comic book, and that graphic shit was *hot* right now.

'And . . . *action!*' he said.

Then he shot the poor bearded loser in the back of the head, watched him drop like a heavy sack to the bathroom floor. Lie there – nothing moving. The blast roared through his head in the tiled room, louder than he'd dreamed it would be.

'Hey – what the? What happened? *Hey!*' he heard, and the Storyteller whirled around as if there was an audience watching him in the men's room.

Two guys from the Sutton Theater crew had entered behind him. What were the odds of that happening? And how much had they seen?

'Heart attack,' he said, blurted it out, tried to sound convincing. 'Man just fell over at the urinal. Help me get him up. Poor guy. He's bleeding!'

No panic, no emotion, no second thoughts whatsoever. Everything was pure instinct now, right, wrong or indifferent.

He raised his gun and shot both theater workers as they stood wall-eyed and dorky at the door. He shot them again when they were down on the floor. Just to be careful. Professional.

And now he was really shaking, legs like Jell-o, but trying to walk very calmly out of the men's room.

Then out of the Sutton Theater on to 57th, heading east on foot. Everything outside feeling completely unreal and otherworldly, everything so *bright* and *brassy*.

He'd done it, though. He'd killed three people instead of just one. His first *three* murders. It was just practice, but he'd done it, and you know what – he could do it again.

'Practice makes perfect,' the Storyteller whispered under his breath as he hurried toward his car – *his getaway car, right?* God, this was the best feeling of his life. Of course, that didn't say much for his life up to now, did it?

But watch out from here on, just watch out.

For Mary, Mary, quite contrary.

Of course, he was the only one who got *that*. So far, anyway.

Chapter Two

You think you can kill again in cold blood? he asked himself many times after the New York murders. *You think you can stop this now that you've started? You think?*

The Storyteller waited – almost five months of self-torture, also known as discipline, or professionalism, or maybe cowardice – until it was his time.

Then he arrived in the kill zone again, and this time it wasn't going to be practice. This was the real deal, and it wasn't a stranger who was going to die.

He was just a face in the crowd at the 3:10 showing of *The Village* at the Westwood Village Theater in Los Angeles. There were a number of patrons, which was good news for him, and, he supposed, for the film's star director, M. Night Shyamalan. What kind of name was that? M. Night? Self-conscious phony.

Apparently Patrice Bennett was among the last people in town to see the horror film. Also, Patrice actually deigned to sit in a real movie theater, with real ticket-buyers, for her movie fix. How quaint was that? Well, she was famous for it, wasn't she? It was Patrice's schtick. She'd even bought her ticket ahead of time, which was how he knew she'd be there. The Storyteller had gotten the info out of Patrice's executive assistant, Marjorie Seger. *Loose lips sink ships, Marjorie. But thank you, Marjorie.*

So this wasn't target practice any more, and everything had to be just right, and it would be. Never a doubt. The story was already written in his head.

For one thing, he couldn't be spotted by anyone in the theater. So he went to the twelve o'clock; then, when the show let out, he waited around in a bathroom stall until the 3:10. Nail-biting, nerve-thwacking ordeal, but not that bad really. Especially since if he was spotted, he'd simply abort the mission.

But the Storyteller wasn't seen – at least he didn't think so – and he didn't see anyone he knew.

Now, the theater had more than a hundred viewers – or rather, *suspects*, right? At least a dozen of them were perfect for his purposes.

Most important – his gun had a silencer on it. Something he'd learned from the thrill-packed run-through in New York City.

Patrice sat in the balcony. *Works for me, Patsy*, he thought. *You're being way too thoughtful, especially for you, you über-bitch.*

He was watching her from across the aisle and a few rows behind. This was so delicious – he wanted the luxurious anticipation of revenge to go on and on. Except that he also wanted to pull the trigger and get the hell out of the Westwood Theater before something went wrong. But what could go wrong, right?

When Joaquin Phoenix got stabbed by Adrien Brody, he calmly rose from his seat and went directly to Patrice's aisle. He never hesitated for an instant.

'Excuse me. Sorry,' he said, and started to make his way past her, actually *over* her bare, skinny legs, which weren't very impressive for such an important woman in Hollywood.

'Jesus Christ, will you watch it,' she complained, which was just like her, so unnecessarily nasty and imperial-sounding.

'Not exactly who *you* can expect to see next. Not *Jesus*,' he quipped, and wondered if Patrice got his little joke. Probably not. Studio heads didn't get subtlety.

He shot her twice – once in the heart and once right between her totally shocked, blown-away eyes. There was no such thing as too dead when it came to this kind of power-mad psycho. Patrice could probably come back at you from the grave, like that reverse trapdoor ending in the original *Carrie,* Stephen King's first story to reach the silver screen.

Then he made his perfect escape.

Just like in the movies, hey.

The story had begun.

Cross

James Patterson

Alex Cross was a rising star in the Washington, DC, Police Department when an unknown shooter killed his wife, Maria, in front of him.

Years later, having left the FBI and returned to practising psychology in Washington DC, Alex finally feels his life is in order . . . Until his former partner, John Sampson, calls in a favour. John's tracking a serial rapist in Georgetown and he needs Alex to help find this brutal predator.

When the case triggers a connection to Maria's death, could Alex have a chance to catch his wife's murderer? Will this be justice at long last? Or the endgame in his own deadly obsession?

CROSS is the ultimate, high-velocity, high-emotion thriller, and the one Alex Cross's fans waited years to read.

'This story has elements of Hitchcock's *Vertigo*, and its page-turning quality is in a class of its own' *Independent*

'A fast-paced, electric story that is utterly believable' *Booklist*

'Unputdownable. It will sell millions' *The Times*

978 0 7553 4940 1

headline

Double Cross

James Patterson

Just when Alex Cross's life is calming down, he's drawn back into the game to confront the Audience Killer – a psychotic genius who stages his killings as public spectacles in Washington, DC, and broadcasts them live on the net.

In Colorado, another murdering mastermind is planning a triumphant return. From his maximum-security prison cell, Kyle Craig has spent years plotting his escape and revenge. Craig prefers to work alone, but if joining forces with DC's Audience Killer helps him to get the man who put him away then so be it.

Both are after the same detective – Alex Cross.

From the man the *Sunday Telegraph* called 'the master of the suspense genre', DOUBLE CROSS has the pulse-racing momentum and electrifying thrills that have made James Patterson a No. 1 bestselling storyteller all over the world.

'James Patterson does everything but stick our finger in a light socket to give us a buzz' *New York Times*

'A novel which makes for sleepless nights' *Daily Express*

'Pacy, sexy, high-octane stuff' *Guardian*

978 0 7553 4941 8

headline

Cat and Mouse

James Patterson

First came the stunning bestseller, ALONG CAME A SPIDER, which introduced its memorable hero, Washington, DC, detective and psychiatrist Alex Cross. Then the explosive novels KISS THE GIRLS and JACK AND JILL proved that no one can write a more compelling thriller than James Patterson – the master of the non-stop nightmare. Now he brings us CAT AND MOUSE.

Psychopath Gary Soneji is back – filled with hatred and obsessed with gaining revenge on detective Alex Cross. Soneji seems determined to go down in a blaze of glory and he wants Alex Cross to be there. Will this be the final showdown?

CAT AND MOUSE is a powerful and exciting thriller with the electrifying page-turning quality that is the hallmark of megaselling author James Patterson.

'A fast-moving thriller . . . a good time is had by all'
Daily Telegraph

'Patterson does everything but stick our finger in a light socket to give us a buzz' *New York Times*

'Keeps the pedal down on the action and suspense'
Washington Times

978 0 7553 4932 6

headline

Pop Goes the Weasel

James Patterson

'It's all just a game, darling. I play with three other men. Their names are FAMINE, WAR and CONQUEROR. My name is DEATH. You're a very lucky girl – I'm the best player of all.'

Geoffrey Shafer: a man who never loses, he is prepared to play the game of games for the highest stakes of all.

Alex Cross: senior Washington, DC, homicide detective, he is determined, whatever the consequences, to unmask the man he has nicknamed the Weasel, the prime suspect for a spate of killings that Cross has been forbidden to investigate.

In POP GOES THE WEASEL, James Patterson has created a formidable villain every reader will see in the shadows when the lights are out, a tender love story, a plot powered by relentless suspense and psychological thrills kicked up to an all-time high.

'A novel which makes for sleepless nights' *Daily Express*

'Another brilliant tour de force' *Books* Magazine

'Patterson does it again. POP GOES THE WEASEL brings back his Washington, DC, detective, a crazed villain, and a page-turning plot. The man is a master of this genre' *USA Today*

978 0 7553 4933 3

headline

Roses Are Red

James Patterson

A series of meticulously planned bank robberies ends in murder, and Washington, DC, detective Alex Cross must pit his wits against the bizarre and sadistic mastermind behind the crimes. Although torn between dedication to his job and commitment to his family, Cross cannot ignore the case, despite the risks he knows will come with hunting down a killer – and the heartbreaking cost.

James Patterson's bestseller takes us from deep inside the crazy world of a psychopath's masquerade right to the heart of fiction's most brilliant detective. Alex Cross is back in an explosive tale where mind games lead to violence and the slightest mistake will be punished with death.

'Makes Kay Scarpetta's lot look positively fairytale' *Mirror*

'The author's sure-fire tactics have us turning those pages with ever-increasing speed' *Good Book Guide*

'Patterson has a way with plot twists that freshens the material and keeps the adrenaline level high' *Publishers Weekly*

978 0 7553 4934 0

headline

Honeymoon

James Patterson and Howard Roughan

All writers have a book that they know is their very best, ever. James Patterson invites you along to his.

When FBI Agent John O'Hara first meets Nora Sinclair, she seems perfect. She has the career. The charisma. The tantalising sex appeal. The whole extraordinary package – Nora doesn't just attract men, she enthrals them. She's worked hard for this life and she will never give it up.

So why is the FBI so interested in Miss Sinclair? Mysterious things keep happening to the men in her life. And when Agent O'Hara looks more closely he sees something dangerous about Nora – something that lures him at the same time as it fills him with fear. And the more time he spends with her the less he knows whether he is pursuing justice or his own fatal obsession.

With the irresistible attraction of the greatest Hitchcock thrillers, HONEYMOON is a sizzling, twisting tale of a woman with a deadly appetite and the men who dare to fall for her. In his sexiest, scariest novel yet, JAMES PATTERSON deftly confirms why he is the world's bestselling thriller writer.

Praise for HONEYMOON:

'HONEYMOON is all pacy, sexy, high-octane stuff'
Guardian

'O'Hara and particularly Nora stand as two of Patterson's most complex characters yet . . . This is one canny thriller and Patterson's millions of fans will be most pleased'
Publishers Weekly

978 0 7553 0577 3

headline